SLAUGHTERED AS THEY SLEPT

An absolutely gripping killer thriller full of twists

STEVE PARKER

Detectives Paterson & Clocks Series Book 9

Joffe Books, London
www.joffebooks.com

First published in Great Britain in 2023

Cover art by Nebojša Zorić

ISBN: 978-1-80405-765-0

As always, for Caz.
Debbie, June and John. Thank you for your love and support.

Dedicated to MT/MD 'A' Relief
You know who you are.

CHAPTER ONE

Running along the balcony, PC Johnson screamed at the neighbours gathered outside number 42. 'Get back! Get back!' Heads turned as he and his colleague, PC Summers, ran toward them from the stairwell.

'Move!' Johnson said when they reached the door. He could hear the place was being trashed: banging, shouting, screaming, glass smashing.

Summers grabbed at his radio. 'Urgent assistance! Forty-two Leman House. Male berserk inside. Female screams.'

'Who's inside?' said Johnson to the group of neighbours.

'Dunno, mate,' said one of them. 'She lives alone.'

'Shit! Okay.' He pressed the talk button on his radio. 'Mike Delta. Believe life at risk. Forcing entry. Assistance required.' He hooked the radio back into its holder. 'Everyone, back. Get back!'

The noise from inside had subsided and there was silence. Johnson frowned. That was not a good sign.

He booted the door. A loud bang echoed along the balcony as his foot connected. The door held. He booted again. Summers joined in with the booting. A few kicks later and the frame splintered, then gave way. The door flew inward and bounced off the wall inside.

Johnson ran inside and saw carnage. The windows were smashed, the TV sat broken on the floor, a sofa and two chairs were slashed to ribbons, a coffee table lay upside down and next to it, lying face up on the floor, was a woman. Her lifeless eyes stared up at the ceiling through her blood-soaked hair. Sticking out of her chest was a large crucifix.

PC Summers just stood there, stock still, his mouth open.

Johnson swallowed hard. 'Oh, Christ . . .'

From the corner of his eye, he saw Summers pitch forward.

Buried up to the hilt in Summers's neck was a large knife. Johnson spun around to see the wide eyes of a man staring at him. He felt a sharp pain in his throat, then staggered backward, his hands clutching at the knife deeply embedded in his larynx.

CHAPTER TWO

'Okay, then,' said Johnny Clocks, coming out into the car park. 'I understand you're getting married, is that right?'

David Hollins, the driver of fast-response vehicle Mike One, nodded.

'An' Ray tells me you're looking for advice?'

Hollins nodded again.

Clocks sniffed. 'From me?'

'Yep.'

'An' you're not takin' the piss out of me?'

'No. Asking you straight. Why would I be taking the piss out of you?'

Clocks shrugged. 'Well, people don't often ask me for advice about anythin', let alone women, so you can see where I'm comin' from.'

Hollins smiled. 'Genuine. I know you've not been married that long, so I thought you'd be the best one to ask.'

'Okay, lemme think . . .' Clocks looked up to the sky. It was starting to rain. 'Don't do it.'

'Bingo!' said Paterson. He looked at Hollins. 'Pay up.'

Hollins grinned.

'What?' said Clocks. 'What? What's goin' on?'

'I bet him a fiver you'd say that.'

'You pair of bastards! I thought you were genuine.'

'I know,' said Paterson. 'And I'm due a fiver off of your Lyndsey too. She said you wouldn't say that.'

Clocks looked bewildered. 'Wait a minute. Me missus is in on it too?'

Paterson nodded. 'Yeah. But she thought you'd tell him to go ahead because you were both so happy.' He smiled as Hollins handed over the fiver. 'Don't look so upset, Clocksy. At least she thought you'd say the right thing. She clearly has faith in you and the great institution that is marriage.'

'Yeah. I guess. But you're a knob.'

'I know.'

'Ray . . .'

'What?'

'If you go collect that fiver off of her, I'm in the shit, ain't I?'

'Yep. Should have said the right thing.'

'I'll give you a tenner if you keep yer trap shut. She'll murder me if she finds out.'

'How much?'

'Twenny, then.' Clocks screwed his face up and shook his head. 'Come on. Twenny.'

'Make it fift—'

All three turned their heads toward the radio operator of Mike One, who was talking into the mouthpiece, voice raised. Richie Bradburn's door was open wide. He'd been sitting in the car, monitoring the radio for calls and drinking coffee. Hollins shook the remains of his drink onto the ground and jogged over. He could tell something was up by the tone of his partner's voice.

'Show Mike One attending,' said Bradburn. He put the radio back into its cradle on the dashboard and lobbed his polystyrene cup into an open bin. 'David! Urgent assistance!'

Hollins broke into a run. Paterson and Clocks chucked their cups and joined him. All three piled into the car.

Hollins started the car at the same time as Bradburn hit the two-tones and lights. The radio was crackling with voices of other units all responding to the assistance call.

'What we got?' said Paterson.

'Not sure. Two of our boys called for help. Gone to a domestic. Sounds bad. Lots of shouting and screaming in the background.'

Hollins gunned the engine and pushed Mike One out of the yard and into the night streets. He slung a left into Queen Elizabeth Street, another into Tower Bridge Road and then accelerated, swerving around the traffic that was busy pulling over and out of their way.

'Mike Delta from Mike One. ETA four minutes,' said Bradburn into his radio.

'*Thank you, Mike One,*' said the CAD operator. '*For your info, I can't raise the officers at scene.*'

'Understood,' said Bradburn.

Hollins shot through the traffic lights at Tooley Street and floored it just as the lights at the junction with Druid Street turned red against him. From the left, a vehicle started to pull away on the amber. He kept going.

Bradburn flinched as the car coming in on his left swung a last-second hard right and missed Mike One by a foot. Hollins kept the car straight.

'Fuck me, son!' said Clocks from the back seat. 'That was bit close.'

Hollins said nothing.

'I know it's an urgent shout but if you get us killed, we're not gonna be any use to anyone, are we?'

'Shh,' was the only sound Hollins made.

'Shh? Did you just fuckin' *shh* me? Or was that the delayed sound of your pants fillin' up at the stupid fuckin' thing you just did?'

'Sir . . .' Hollins's eyes stayed glued to the road. 'With respect, shut up. I'm concentrating.'

Clocks looked over at Paterson, who was grinning. 'What you smilin' at?'

'Nothing.'

'Yes you are. Let's 'ave it, then.'

'It's just the cheek of it.'

'What? Cheek of what?'

'Cheek of you telling a Class One advanced driver how to drive.'

'Someone's got to.'

'Maybe—'

Hollins threw the car into a hard right, pushing Paterson into Clocks and squashing him up against the door. Clocks's head banged against the window and he let out a yelp.

'Fuck! Will you slow down?' Clocks yelled. 'I've banged me nut!'

Hollins ignored him.

'As I was saying,' said Paterson.

'Mike Delta. Two minutes out,' said Bradburn, ignoring the conversation in the back.

'You're having a go at an advanced driver when you drive like shit.'

Clocks looked genuinely hurt. 'Shit? Me?'

'Yeah, you. Remember France? You stacked a three-million-pound car.'

'Not my fault,' said Clocks. He looked out of the window. 'You were there. Snail jumped out at me. Nothing I could do,' he mumbled.

'Sirs,' said Hollins. 'Again. With respect. Shut up. You're like an old married couple bickering on in the back. I can't think.'

Clocks wobbled his head. 'Alright. Don't go on.'

'Mike One on scene,' said Bradburn into the radio. He pushed his door half-open and readied himself to bail out once the car stopped. Paterson and Clocks did likewise.

'Where we goin'?' said Clocks.

'Top floor,' said Bradburn.

'Bollocks! It's always the top floor,' said Clocks shaking his head.

The car skidded to a halt and all four leaped out and broke into a run. Paterson was first to reach the stairwell, followed by Bradburn then Hollins. Clocks was last.

Paterson took the stairs two at a time and was on the fourth-floor balcony in less than a minute, running toward the commotion. He saw the neighbours crowding around the door, a look of horror on one or two faces. 'Police! Move!'

The small group parted as he hurtled toward them. One man raised his hand. 'Be careful, mate! Careful! I think he's got a knife!'

Paterson drew up to the door and poked his head inside. He saw a figure lying face down in what he took to be the living room, and the legs of another whose torso was obscured by the door. He stepped in.

Bradburn and Hollins rushed in behind him. Paterson held up his hand to stop them. He inched forward toward the living room. 'Police!' he shouted into the stillness.

A panting Johnny Clocks made it into the hallway. 'Ray! Careful!' He fell against the wall to catch his breath.

Hollins looked back out at the neighbours. 'Who's in here?' he said to a woman.

'Dunno, love. Whoever it was, no one ain't come this way out.'

'Guv! Suspect still inside!' he called to Paterson.

Paterson nodded and edged forward. With his senses sharp, he drew level with a staircase on his left. To the right, a door was closed. He was comfortable in passing it; anyone inside would have to make a noise to open the door and it would take them a second or two. That was all the time the uniforms and Clocks would need to be on any assailant.

Slowly, he approached the living room door and craned his neck left and right to see around it for a view inside. The body on the floor prevented him kicking the door open.

Moving closer gave him a view he did not want to see. Both bodies were uniformed police officers. He grimaced and swallowed hard.

Ahead of him were the bare legs of a woman, her feet pointing outward among the wreckage. She was either unconscious or dead. His money was on the latter. 'Fuck!' he whispered to himself. Cautiously, he entered sideways, his back to the wall. He stepped over the first body. A quick glance around the room showed him that it was empty of an assailant.

From outside came the sound of several two-tone sirens. Extra help was coming. He heard feet running along the balcony. The extra help was seconds away.

'Three bodies. No suspect,' he said. 'Let's get more help here. We need to search this place from top to bottom. You two,' he said to the crew of Mike One, 'stay out of there. Crime scene. No one goes in, understood?'

Paterson was aware that these two experienced officers knew the ropes but the last thing he wanted was for them to see their two dead colleagues and definitely not like this. There would be time for grief and rage later.

Clocks stood in the hallway watching Paterson and controlling a new group of uniformed officers desperate to get inside and help their colleagues. 'Wait! Just wait, boys.' The tinkling sound of glass breaking followed by a loud bang came from somewhere upstairs. Clocks turned and looked up into the darkened stairwell for a second before charging up it. 'Window! He's runnin'!'

Paterson pushed Hollins and Bradburn aside. 'Get units outside. Surround the block! John . . . wait!'

At the top of the stairs, Clocks held his forearms in front of his face and body, a trick Paterson had showed him to protect himself against anyone swinging a knife or bat at him. Satisfied that was not going to happen, he darted toward the nearest door. It was open. Paterson was right behind him.

'Careful, John.'

Clocks gave a single nod then stepped inside. 'Oh, fuck me blind . . .'

'What?'

'Dead kid. Move!'

They turned and headed toward the next room, another bedroom. Paterson pushed Clocks aside and entered. It was a child's nursery. A window was wide open and a raggy net curtain fluttered in the breeze. He ran toward it oblivious to the room and its contents. He thrust his head through the open window and looked out onto a small, thin roof bordered by a low wall. Although small, it was wide enough for a human to traverse. In the distance, a figure was running with two dogs keeping pace. Paterson climbed onto the dressing table that stood underneath the window, ready to give chase.

'Oh no. No, no, no, no, no. No! God no!'

Alarmed at his friend's voice, Paterson turned to an ashen-faced Clocks. He followed his gaze into the small cot. His legs wobbled at the sight of a baby lying in a pool of blood, an ugly red gash across its throat.

'Oh, fuck.' He pushed his hair back tight against his head, struggling to take in all that had occurred in this small two-bedroomed flat. The two men looked at each other, helpless, neither knowing quite what to do. A few seconds passed then Paterson lifted his head, his face impassive, his eyes dark. He turned away from Clocks and the baby and scrambled out onto the roof.

Clocks ran to the window. 'Ray! Ray! The fuck . . .' It didn't matter where he was going, Clocks was going with him. He scrambled onto the dresser and called out. 'Get up here! Need some 'elp!' And then he was gone.

CHAPTER THREE

Paterson ran after the escaping silhouette, oblivious to the danger. One slip would see him tumble over the low wall that edged the side of the roof to his death, sixty feet below. The thought never entered his head. All he cared about was catching the running man and his two dogs.

* * *

'Ray! Fuck's sake, be careful!' Clocks eased his way out onto the roof. To his left, Paterson was running fast. He looked down and to his right and saw the small figures of his colleagues dashing about in the street below. Two ambulances had now arrived, their crews frantically setting up gurneys for transporting the injured. A thought flashed through his mind: *We're way beyond that, fellahs.*

* * *

The suspect was a good hundred yards ahead of Paterson. He watched in amazement as the man ran atop the low wall, bypassing the roof altogether. The wall was less than a foot wide, yet the man was running as if he was on solid ground.

The only person he knew with that sort of ability and nerve was Liam Bailey, the White Ghost. What he wouldn't give to have Bailey with him now.

Paterson could see a wall ahead of him — the end of the block. There was nowhere else for the man to go but up and over the pitched roof to his left. He doubted he would be able to get a grip. Rain had started to fall and the tiles would be slippery. Too slippery to take a man running up them.

This is it, then. Nowhere left to run, you bastard. Just the dogs to contend with first. Then I'm coming for you.

No sooner had the thought passed through his mind than his mouth fell open and he slowed his pace. The man carried on running. And running. And ran straight off the edge of the roof. The dogs followed suit. None of them broke their stride. Paterson sped up again until he was at the edge. He peered over. Ten feet below him, the suspect was running again, dogs in tow.

Paterson looked on as the man put distance between them.

He'd long had a fear of heights but had worked hard to overcome it. For the most part he had, but to jump down from this height agitated him.

Clocks caught up with Paterson and huffed. 'Where's 'e gawn then?'

Paterson ignored him, weighing up his chances of landing badly against his rage and desire to catch this man. Clocks took a tentative look over the low wall.

'Yeah, right. Fuck that. That ain't 'appenin'.'

Paterson climbed onto the wall in front of him.

'Ray! What'cha doin'? Get the fuck down 'ere.'

'He's mine, John.' Paterson took a couple of deep breaths.

'Don't be a twat! Get offa there 'fore you fall.'

Paterson stepped off the wall.

'Ray!'

He landed heavily and forced his body to fall sideways against the pitched roof. He righted himself and took off again.

* * *

11

Oh, you silly-born bastard! Clocks said to himself. *You think I'm doin' that, you've got another think comin', me ol' son. Hmm, hmm. Ain't doin' that. Fuck no.*

Clocks watched his friend race off into the darkness. 'Ah, bollocks. No good'll come of this, I fuckin' know it. Still, what's a girl to do, eh?' He sat on the wall and swung his legs over. He turned himself sideways and lowered himself until he was hanging off it by his fingertips. His feet scrabbled for any sort of purchase on the wall.

'This is a bad id—' His fingers gave up the fight and he dropped. He landed heavily on his feet and banged his head against the roof as he fell sideways. 'Shit!' He pulled himself upright and turned around. There was no sign of Paterson. He broke into an awkward, unbalanced run, making sure to keep himself away from the edge.

* * *

Paterson ran as fast as he could, but he couldn't get near his man, who had now opened up a good two-hundred-yard lead ahead of him. He took comfort in the fact this chase would have to end soon. There weren't that many blocks left to run and he doubted that this man, as agile as he was, was going to jump to the ground from this height. He'd get him.

The man it seemed, had other ideas. He stopped, turned and looked in Paterson's direction. 'Stop him!' he said. The dogs dropped low and took off toward Paterson. They were fast. *Very* fast.

'Oh, fuck!' Paterson reached instinctively for his side-arm. He didn't have it.

The dogs closed in.

A hundred yards.

Seventy-five.

Paterson saw them more clearly now. Face like a German Shepherd, but smaller. He tore off his jacket, wrapped it around his left arm and drew back his right fist.

Thirty yards.

Paterson took a sideways stance. This was going to be bad.

Ten yards.

He dropped into a crouch.

The first dog leaped at him. Its jaws clamped down on his padded forearm. He threw himself backwards against the pitched roof seconds before the second dog launched itself toward him. It failed to find its mark.

Paterson kicked out and, mid-air, caught the dog square in the ribs, sending it flying off the roof. The man let out a painful scream as he watched his dog sail off the building and crash to the ground.

Paterson was still in trouble. The dog that had clamped onto his arm was growling and tugging at it. He pulled himself up straight and punched the dog in the head. No effect. He hit it again. The dog bit down harder. He yelled out in pain. This thing was not going to let him go.

A sharp whistle from the man caused the dog to immediately release him. It turned and ran toward its master. Paterson looked on as the man turned and stepped off the building. Without hesitation, the dog leaped off behind him.

Clocks came half trotting, half walking along the balcony. Paterson was unravelling the jacket from his arm.

'You alright, mate?' said Clocks.

Paterson examined his arm. Faint teeth marks were clearly visible and it would bruise, but the jacket had done its job and saved both skin and bone from breaking.

He nodded. 'I'll live.'

''Ere. Did I see a flyin' dog or was I imaginin' things?'

Paterson peered over the roof. The dog lay dead on the concrete.

'You did. The other one had my arm.'

'Fuck!'

'Fuck, indeed.'

'Did it bite yer?'

'No. It brought me one of its toys to play with.'

'Aw. They're cute like that. Was it a teddy?'

'Come on.' Paterson broke into a half run. Reaching the edge where the man had jumped, he looked for him on the street below. He shook his head. 'Bastard's gone, John. Gone. Thought I had him.'

'Well, you might 'ave got 'im if you weren't playin' about with 'is little friends. I mean, I know you like a dog. Gawd knows you've 'ad more than your fair share of ol' bow-wows in yer time. P'raps they thought they'd get their own back an' 'ave you for a change.'

Paterson sighed. 'I'm going to get a shit ton of dog jokes now, aren't I?'

'There is that possibility, yes. Come on. We best get back to the nick and set everything up to catch this nutter. I think one of these windows leads to the old dryin' rooms.'

'Drying rooms?'

'Yeah. These old flats 'ad a large roof space, bit like an attic, with washin' lines in 'em. People would come up with their wet washin' and 'ang it up to dry. We'll be able to get down the stairs, 'opefully.'

'Sounds like a plan.'

'Doesn't it?' Clocks turned away, patted his thigh and whistled. 'C'mon, Raymie. There's a good boy. Gooood booooyy.'

CHAPTER FOUR

Paterson was seated at his desk and on his second cup of strong coffee when Johnny Clocks poked his head around the office door.

'Gang's all 'ere, guv.'

Paterson nodded. 'Let me finish this.'

Clocks held his hand up. 'Take yer time. They'll all be fannyin' about for a few minutes anyway.' He closed the door behind him.

Paterson rubbed his forehead. The second he closed his eyes, the whole crime scene flashed in front of him. Each room, each body and then the rooftop chase. He shook his head. *How is someone that confident? That sure of their footing sixty feet up?*

Nothing made sense about tonight. He drained the coffee cup, checked his watch: 11.48 p.m. He rose from his seat and stepped out into the main office to an unusually subdued team of detectives. He was aware that Clocks would have given them a basic heads up when he called them in from home. Now he had to tell them the horrific news.

'Right, you lot!' Clocks said. 'Phones on silent, gather round, notebooks out. This is gonna be a bloody long night for us all. Before we begin, a big welcome back to Jackie. Good to see you back with us, luv. Not good to see you failed to make the teas for everyone, but it's yer first day back with us so I'll forgive yer. This time.'

Jackie Hartnett, who'd been on extended sick leave after being stabbed in the throat, smiled at Clocks and gave him the finger. At the time of her assault, Paterson and Clocks both thought they'd lost her, but she somehow clung to life until the surgeons took over that responsibility. Three operations later, her voice had recovered to some degree but it was still painful if she overused it. Psychologically, she still had a fair way to go.

'Yeah, welcome back, Jack,' said Paterson. 'Straight into the fire, eh?'

The detectives shuffled around in their seats, pulled out their pens and flicked open their notebooks.

Paterson picked up the remote control of the large monitor that hung from the back wall. 'Okay, then. First . . . evening all. Apologies for pulling you away from your families, but we have a really bad situation here. I don't know what Clocksy's told you, but we have ourselves a five-murder crime scene. We were standing in the yard chatting to the crew of Mike One when we got an urgent assistance shout. We piled in the back and went for the ride.

'When we got there, it was all over. We found five bodies. Two in the doorway to the living room, and this woman —' Paterson clicked a button on the remote — 'whom we have yet to positively identify.'

'Jesus!' said Michael 'Monkey' Harris. 'Is that . . . is that what I think it is?'

Paterson nodded. 'If you're thinking it's a crucifix jammed into her chest, you'd be right. Can't be sure yet, but it was most likely what killed her.'

'I'm not fucking surprised.' Monkey began scribbling in his notepad.

'She had a couple of kids in the flat. A small boy, looked to be about six, seven maybe.' *Click.* 'Murdered in his bed.'

'Oh, fuckin' hell,' said Ronnie 'Dusty' Doneghan. Sticking out of the child's throat was another crucifix.

'The initial forensic report tells me it was rammed in with such force, it came out of his neck. Don't get too many crosses with a pointed end. This one had.'

There was a lot of shaking heads.

Click.

'And . . . and a . . .' His voice faltered. 'A baby. Probably less than a year old, I would guess.'

The detectives, battle-scarred veterans, all grimaced. Of all the crimes police officers have to deal with, the murder of a baby is the worst. A child killer is the one thing they will willingly abandon their families and social life for and will move heaven and earth to find.

Paterson flashed up the picture of the baby. A few officers fought to hold back tears at the sight.

'As I said . . . a long night ahead of us.'

'Hang on, guv. You said *five* bodies. Who's the other two?'

Paterson looked over at Clocks. It was obvious from the question that Clocks hadn't told them when he called. He sighed.

'Unfortunately, we lost two of our own. PCs Summers and Johnson.'

Now the room was ready to lose it altogether.

Monkey Harris threw his pen onto the desk. 'Fuck! Fuck!'

'Did you know them, Monkey?' said Paterson.

He wiped his face with his hand. 'Summers. Good man. Jesus.'

Paterson pressed the button and looked at the photo that showed the interior of the room in its entirety. Summers and Johnson could clearly be seen. One face down, one face up. Both with knives sticking out of them. Monkey closed his notebook and his eyes.

'We don't know for sure what happened here, but they were the first officers on scene. Initial statements from neighbours say that they forced entry after hearing all the commotion from inside. The flat went quiet when they broke in and they never came back out.

'Obviously we don't know for sure what happened in there, but my best guess is that they were rooted to the spot at the scene in front of them and this bastard crept up behind. Summers was stabbed in the neck. Johnson must have turned and got it in the throat.'

'We know who this prick is, guv?' Jackie's voice was deep and raspy.

Paterson shook his head. 'Turned out, though, that he was still in the flat. He bailed out onto the roof and we both went after him.' He nodded toward Clocks. 'Didn't get near him. Man had no fear of heights. Anyone know Leman House?'

A few heads nodded.

'Well, on the roof, to the right is a low wall that I would think acts as some form of protection from stepping off the edge if anyone is doing any sort of repair work on the roof. This bastard ran along the top of the wall. He didn't falter once. That takes extreme nerve and balance to pull off.'

'An' 'e 'ad two fuck-off, crazy-arse dogs too,' Clocks piped in. 'Those mad fuckers were right off their nuts an' all. Where 'e went, they went. An' they didn't skip a beat neither.'

'True. This man jumped from one roof to another without hesitation and the dogs did the same. I tried to follow but . . .'

'The suspect set the dogs on the guv. When I came runnin' 'e'd treated one of 'em to a flyin' lesson. The other was runnin' away.'

'Not before it tried to eat my arm,' Paterson reminded him.

'Dogs? Who takes a coupla dogs with 'em while they go out murdering?' said DC Tommy Gunn.

'P'raps he couldn't get a sitter for 'em,' said Clocks. 'Who the fuck knows?'

'What sort of dogs were they, guv?' said Monkey.

'One of the uniforms on scene, a dog lover, said they were Belgian Malinois.'

'Fuck's that when it's at home?'

'That,' said Clocks. 'Is a fuckin' lunatic of a dog, Monkey, my son. Watched a coupla vids on YouTube on the way back to the office. Bastards can run up walls, jump about fifteen feet in the air and don't know what fear means by the looks of it. Basically, it's the dog the Devil would own if he wanted to be a right 'ard bastard an' try to start a punch up 'ere in Bermondsey on a Friday night.'

Paterson grinned. 'Yeah. They're a tad on the athletic side. Anyway. The murdered officers, they were just in the wrong place at the wrong time, poor bastards. What we need to know, is what this man was doing in that flat. Why did he pick this family to butcher? Were they related? Ex-hubby? Father of these kids? If so, what pissed him off so much that he'd go to this level of barbarity?'

'Monkey. Get on to the local nut'ouses an' see if one of 'em didn't come 'ome for 'is tea tonight,' said Clocks.

'Shouldn't call them nuthouses, sir.' DC Colin Yorkshire was the most disliked but, without question, the most competent detective Paterson had on the squad. It was a constant source of amusement to the squad that DC Yorkshire actually came from Yorkshire and was immediately given the nickname 'Tetley' after the famous tea manufacturer based in that part of the world.

Clocks rolled his eyes. 'I know I shouldn't, Tetley. You're right. Monkey . . . I want you to check on all the homes for the *mentally bewildered* an' see if one of 'em didn't come 'ome for 'is tea tonight. That alright, Tetley, you politically correct fucker, you?'

'Not really, no. But it'll do, sir. It's a slight improvement.'

'Oh, good. I do love to improve meself.' Clocks faked a loud cough and finished it off with the word 'wanker'.

Yorkshire eyed his boss with contempt.

'Sir?' said Jackie. 'The use of crucifixes . . . do we know if *she* was particularly religious? Anything around the flat that would suggest she was? More crucifixes on the walls, pictures of Jesus, that sort of thing?'

'Don't think they 'ad cameras in Jesus's day, luv,' said Clocks.

Jackie shook her head. 'Paintings. I meant paintings.'

Paterson shrugged. 'No idea. I didn't notice anything too over the top when we were there, but we were a bit tucked up. Why?'

'Well, clearly the whole thing smacks of having a religious element, don't you think?'

'You thinking a religious nutter, then, Jackie?' said Doneghan.

'Not unreasonable, is it?' she said.

'Hmm,' said Paterson. 'Not a bad place to start. Okay, everyone. Add churches and any other places we can find that has something to do with the Christian faith.'

'What about other religions?' said Clocks.

'Not too many of them are cross wavers, are they?'

'Dunno. Don't know much about religion 'cept that it's all a bunch of stupid little fairy stories that kings made up in collusion with the church to control the masses. Helped to keep 'em in poverty an' servitude while promisin' 'em a better "afterlife" if they also coughed up a good lump of their wages.'

The room went silent.

'Anyway . . .' said Paterson. 'We'll stick to the Christians first and widen up if we draw a blank. The religious angle is a good starting point. Good to have you back, Jackie. We missed you.'

She smiled.

'We did indeed, babe,' said Clocks. 'Now, be a good gel an' go put the kettle on. You must be well out of practice by now.'

CHAPTER FIVE

Paterson's backside had barely touched his office seat when his desk phone rang. He picked up the receiver and listened to the female voice on the other end.

'Where?' he said. 'When?' He nodded and slammed the phone down. Jumping out of his seat, he ran for the door. 'Everyone! He's been spotted! Move it!' He ran past them all and fished his cars keys out of his pocket.

'The fuck . . . ?' said Clocks.

The office exploded into action. Officers made a grab for their coats, books and car keys before scrambling for the door. The entire place emptied as they crashed their way down the old concrete stairs of Tower Bridge Police Station to burst out into the yard and jump into their cars.

'Grange Road!' Paterson shouted.

Clocks jumped in with Paterson. 'Whereabouts in Grange Road?'

'Spotted on top of Grange House. Complete with dog.' Paterson started up his car and slammed the accelerator to the floor. His tyres skidded on the wet tarmac before they bit.

Clocks hit a button to switch on the grille lights then dialled the control room on his phone. 'DI Clocks 'ere. That shout to Grange 'ouse. We're on our way.'

21

'*DI Clocks, thank you.*' It was the voice of civilian radio operator Ross Brand.

'Anyone else goin', tell 'em *silent approach*. No sirens. Nothing.'

'*Understood, sir.*' Brand got straight on the radio. '*All units attending Grange House . . . Silent approach requested by DI Clocks. Acknowledge.*'

'*Mike Two, received.*'

'*Mike Delta Four Five, received.*'

'*Mike Delta Two. Understood.*'

'*Be careful, sir,*' said Brand.

'Cheers, Russ,' said Clocks. 'Not me you need to be worried about, though. Keep me on the line.'

Paterson hurtled across the first and second junctions he came to, overtaking a few cars as he went. On the wrong side of the road, he narrowly missed a container lorry heading toward him. Clocks stared impassively out of the front window. He had faith in Paterson's driving ability.

Paterson threw the car left, then right, sped on for half a mile, kissed the brakes more often than he wanted to and narrowly missed a post office van that was backing out of a side street. Clocks killed the grille lights and spoke into the phone again.

'Russ . . . any update?'

'*Informant says, he's just standing on the roof, and sort of gesturing, like one of those WWF wrestlers. Every so often he roars.*'

'Roars? What is 'e? A fuckin' lion?'

'Probably still got the hump because I killed his devil dog,' said Paterson. He pulled the car against the kerb. Both men climbed out and looked up. Their suspect was standing defiant, arms wide and yelling at them in gibberish.

'Show us on scene and dealin', Russ.' Clocks hung up. 'What's he sayin'?'

Paterson shrugged. 'Dunno. Perhaps it's tongues.'

Clocks looked at him. 'What? What's tongues, then, when it's at 'ome? What language is that? What country is that from then?'

Paterson sighed. 'Tongueania.'

Clocks frowned. 'What? Well, where's *that*, then, when it's at 'ome?'

'It's near the Russian border. Turn left at Australia.'

Clocks squinted at him. 'Yeah? Never 'eard of it.'

'Not many people have heard of it. It's only small. To be honest, so far it's only me. And now you. So, keep it quiet or everyone will want to go there and fuck it up as a holiday destination.'

'You're tuggin' me todger, ain'tcha?'

'Yep. I am indeed.'

'There's no such place is there?'

'Nope.'

A middle-aged man in a security guard uniform hurried over to them. 'You police?'

'No,' said Clocks. 'We're the fire brigade in plain clothes. We're the ones you call when you don't want the fire to know we're 'ere.'

The guard pulled a face at him. 'Alright. Only asked, mate. Sorry.'

'Take no notice of him,' said Paterson. 'We've had a bad night so far and it's either going to get a lot worse or a lot better depending on if we manage to nick this guy.'

The rest of the squad joined them and they all crowded around the security guard eager to hear what he had to say.

'How'd 'e get up there, mate?' said Clocks.

'Dunno. Was doing me rounds and I noticed that one of the windows on the first floor had been smashed.'

'Well, that'll be it, won't it?'

The guard glared at Clocks. 'Is he always this rude, mate?' he said to Paterson.

'Oh, yeah. Don't take it personal. How do we get up onto the roof?'

'Wasn't being rude, mate,' said Clocks. 'Just sayin', is all. Everyone's so soddin' touchy these days.'

'I'll show you,' said the guard. 'C'mon.'

Clocks saw Monkey Harris bend down and pick up a brick. 'What yer doin' Monkey?'

'Wonderin' if I could chuck this at him. Knock him down from there.'

Clocks stopped and looked at him. 'What? 'Ang on . . . You tellin' me you can chuck that brick up three floors an', with deadly accuracy, 'it 'im on the nut and knock him off the roof? He's not a fuckin' coconut, is 'e? We're not at the funfair, for chrissakes.' Clocks shook his head. The others in the group all chuckled at the exchange.

'You're on another planet, mate,' said Clocks as he walked away still shaking his head. 'I think you need a bit of the ol' early retirement, cocker.' He followed Paterson inside.

'Up these stairs here,' said the guard. 'Turn left at the top and when you get to the third floor you'll see a metal ladder attached to the wall. Climb up and open the hatch. That'll put you straight on the roof.'

* * *

In the street, uniformed police cars were pulling up.

'Got a plan, Monkey? Other than chucking bricks at him?' said Yorkshire.

Monkey whirled around. 'Funny little prick, ain't yer? You got a plan, then?'

Yorkshire nodded. One of the officers stepped out of his vehicle and Yorkshire approached him. 'Officer . . . get on the radio and call the fire brigade for us. Tell them we need a vehicle with some sort of high-access ladder.'

'On it,' said the PC.

Yorkshire returned to the group. 'That might do it.'

Monkey shook his head. *Cocky little fucker.* 'Right. Spread out. Take a plod each with you. I want four around the back of the building in case he gives the guv's the slip. Nick 'im if you can but bear in mind how dangerous he is.'

The team nodded their agreement and set off to grab a uniformed officer each.

'We going in with them, Monkey?' said Doneghan, nodding toward the door.

24

'Nope. We'll hang fire here just in case the fucker makes it out.'

'What? Against the Met's best two psycho's? I don't think so.'

'Fair point,' said Monkey.

'Can I ask you a question?'

Monkey looked over at him. 'Yeah. Course you can.'

'Were you *seriously* going to lob that brick at him?'

Monkey chuckled. 'Fuck off!'

CHAPTER SIX

Clocks pointed to the hatch. 'You go first, mate.'

'What?' said the guard.

'Go on. Chop, chop. Step lively, son.'

'I'm not goin' up there.'

'Why not? You're the security for this place, ain'tcha?'

'Yeah, but they don't pay me to go up after lunatics.'

'That's a fair point, mate. I don't suppose they do. Right. Step aside. Show the dog the rabbit.'

Paterson's phone rang. 'Go on, Dusty,' he said. 'Okay. Hang fire.'

'Whassup?' said Clocks.

'The fire brigade's here.'

'Yeah? The ol' smash an' squirt boys. Who called them?'

'Don't know, but they're pulling up as we speak.'

'What d'you wanna do?'

'Makes sense to see what they can offer us. Might have a big ladder we can go up on.'

Clocks nodded. 'Yeah. Maybe. And with a bit of luck our man can kick us off the fuckin' thing when we get near him.'

Paterson headed back to the stairs. 'You're always so negative, John. What else can we use?'

Clocks cocked his head for a second. 'Goddit. 'Oses! Big ol' 'oses.' He jogged after Paterson. 'Bagsy I get to blow the fucker off the roof.'

Paterson started down the stairs the same way he came up, two at a time. 'Uh, uh. I'm the boss. I get first shot.'

Clocks sighed and tried jumping the stairs three at a time. After a few stumbles, he caught up with Paterson, who was talking to the senior fire officer, Matt Ridley. Paterson brought him up to speed and put the fire hose proposition to him.

Ridley shook his head. 'I can't let you use the hose on him, boys.'

Clocks frowned. 'Why's that?'

'Health and safety.'

Paterson looked at him, unsure if he was hearing him right. 'Health and safety? Did you not hear me or understand what I've just told you about this man?'

'I'm sorry. It's more than my job's worth. You could kill him.'

'And?' said Clocks. Paterson glanced over at him. He could see Clocks wasn't taking this refusal too well.

'What d'you mean, *and*?' said Ridley.

'And? If 'e falls, 'e falls. Who gives a shit? You give a shit, guv?'

Paterson shook his head. 'I don't give a — what is it you say, John? — a tiny rat's arse if he falls.'

'That'll kill him.'

'Well, no. The sudden stop at the bottom will but not the water or the fall. So, technically, it'll be the ground that kills 'im.'

'Look. I'll do my job and get you up there. You do your job and talk to him.' The man's face began to redden. 'Get him to surrender. Okay?'

'Jesus wept,' said Clocks. 'What is this world comin' to? I remember a time us emergency services used to back each other up, no question.'

'Yeah, well, the seventies are long gone.'

'An' don't I bleedin' know it.'

Paterson grinned. 'We don't mean it, mate. We're just pissed off with this man and what he's done. We won't kill him. Jesus.'

Ridley eyed Paterson up. He didn't look convinced.

'Right,' said Clocks. 'Sort out a ladder for me, then.'

'Do you one better than that. How's about an aerial appliance?'

'A what?'

'An aerial appliance.'

Clocks looked confused. 'What's that? Sounds like some sort of dildo for that Disney mermaid. But, thinkin' about it, where the fuck would she stick it?'

Paterson turned around. He didn't want Ridley to see him laughing if he could help it.

'Actually,' said Ridley, 'what I meant was, putting you both up on a platform. That's what an aerial appliance is.' He called over to his crew and told them to prepare the platform.

'Sweet,' said Clocks. 'Always fancied a go in one of them.'

The two colleagues walked toward the fire engine. A very short, rotund fireman was pressing different buttons to turn the platform around.

Clocks spotted him straightaway. 'Oh, 'ave a look, Ray. It's only Bridget the Midget. I wondered what 'appened to 'er.'

Paterson chuckled. 'John. Don't.'

'What?'

'You can't say *midget*.'

'I just did.'

'I know. But you shouldn't. It's offensive.'

'Okay then. Dwarf. That better?'

'Not really, no. They prefer to be called *little people*.'

'Do they? I'da thought that was a bit too obvious.'

Clocks fell silent.

'What are you thinking, John? Spit it out.'

'Well, I was thinkin' that's me fucked in the sweetie shops, then, innit?'

'What?'

'I mean, I like a bag of Midget Gems from time to time. But, according to the new world we live in, it seems that I now 'ave to ask for a bag of little people gems. I think I'm likely to slip up there an' probably offend the shopkeeper. Especially if 'e's got any midgets — sorry — little people in 'is family.'

Paterson saw the fireman glare over at them.

'Heads up, John. He's not happy.'

'I can see that. What one is 'e, then? Doc? Sneezy?'

Paterson burst out laughing. 'You bastard!'

Clocks grinned all over his face.

'All right, lads? What's so funny, then?' said the fireman. Both men shook their heads.

'Nothing,' said Paterson. 'Why?'

'Just curious. I got the impression you were taking the piss out of me for some reason. Were you?'

'Hold up,' said Paterson. 'Why would we do that? Don't even know you, mate. Bit on the sensitive side there, fellah.'

'Well, he said something that made you laugh.'

'So? He makes me laugh about a lot of things. What makes you think it's about you? Could have been a million and one things we laughed about.'

'Oh, yeah. Would it have been the one about my height by any chance?'

Clocks rolled his eyes. 'What height's that? You ain't got none, 'ave yer?'

The fireman scowled at him.

'Look. To be honest, I did 'appen to notice you're a bit on the small side an', bein' the dick that I am, I remarked to my guv'nor 'ere, that I wondered if you're one of Snow White's mates.'

Paterson was horrified. *Oh no! Fucking hell, John . . .*

The fireman took his finger off the button. 'What'd you say to me, mate?'

'I said . . .'

'I heard what you said. You're fucking out of order.'

Clocks nodded. 'You're right, mate. I am an' I'm sorry, alright? It's just that it caught me on the 'op, you bein' a bit on the small side. Didn't mean to offend you but . . . 'Ere, serious question for yer . . . They done away with 'ow tall you've gotta be to get in these days? I thought you 'ad to be, like, six foot minimum to get into Trumpton.'

'Trumpton? The fuck is that?'

Clocks chortled. 'You're young ain'tcha? What are you? Under thirty, I'll bet. Used to be a TV show back in the . . . past. A kid's animated TV show. Trumpton was a little village with a fire brigade in it. They'd all line up and the guv'nor would do a roll call. Pugh, Pugh, Barney McGrew, Cuthbert, Dibble and Grub. Catchy little number when you're only two or three. Or forty-seven.'

'You know what, mate? You're an obnoxious prick. I'd keep your mouth shut before I fill it for you.'

Clocks smiled. 'Well, that ain't gonna be easy, is it? You can't fuckin' reach it for starters, can yer?'

The fireman turned on him. 'One more *fucking* word out of you and I swear to God . . .'

Paterson was on the point of losing it altogether.

Clocks held his hands up, palms out. 'Alright, take it easy, mate. Only funnin' with yer. I'm sorry. Look, we've got a little fellah like you in the nick. Only five foot five, 'e is, an' we all call 'im Laptop.'

The fireman stopped his move. 'What?'

'We call 'im Laptop'.

'Why?'

''Cos 'e's a small PC.'

Paterson lost it then. The fireman chuckled.

'Got some balls on you, mate,' he said. 'You don't know me, but you came straight out swinging. I like that.'

Paterson was busy wiping his eyes on his handkerchief.

'I'm sorry, fellah. It's been a rough night. I'm only joking with yer. No offence intended. Gotta 'ave a laugh, ain't yer?'

From above them, the man howled and set the dog off barking.

'Oh! I was 'avin' so much fun, I forgot about 'im. Can you get us up there, mate?'

'Yep. Two minutes and up you go.'

CHAPTER SEVEN

Paterson pulled himself together, folded the handkerchief and slipped it in the inside pocket of his jacket. 'Sometimes, Clocksy . . . sometimes you amuse me.'

Clocks smiled. 'I amuse you all the time, but you won't roll with it. Still a bit too bunched up in the ol' politically correct department. Don't worry though. I'll get you there if it's the last thing I do.'

Paterson nodded. 'I hope so, mate. Life must be a lot easier when you look at it the way you do.'

In fact, Clocks was worried about his friend. Truth be told, he'd been worried for a long time. His wife, Lyndsey, had spoken to him about Paterson's deteriorating behaviour a while back and he'd fobbed her off by saying that he was under immense pressure. It was true, of course. They both were. To cope, he'd started drinking and Paterson was sniffing the odd line of cocaine here and there. Marrying Lyndsey had straightened him up a bit, but he still had nightmares, night sweats and the odd, very well-hidden, panic attack. He used humour and the odd bout of gratuitous violence to cover up his insecurities, but they were there.

Paterson, though, had no one to go home to. No one to talk to, to unburden himself to. Since his wife was butchered by a serial killer, he'd had the odd casual relationship but nothing serious, and Clocks worried that he was slipping faster and faster down a very dangerous path. Their last case had pushed Clocks's worries to a new level. Paterson, frustrated that the villain he was chasing, an international organ trafficker, kept giving them the slip, took matters into his own hands and literally smoked her out. He had set fire to all the clinics she owned in India on a rampage that brought universal condemnation from everyone — except Clocks, who figured it was a smart and reasonable move under the circumstances.

But things dipped further south when Paterson hired a team of 'operatives' to assassinate the woman and her two business partners. What shocked Clocks most was the callousness in Paterson's demeanour. No qualms at all. The kill team broadcast the entire operation to Paterson's home TV and he calmly gave the order to kill all three without batting an eyelid.

That was the moment Clocks grasped the fact that his friend was becoming ever more dangerous and definitely homicidal, but he was unsure of how best to proceed. Paterson was his best friend. His brother. The only man he'd ever poured his heart out to, told him his deepest fears, his hopes and dreams. And they'd been through so much shit together, fought some of the worst villains this sick society had to offer and took on the authorities that did their best to have them arrested and sent to jail. They would happily die for each other. Friendships and loyalties rarely ran so deep, and Clocks just couldn't bring himself to see this man come to grief. Whatever happened to Paterson, it would never be by his hand. Never.

'You alright goin' up on this platform, Ray?'

'Yep. Why wouldn't I be?'

'I know you're not a fan of heights.'

'I'm alright. Better than I was. I've been working it out in my head. Got a few mind techniques in my bag of tricks. I chased this fucker along the roof, didn't I?'

'You did. Yeah. Okay. Fair enough.'

'Ready for you,' said Ridley.

Clocks looked up at the raving man and his barking dog. 'What *is* the plan when we get up there?'

Paterson shrugged. 'Throw him off, I suppose.'

CHAPTER EIGHT

Paterson set his jaw and fixed his eyes on the man. Younger than Paterson. Mid-to-late twenties. Athletic build. Long greasy hair, parted in the middle and hanging down across his face. His eyes were two dots of pure white. Contacts. Had to be. The nose was upturned, like a bat. Paterson had seen this before. Tape. A crude but effective way of changing the features. This man didn't want to be recognised.

The platform juddered and swayed into life and Paterson took several deep breaths as he and Clocks left the ground behind them. A couple of years before, he would have broken out in a sweat and his legs would have gone from under him. A lot of work on his fear had got him to the point where he had better control of himself now. He put his hands behind his back, copper-on-the-beat style. Clocks looked over the side, then back up at the man on the roof.

'Fuckin' 'ell, Ray! 'Ave a look at 'im! What the bleedin' 'ell is goin' on there?'

Paterson said nothing.

'Oi! Give it up, mate. There's nowhere fer you to go,' Clocks shouted.

The man crouched low, legs wide, and screamed at them in an unintelligible form of gibberish. Clocks grinned. A good old kicking it was, then.

34

The nearer they got to the roof, the more agitated the dog grew. The platform juddered to a halt, a foot or so lower than the roof. The dog went ballistic, barking excitedly and waiting for the command to jump at either one of them.

It never came. 'Quiet!' the man said, his voice low, harsh. He didn't need to shout to command his dog. It knew its place. Restless, the dog sat and watched, licking its mouth and never taking its eyes from Paterson.

The two men stared at each other, neither speaking.

'Oi, nut-nut!' said Clocks. 'Time to come down now, before I 'ave to climb over there and nick you.'

The man ignored him, fixated on Paterson. Clocks pulled out his phone and opened up the camera app. 'Oi! Say, "Who's a fuckwit?"' He snapped a couple of photos. The man continued to stare at Paterson.

'What you two doin'? Seein' who's got the maddest eyes?'

Both ignored him. The man rocked his head from side to side but his eyes remained still, burning into Paterson.

'Fuck me. Ray, you need to be careful 'ere. I read somethin' once that said that the way to get someone to fall in love with yer was to stare into their eyes for a bit longer than normal. Thirty seconds, I think it was. If that's true, you two are gonna be movin' in an' 'avin' a coupla kids together at this rate.'

The man's head turned slowly toward Clocks and then lunged at him sharply and hissed.

'Shit!' Clocks drew his fist back.

'What . . . are . . . *you*?' The man's voice was like a loud whisper, but guttural, almost demonic.

Clocks sniffed. 'What am I? That's a dumb-arse question, innit?' He tossed a pair of handcuffs next to the man's feet. 'I'm the bloke that's gonna fuck you up an' put you away for the rest of yer natural. Now, be a good nutter an' put those 'andcuffs on. Then we can drag you in 'ere, give you a fuckin' good clump, 'ave yer dog put down, an' then go an' get a big ol' fry-up in Wetherspoons. I'm bloody starvin' like Marvin. C'mon, let's 'ave yer.' Clocks beckoned him forward.

Saliva fell like strings of slimy glue from the man's mouth as he showed them his tongue. Paterson raised an eyebrow. Clocks grimaced.

'Fuckin' ell, geezer. What's that all about? Dribblin' all down yer chin. Disgustin', that is.'

The man turned back to Paterson, who was still staring, still with one eyebrow raised.

'What . . . are . . . *you*?' the man hissed at him.

'Me? Oh, I'm your worst fucking nightmare.'

The man smiled. More drool fell from his chin. 'What . . . are . . . you?'

'I am sin. You?'

Clocks was baffled. It was an odd thing to say, even for Paterson.

The man jerked upward to his full height before half bending and screaming. 'Devil!' He pointed a bloody finger at Paterson. 'I will wipe the filth from you. I . . . will . . . cleanse you, demon!'

Paterson nodded. 'That's nice of you. Shall we do that now? Come over here and you can try your luck.'

Eyes wide, the man rocked his head from side to side again. 'You will kneel before the Angel of Light, demon. Kneel!'

'Er, no,' said Paterson. 'That won't be happening. Not now. Not ever.'

Clocks backed up as far as he could go in the platform's cradle. This was really odd.

'I suggest you give yourself up before things get a bit tricky for you.'

'You would threaten me, Devil?'

'I don't usually. I'm more of a deliver-on-my-promises kind of guy but, in your case, yeah, I'm threatening you. Up to you which way this goes.'

'Ray . . .' said Clocks.

Paterson kept his eyes on his opponent. 'Not now, John. I'm busy getting the Angel of Light here to surrender.'

'Oh. Okay, then. Sorry. 'Ow's that goin'?'

'Not too well at the moment. I think it's going to take a bit longer than I first thought. We'll see.'

Clocks folded his arms. 'No rush. Take yer time.' He looked at the dog. 'Alright there, Fluffy? Won't be long before we have yer shot, yer vicious little bastard. Good boy.'

The man crouched low again and screeched at Paterson. 'Soon, Devil, soon!' Then he turned and ran. The dog ran with him.

'Oh, fuck!' said Clocks.

Paterson put one leg on the top of the cradle and pushed himself up and forwards, clearing the gap between cradle and roof with ease. He took off after the man. *Not this time, fucker.*

Clocks scrambled over the cradle and followed the two men.

This roof was flat. The man had no balance advantage here. Paterson closed in, reached out and grabbed the man's coat collar. The dog barked as his master slipped out of the jacket with ease and continued to run. Paterson threw the coat and ran on, eyes locked on his target.

The man suddenly leaped sideways off the roof. Paterson struggled to break his momentum but was able to see the man land and roll ten feet down the roof of another building. The dog followed, landing easily.

Without thinking, Paterson jumped. 'Fuck!' He hit the ground with a lot less elegance and fell forwards, tumbling to a halt up against a fire exit door. With a shake of his head, he pulled himself up and took off after the man again.

Chasing the man to the edge of the roof, he watched with a mixture of rage and amazement as once again, the man ran straight off the edge. But Paterson wasn't going to let this go. He did the same with no idea what was waiting for him below. It was a tree. He shut his eyes and braced for impact. Smashing through the thin branches he let out a large grunt after hitting his leg on a thicker branch. Tumbling on through the foliage he landed with a sickening thump onto his back.

Struggling for breath, bruised and shaken, he pulled himself upright and looked around for his man. It took a second to spot him disappearing around a corner. Realising he'd managed to escape the fall without breaking anything, Paterson stumbled after him.

Rounding the corner, he jerked to a halt. Crouched low, the man and his dog were waiting for him. Paterson saw why: he'd run himself into a dead end. Behind him, a solid brick wall, fifteen feet high with no way to climb it. Either side stood two deserted office blocks. Both had the ground-floor windows covered by solid steel plates. Each one bore bright yellow stickers: *Latham Security. 24 Hours.* Any drainpipes there may once have been had been broken and stolen long ago. A few old and rotted wooden doors lay at odd angles against one wall and two industrial bins stood against the other. Nowhere to climb. Nowhere to hide. Nowhere to run.

The dog growled and began to advance on him slowly, teeth bared, defending its master. Paterson looked around for a weapon of some sort. A discarded bottle lay on the ground barely a yard away. He snatched it up and smashed it.

The dog was closer, snarling, drooling. Paterson would only get one go at this. If he blew it, he was done for. The dog would tear him to shreds.

'Call it off!' he called. 'Don't make me kill it like I did the other one!'

'What is . . . the life . . . of a dog . . . to one like you, Devil?'

'I like dogs! Your two are a bit shit, though, got to admit. Not their fault. It's always the owner.' Paterson readied himself, crouching to stand his ground. The dog leaped. Paterson dropped onto his back and thrust the broken bottle upward. The dog shrieked as the glass raked its stomach. It landed and turned, in pain and now enraged, in a fight for its life, its entrails hanging out.

Covered in blood and intestine juice, Paterson was worried. He hadn't finished off the dog and, to face it, he had to turn his back on the man. The dog moved to its left, growling and whimpering as it eyed Paterson. Behind him, the man bellowed loudly.

Paterson's head snapped up as a police car, lights flashing, came screeching around the corner. It skidded to a halt and Johnny Clocks bailed out, running toward them with a Glock 17 in his hand.

The dog turned to face this new threat. Clocks kept coming and fired seven shots at the dog. Three hit it, killing it instantly.

'Down boy!' he shouted as he ran past Paterson.

Paterson turned and watched his partner running toward the man.

He fired. The man jumped to the side. Clocks's shot went wide. He fired again. The man jumped up onto an industrial bin, leaped onto a parked car, jumped off again and rolled across the pavement. Clocks fired again. Missed.

The man was up and running now, toward Paterson. Paterson threw the bottle down and grinned.

The man kept running, suddenly jumped high sideways, hit the wall with one foot and dodged past Paterson.

'Shit!'

Clocks fired again, narrowly missing Paterson. The shot hit the windscreen of the police car, splintering the safety glass into thousands of tiny pieces. 'Oops!' he said. The ashen-faced driver of the car sat stock still, his eyes wide, his mouth open, his body showered with glass.

'Sorry!' said Clocks as he and Paterson ran past him.

Clocks fired two more shots. Both missed, never coming close. The man scrambled up a wall. And then he was gone.

'Fuckety-fuck!' said Clocks. 'Where'd the bouncy little shit go?'

Paterson stared into the darkness and listened to the man's footsteps fading into the distance. 'Not where I was planning on sending him.'

CHAPTER NINE

The boys headed back toward their car. Paterson kept himself three steps ahead of Clocks. He got to his car, wrenched open the door, dropped down into his seat and slammed the door with a loud *thunk*. Clocks let himself in through the passenger side and closed the door gently. He looked across at his boss, who was staring out of the window, elbow on the arm rest and banging a knuckle against his teeth.

Clocks kept quiet for a change.

'Nearly got the fucker,' Paterson said through gritted teeth. 'Nearly had him.'

'We'll get 'im, Ray. They all come again, mate. You know that.'

'Hmm. Yeah. Trouble is, all the time he's out there, the bastard can kill again.'

'Well, we can't know that for sure. One thing at a time, eh?' Let's find out about all this God an' Devil stuff you two were chattin' about back on that platform. C'mon. What was that all about, then?'

'I was running with Jackie's theory that this is religiously motivated. To be honest with you, I was just trying to figure out which side of the equation he thinks he's on. The good or the bad.'

'God, yeah?' That's what 'e said, weren't it? Thinks 'e's an angel. Twat.'

'Lucifer was an angel, John. Cast out by God when he challenged his authority. Had the hump that God wasn't doing things the right way so branched out on his own. Well, not entirely on his own. Took a few of his mate angels with him. Caused the first war. The war in heaven.'

Clocks wrinkled his nose. 'War in Devon? When was that then?'

'Not Devon. Heaven, John. Heaven. Listen in.'

'I thought it sounded funny. I 'ad a vision of it all kickin' off 'cos they'd run out of pasties or cream teas or somethin'.' Clocks sniffed. 'I went there once when I was a kid. On me 'oliday, I was. Some shitty ol' caravan in a field near a sheer drop somewhere. D'you know the locals have all got webbed toes an' fingers?'

Paterson sighed.

'I'm serious, mate. It's always, *always*, rainin' there, and to survive the floods they evolved into part fish. Same as the people up north. Yorkshire, mostly. Where Tetley comes from. 'Ave you not noticed 'is 'ands? You 'ave a crafty peek when we get back to the nick. An' 'e smells of kipper. Dead giveaway, that is.'

Paterson shook his head. 'Anyway, let's leave Johnny Clocksville for a minute and get back to your question. Clearly, this man believes he's doing the work of God, so we've got to find out why he's doing that and what it was about the woman and her two children that caused him to do what he did to them.'

'And the two cops, of course.'

'I've already told you, I think they just happened to be in the wrong place at the wrong time and got in his way while he was trying to escape. He probably figured he couldn't overpower the two of them, maybe didn't want to even chance it and maybe didn't even want to try. Who knows how these people think? Lord knows we've dealt with enough of the mentally disturbed in our time.'

41

Clocks nodded. 'Hmm. So, look . . . all this runnin' and jumpin' and bouncing off walls an' shit. 'Ow's 'e manage to do all that?'

'Parkour.'

'Come again?'

'Parkour. Don't tell me you've not heard of it.'

Clocks shrugged. 'I 'ave not. You'd think I would 'ave by the sound of your incredulous tone, an' yet I ain't.'

'Okay. It's an activity of moving rapidly through an area, usually in cities and towns, and negotiating obstacles by running, jumping and climbing. Did you ever see James Bond? The one where at the beginning he chases after the bomber and they end up on a building site. The bloke he's chasing there jumps about all over the place?'

'Oh, yeah. Yeah, I remember that. Bit lively, that fellah.'

'Well, that's parkour. It's from the French and means *obstacle course*.'

'French? Sounds about right, dunnit? Trust them to find new and improved ways to run away.'

'Don't start on that again, John.'

'What? I'm just sayin'.'

'Leave it be, mate. We have to get back to the nick and sort this shit out.'

'Can we just quickly swing by the car whose window I shot out? Wanna see 'ow the driver's doin.' Looked a bit shaken.'

'Not surprised. You could've killed him.'

'Yeah, I know. Think I should say sorry?'

Paterson started the car and pulled away, calmer now.

'Er, yeah. I do think you should say sorry. Don't want him putting in a complaint.'

Clocks shrugged. 'That's alright. I'll just deny it an' say a stone flew up and 'it the window. Can't prove it, can they?'

'Can if the bullet lodged somewhere in the car.'

'Oh fuck. Didn't think of that.'

'So, let's go and say sorry and hope it didn't.'

Paterson drove back to the scene. Ahead of him, the driver was busy talking to the duty inspector, Stuart Norris.

'That's a stroke,' said Clocks. 'It's No Nuts.'

Stuart 'No Nuts' Norris was the sort of man that was nowhere to be seen whenever things went south. He was either 'unavailable' or 'non-contactable', and this had earned him his nickname among those at the sharp end. No love was lost between him and Paterson and Clocks.

Paterson pulled up next to the two officers. Clocks leaned out of his window. 'Alright, No Nuts? 'Ow's it 'angin, then?'

'What the fuck is wrong with you Clocks? What'd you think you're doing, running around the streets discharging a firearm willy-nilly. And don't call me No Nuts!'

Clocks grinned. 'You said "willy".'

'Grow up, man! This is bloody serious. You could have killed this officer.'

'Didn't though, did I? An' for your information, I wasn't just runnin' around, I was chasing a lunatic. You know what that's like — well, *you* probably don't — that's why they call you No Nuts, innit? Or is it because you literally 'ave no nuts? Like one of them, whatcha call 'em? Enochs.'

'Eunuchs,' said Paterson.

'I said that, didn't I?'

'Nope. You said "Enochs".'

'Same thing.'

'No, it's not.'

If looks could kill, Clocks would have been six feet under from the icy death stare Norris gave him.

'Look, knock it off, Clocks! This isn't funny.'

'What? You not 'avin' any bollocks is a fuckin' hoot, mate.'

'Could be suffering from unilateral or bilateral cryptorchidism, I suppose,' said Paterson. Clocks and Norris both looked at him.

Clocks frowned. 'Come again? A what-what?'

'Unilateral or bilateral cryptorchidism. It's a medical term for having either one or two undescended testicles. Would explain the absence.'

Clocks turned to Norris. 'Yeah. What Dr Paterson said. You got that then, No Nuts? Yer balls not dropped? They still tucked up in yer little pot belly?'

'Oh, yeah. You two are really, really funny. What a laugh you both are. Well, just for your information, I've got both my balls, thank you.'

'Get out of it,' said Clocks. 'We both know your missus 'as got 'em in a biscuit tin at 'ome, keepin' 'em safe for 'er little soldier.'

'Just shut up, Clocks.'

Clocks grinned at him. 'An' just for *your* information, I didn't discharge a firearm, I *shot* it. A discharge is what men an' women get in their underclackers when they're gettin' on a bit.'

'Get out of the car, Clocks.'

'What? Why's that?'

'I've had enough of you.'

'An' . . . you wanna fight me?'

Norris looked shocked. 'What? No. I'm not an animal. I wanted to talk to you face to face.'

'You are. I'm just sitting in the car.'

'It's not the same.'

'Yeah it is. Me face don't change when I stand up, does it?'

'Forget it, Clocks. You're a bloody child.'

'Oh, I get what this is about. I get it. You're on yer period again? That's what it is, innit? You've got the drips. I thought I saw you in Boots the other day with a box of tampons in yer basket.'

'Don't be so damn offensive and stupid, Clocks. You're not as bloody funny as you think you are!'

'What? Oh, come on. I am. You know I am, Stewie, ol' chap.'

'Sir,' Norris said to Paterson. 'What is wrong with the two of you? Why do you not take anything seriously? You're a senior officer — his commanding officer. The two of you are bringing the reputation of the Metropolitan Police Service into disrepute all the bloody time. It has to stop.'

'To be fair, Stuart,' Paterson replied, 'the reputation of the Met has been shot to pieces for a long time. Not sure that's entirely down to us.'

'You have got to sort this man out once and for all. He's a menace to society.'

Paterson sighed. He didn't have a lot of time for this man. 'No he's not. He's just a bit . . . feisty.'

'Feisty? *Feisty?* He's mad.'

'Bit harsh, Stuart, but then, I suppose we all are to a degree, otherwise we wouldn't be doing this job, would we?'

'No offence, sir, but that's a ridiculous thing to say.'

'None taken. But I can sense you're not in the mood to be reasonable, so what's the plan? You going to be a pain in the arse about this? Hmm?'

Norris frowned.

'Has the bullet lodged in the car anywhere? Is it laying around inside? Seats? Footwells? Have you looked?' said Paterson.

Norris shook his head. 'Yes, I've looked. Not that I can see. Seems it went through the windscreen at an angle and exited through the open side window. Sheer bloody luck.'

Clocks looked out at the driver of the car and smiled. 'I'm really sorry, mate. Caught up in the 'eat of the moment. You know what it's like when you're on a chase. Adrenaline an' shit. We good, pal?'

The officer nodded. 'It's okay, guv. Coulda been a lot worse. I appreciate the apology.'

Norris frowned. His chance of taking things further just diminished.

'There we go then, Stuart,' said Paterson. 'It seems the officer here has accepted Clocks's apology. Can we keep this between us, then? Maybe put it down to a stone flicking up through the window? That would be the decent thing to do. Yes?'

Norris shook his head and sighed loudly. 'Fine! I know it was an accident. But no more. You understand me, sir? No more. This can't be allowed to happen again.'

'Stuart,' said Paterson. 'You're a gentleman. Thank you. That's one I owe you.'

'Then sort yourselves out, sir. That's what I want. Sort yourselves out.'

Paterson smiled then roared off into the night, leaving Inspector Norris standing on the kerb.

CHAPTER TEN

Back at the office, Paterson broke out the bottle of vodka he kept in his desk drawer and poured himself and Clocks a large one each.

'Got any ice?'

Paterson looked down into his drawer. 'Yeah. How much you want?'

Clocks grinned. 'Nice one, Ray. See, you're gettin' the 'ang of sarcasm. Good man.'

Paterson swung his feet up on the desk and took a gulp of his drink.

Clocks dropped heavily into a chair. 'So, what now, Ray?'

'Don't know for sure but, given that this man thinks he's somehow doing God's work and we think that our victim was in some part religious, I think we need to go knocking on the door of the church to see if they have any idea who he is.'

'The church?'

'Yeah.' Paterson glanced up at the clock in his office. 'We'll grab a few hours kip here and nip over to the little one around the corner at about nine. What's it called? St James's? Yeah. St James's. We can have a little chat with the vicar and maybe he or she can enlighten us. Sound like a plan?'

Clocks nodded. 'It does. But, just to be clear, we're goin' to a church even though you know I don't like 'em?'

'You don't have to. I'll go.'

Clocks put his glass down. 'I'm not sayin' I'm not goin'. It's just that you know me an' religion don't mix. I don't 'ave any time for all this God nonsense. There's no such thing. There's here an' there's not. No afterlife, no 'eaven, no nothin'. It's light's out, goodnight, thanks for comin'.'

Paterson raised an eyebrow. 'I know. You've said. Many times. But you have to understand . . . religion gives great comfort to millions of people and has done for millennia. And I'm not just talking about Christianity here. People have always needed to believe in something greater than themselves. Their lives were usually so shit that they had to believe there was more, and dying offered them an end to human suffering and the promise of paradise.'

'I know that. But 'as it done any real good? No. Far as I can see all religion's ever done is cause sufferin' one way or another. 'istory's rife with people killin' 'emselves in some sort of fuckin' 'oly war or somethin'. Just an excuse to do bad shit an' justify it by sayin' God wants it. Well, fuck that. I don't buy that shit!

'The church does a lotta pontificatin' and bangin' on about 'ow we should all be 'elpin' the poor people, but I don't see the Pope floggin' off any treasures to 'elp 'em. Fucker's banged up in 'is big gold 'ouse with a shit ton of Van Gogh's an' Banksy's an' other priceless stuff 'angin' on the walls. Don't see 'im on the charity 'elplines or doin' stuff with that . . . what's that little one-eyed bear called . . . ? Spotty bandage over his mince pie?'

'Pudsey?'

'Pudsey. That's the fellah. Charity bear. Children in Need. Never see the Pope rollin' up 'is cassock an' gettin' stuck in with 'elpin' all the little African kids get clean water or go to school, do yer? No, you don't. Probably busy writing a new manual for new recruits to the church on 'ow to get away with sexually assaultin' kiddies.'

He drained his glass and held it out. Paterson poured him another, slightly smaller. Clocks wiggled his glass until Paterson poured out a drop more.

'Is this gonna be a long rant, Clocksy? Only, I think we should get a couple of hours sleep before you get going on one.'

Clocks took a swig. 'I'm not rantin', Ray. I'm just sayin'. Religion 'as a lot to answer for. Some serious shit gone bad in the name of religion.'

'I know.' Paterson stood up and wandered over to the small sofa bed he kept. 'I'm going to kip. Where you going?'

Clocks shrugged. 'I'll pull a few chairs together. Don't worry about it. It's not for long.'

'Okay.'

Clocks started dragging two padded chairs toward him. 'An' then there's what they did to unmarried women. Bloody evil, them nuns. Nothin' like the Julie Andrews version, that lot. An' then there's all the bummin' the vicars do to the choir boys. Dirty, no-good bastards. An' what's the church do about it? Fuck all, mate. Cover it up. Should all be fuckin' shot, the lot of 'em.'

'Goodnight, John.' Paterson flicked off the office light before lying down.

'Night, night.' Clocks manoeuvred himself onto the two chairs, downed his vodka and wriggled himself into a sleeping position. 'Oh, fuck me!'

'What's the matter now?'

'I need a piss.'

'*Of course* you do.'

Clocks struggled to get himself up and headed toward the door. 'I can see meself 'avin' a word with this bishop fellah later on. Y'know that, don'tcha?'

Paterson sighed. 'Vicar. It'll be a vicar. And I'm sure you will.'

CHAPTER ELEVEN

Paterson dozed fitfully throughout the three and a half hours of rest they snatched. His mind just wouldn't settle down. Images of the dead family flicked in and out of his memory, as did the killer's face, his dead dogs and the rooftop chases. He beat himself up for not being agile or fast enough to have caught him, but what really angered him was that he hadn't brought a gun when they tore out of the office.

That hadn't been an option. He had authorised Clocks's firearm, but his own use had to be authorised by an officer of at least commander rank, and by the time he'd have got that, their suspect would have been long gone. But still, he imagined himself back in the fire engine cradle looking at the man's face, his eyes, his grin, the drool, the sound of his voice, and then, in a leap from memory to imagination, he saw the killer's face explode as he pulled the trigger.

He saw himself in a final confrontation with this man. Good versus evil. Or was it evil versus evil? The things he'd done . . . A few years before, life was cut and dried. There was good. There was bad. There was right, there was wrong. Simple as that. Until he joined the murder squad and quickly realised life was nowhere near as neat as that. Oh, would that it was!

He'd found himself in too many situations where cut and dried would have got him or Clocks killed. Where very bad people would have walked away scot-free if he hadn't stretched the rules.

He had always been able to justify to himself that what he had done was right but, deep down in the pit of his stomach, he knew it wasn't. He looked across at Clocks, scrunched up in the two chairs, snoring and farting on and off, and he wondered, just as he had done so many times before, whether *he* was to blame for his life collapsing. Perhaps it was Clocks who'd dragged him down to this level . . . but, then again, perhaps not. He knew his life changed the moment he shot serial killer Adam Walker in the head. The man who butchered his wife, Lisa. And then he let Clocks cover it up, saying it was self-defence. Maybe it was at that moment, when he colluded to cover it up to save his own skin, that his life went south. It didn't really matter anymore.

The sound of two of his detectives coming into the office broke him out of his thoughts and, just as tired as he had been when he first lay down, he hoisted himself off the sofa.

'John.'

Clocks squeaked out a little fart and grumbled in his sleep.

He could never understand how Clocks seemed to be able to take everything in his stride. It bothered him sometimes, but really, he envied Clocks. Clocks had his own struggles going on — Paterson knew that — but, somehow, he seemed to push on, to laugh and joke, to function at full throttle. Paterson wished he could be the same.

'John! Up you get. Work to do.'

Clocks stirred and moaned.

He clapped his hands a few times. 'Clocksy! Up! Let's go. Now!'

Clocks struggled to get himself upright, pushing one chair away to stretch his legs out. That was a mistake. With no support under his back, he sank in the middle and made it even more difficult to get himself up. 'Fuck off!' he shouted to the chair. He kicked it away, dropped onto his back, rolled over and pushed himself back up to a sitting position.

'Mornin',' he said.

'Morning, John. Want a cup of tea?'

'Hmm. I do. I could murder a drink. Me mouth's as dry as a dead bird's fanny.' He licked his lips.

'Oh, nice. There's an analogy I could've done without. Thanks.'

'You're welcome. Now, stop bumpin' yer gums and go put the kettle on. Good lad.'

Paterson grinned. 'You do remember that I'm the senior officer in this relationship, don't you?'

Clocks scratched his balls. 'Yep. You never let me forget. But, as there's no crumpet 'ere to make the tea, it's on you. You're the youngest and you volunteered, didn'tcha?'

'Crumpet? Who uses terms like that these days?'

Clocks sniffed. 'I do. Why? What'd you youngsters call 'em, then?'

'Women, John. Women.'

'Same difference.'

Paterson opened the door and narrowly avoided bumping into Jackie carrying two mugs of tea. 'Shit! Sorry. You startled me,' he said.

Jackie grinned at him. 'I know. There you go . . . two teas.'

'Thanks.' Paterson was careful to hold one of the mugs by his fingertips.

'How'd you know we were here?'

She shrugged. 'To be honest, I heard a loud fart and worked out the rest from there.' She nodded at Clocks. 'Guv, tea?'

'Ooh, yeah. Ta, luv. Got any biccies?'

She fished into her jacket pocket and pulled out two snack-size packets of bourbons.

Clocks wrinkled his nose. 'What're these?'

'Bourbons,' she said.

'No Jammie Dodgers, then?'

'Nope. Bourbons.'

He sniffed. 'These are 'orrible. Like little dog turds, these are.'

'All there is.'

Clocks looked at his tea. 'Bit on the dark side, innit? Christ, it's blacker than a witches arse'ole.'

'Bit like your soul.'

'Ooh. That 'urts. I thought you loved me?'

'I do but you're a pain in the arse.'

'I could be a pain in *your* arse if you wanted me to be.' He winked.

'You *want* me to go to HR, don't you?'

He grinned and shrugged. 'Listen . . . if you're goin' there now, can you do me a favour an' get me a bacon san'wich from the canteen? Ray'll 'ave 'is usual plant-based, grass-flavoured, cow-shittin' quinoa bollocks on a lump of rye, whatever that is.'

Jackie pasted a big smile on her face. 'Nope. You want it, you get it. Oh, tell you what, I'll ask Helen, the HR supervisor. I'm sure she'll pick one up for you.' With that, she turned and walked back into the office.

Clocks grinned and called out to her. 'Will she? That's good of 'er! Can you tell 'er not to go mad with the tomato sauce? I bleedin' 'ate it when it squidges out the sides!'

Jackie slid behind her desk, shaking her head.

'Can't get the staff anymore, Ray. Time was a bird'd go an' get you a san'wich no questions asked, 'appy to do it. No backchat, no bangin' on about women's rights, no runnin' off to HR 'cos you asked them to do you a fry-up on night duty. World's gone to bleedin' rat shit, mate, I'm tellin' yer. Question . . . 'ow'd she know we were in 'ere an' 'ow'd she know we wanted a drink?'

Paterson attempted to smooth a crease out of his shirt and tucked it into his trousers. 'She told you. She heard you fart. Loudly.'

'Yeah? Good detective, that one. Told yer, didn't I?'

'No. If I remember rightly, you once told me she was useless and would struggle to find a pair of tits smack in the middle of a lesbian orgy.'

'Did I? That don't sound like me. I would never disrespect a woman like that.'

'Hmm.'

Jackie walked back into Paterson's office, notebook in hand.

'Look. You both awake yet? Got some info on our vics.'

Paterson nodded.

'I will be once you've got me a bacon sarnie,' said Clocks with a smirk.

'Yeah. Do one, guv.'

'Already 'ave, ain't I? Alerted you to our presence, it seems.'

'Go on,' said Paterson.

'Mum's name was Lacey Heaton. Born ninth of September, nineteen ninety-nine.'

'She was only . . . twenty-three?' said Paterson.

'Would appear so,' said Jackie.

'Fuck me. She was a busy girl. 'Ow old was the boy?'

'Five.'

'She 'ad 'im when she was, what, fifteen, sixteen?'

'Close. Eighteen,' said Paterson.

Clocks looked pleased that he'd gotten that close. Maths was never his strong suit.

'And the baby?'

'Eight months.'

Paterson shook his head. 'Where's Dad?'

She shrugged. 'We're working on it. Neighbours say he was last at the flat just after the baby was born and they haven't seen him since.'

'Do we have a name?'

'Danny.'

'That it?'

'For now. We've traced her parents and I'm going to break the news to them later this morning.'

'Want me to do it?' said Paterson.

'No. Better if I do it.'

'Sexist, that is.'

'Shut up, John. Mummy and Daddy don't have time to play with you now.' Paterson sipped at his tea. 'Be a good boy and we'll see how it goes later.'

Clocks smiled. 'Promise?'

'What time are the rest of the troops in?' Paterson said.

'On their way now. Dusty and Monkey are already here.'

'I know. I heard them. Let me know when everybody gets here and we'll have a quick catch-up to see what else has come to light.'

CHAPTER TWELVE

'Okay. Good morning, everybody. I hope you've all had the chance to get some rest.' Paterson looked around the room. Judging from the faces that looked back at him, he deemed it unlikely. He spent the next few minutes bringing them up to speed on the latest events, then turned the floor over to Jackie and watched them scribble Lacey Heaton's name into their notebooks.

'Jackie, we're gonna run with your religion theory until proved otherwise. Believe it or not, Clocksy and I are off to St James's church today to have a word with whoever's in charge, to see if he or she can enlighten us any further as to our suspect.'

A few of the team frowned. Clocks and any member of the clergy was not going to be an easy mix.

'Also, I suspect we'll get a visit from the cops that investigate cops at some point today on account of DI Clocks, who went on a bit of a Wild West rampage last night and shot up this here town of ours.' A few smiled. 'Dead-Eye Dick here narrowly managed to avoid killing one of our own, so I guess that's one thing to be grateful for. The thing to be *un*grateful for is that Inspector Norris had a complete sense of humour failure about it. We think that he may well do the right thing and look after us. Certainly, that's the impression we got but, at the end of the day, it's Norris. Can't trust him to not change his mind.'

Monkey coughed and at the same time said, 'Prick!'

Clocks sniffed. 'Nasty cough you got there, son.'

'Sorry, guv. Happens whenever I hear the names of bottleless bastards that wear the blue and call 'emselves cops. Can't help it. Think it's an allergy.'

Paterson gave him a wry smile. 'If they do show up, can someone tell them we're following up a lead and then give us a call? We'll come back as soon as.'

There were a few nods.

'Does anyone have anything from the neighbours? Any witnesses before or after the event?'

DC Yorkshire put his hand up.

'Tetley!' said Clocks. 'Unless you wanna piss, don't stick yer bleedin' 'and up. Yer not at school, fer chrissake. If you've got summin' to say, just say it.'

DC Yorkshire stared at his senior officer. It was common knowledge that the two men were not overly fond of each other. 'Sorry, sir. I just wanted to say that the immediate next-door neighbour said she didn't see anyone go into Miss Heaton's flat.'

'Would she normally?' said Paterson.

'Quite possibly, sir. She is, by her own admission, a nosy cow and spends a lot of her time in the kitchen looking out at the balcony. She watches who comes and goes, and because Miss Heaton's door is the last stop on the balcony, she would have seen someone walk past.'

'She hear any noise? The door getting kicked in? That sort of thing.'

Yorkshire shook his head. 'Nothing. First she became aware of any problems was with a scream from Miss Heaton's flat. Apparently, that was like a signal for all hell to break loose. And it did, big time. She claims she got on the phone to 999 straightaway. I'm running down the timeline of her claim to see how it lines up with her call and our two officers' time of arrival.'

'Thanks, Tetley,' said Paterson. 'Any forensics yet? Prints?'

Again, DC Yorkshire shook his head. 'Nothing found fingerprint-wise. Shoeprint in blood, yes, but that's not going to be much use unless we can find the shoe and put it on our suspect at the time of the murders.'

'The ol' Cinderella routine, eh?' said Clocks.

Yorkshire looked perplexed.

'We 'ave to find the shoe, in his property, with a blood trace from one of our victims on it and make sure it's his size. Cinderella. A further test or two will give us DNA from skin contact with his socks, and his socks will have left fibre traces inside the shoe. Bingo! Bob's your uncle and Fanny's your aunt,' said Clocks.

'I'm aware of that, sir. I did my courses.'

Clocks looked unhappy. 'So, why'd you ask?'

'I didn't ask, sir.'

'So why'd you look so confused, then?'

'I wasn't confused. I just remembered I had something to tell you and I've been looking for the right time. That was it a minute or two ago. I missed it.'

'Spit it out now, then.'

DC Yorkshire twisted uncomfortably in his chair. 'Your office, sir?'

'I'm sure there's no need for that,' said Paterson. 'Whatever it is, we'll all find out eventually.'

Yorkshire shrugged. 'I'm leaving.'

'Leaving?'

Clocks punched the air. 'Yesssss. Thank you very much.'

'Us? Or the job as a whole?' Paterson was unhappy with Clocks's little display.

'The squad, sir. I recently sat a board for a post in the Sex Crimes Unit . . .'

'Vice squad?' said Clocks.

'Sex Crimes Unit, sir.'

'What'd you put on yer application? I'm a huge wanker that loves to wank so I'd love to join yer little squad an' then I can wank all day?'

DC Yorkshire wrinkled his nose.

'Enough, John,' said Paterson. 'Why didn't you tell me you wanted to leave, Colin?'

'Wasn't sure I'd be successful. If I failed the board, that was it.'

Paterson nodded. 'When'd you find out you'd passed?'

'Yesterday. I would have told you then, but it's been a bit . . . busy.'

'You'll be needing my recommendation, I guess?'

'Yes, sir.'

'I'll be sorry to see you go.'

'I won't,' said Clocks. 'There's the door. Ta. Mind how yer go.'

'The feeling is mutual, DI Clocks,' said Yorkshire. 'I can't say I've been made to feel welcome in my time here.'

'That's because you're a know-it-all knob, mate. If you'd 'ave tried to fit in instead of swannin' around tryin' to show how clever you are and got the beers in once in a blue moon, you'd 'ave fitted in nicely. But, there you go. Too late. So, once again, there's the door. Ta. Mind how yer go.'

Paterson sighed. 'I'll give you a good reference, but just so you know, you're not leaving the squad until this case is cracked. You understand that?'

'Yes, sir. Of course.'

'So, you two . . .' Paterson glanced at Clocks and then turned back to Yorkshire. 'Play nicely. Got it? This job is too big and I don't want any dissent in the team. John?'

Clocks shrugged. 'Yeah. No sweat.'

'Yorkshire?'

'Of course.'

'Good. Everyone . . . you have your jobs. Let's find this mad bastard. John, we're off to the church. Walkie time.'

With the squad slowly filtering out of the office, Clocks put his jacket on. 'D'yer see it?' he said.

'See what?' Paterson patted his jacket down, checking for pen and notebook.

'His fingers. Webbed. Told you.'

CHAPTER THIRTEEN

'I know what I've been meaning to ask you.' Paterson took the stairs down two at a time. Clocks trotted down behind him.

'What's happening about your son? You've not said much about him since we got back from France.'

'I've been meanin' to talk to you about that but . . . I didn't want to.'

Paterson chortled. 'Why not? You couldn't stop talking about him at one point.'

'That's 'cos things were all new and intense.'

Paterson opened the door that led out into the yard and jumped the final three steps. 'What's changed?'

'Got the DNA result back.'

Paterson stopped and turned. 'And?'

'Turns out 'e *is* me boy an' I am gonna be a fuckin' grandad.'

Paterson broke into a smile. 'That's brilliant news, John. You must be happy, yes?'

'No.'

'What? Why?'

'Turns out the fucker's been blaggin' post offices.'

'*You're joking!*'

'Nope. I 'ad a chinwag with 'im. Put 'is 'ands up to it. Only wants me to get 'im off.'

'And you said?'

'You're fuckin' nicked, son.'

'Yeah? Where is he, then?'

'In the wind, mate. Fucker pushed the table over on me an' 'ad it on 'is toes.'

'Shit. You told anyone?'

'Just told you.'

'So, what we going to do about it?'

'First off, we find our killer, then I find 'im, nick 'im an' 'ave 'im carted off to Brixton for a bit of time.'

'Sounds like a plan.'

'Yep.'

'John?'

'What?'

'How thick is he? I mean, who the fuck robs post offices in 2022?'

CHAPTER FOURTEEN

Paterson parked up outside St James's church and had a quick look at the building. It was old, 1800s perhaps, made mostly from red brick that had long lost its vibrancy thanks to a generous coating of London grime. It had somehow managed to survive the Blitz, despite lying close to the old docks, but was now dying a slow death due to lack of parishioners.

'John . . .'

'What?'

'I need you to behave yourself in here.'

'I know. I will. I'm a changed man these days, mate.' Clocks grinned.

'Seriously. We don't have time for your fannying about and winding people up. This is important.'

'I know it is.' Clocks managed to sound slightly offended. 'I said I'd behave. You won't even know I'm there.'

'Hmm. Hope so.'

'Can I ask a question?'

'Go on.'

'Do we actually 'ave an appointment with the boss of this gaff?'

'Nope. Didn't have time to make one. Strike while the iron's hot, eh?'

Clocks shrugged. ''Opefully. We're gonna look pretty dumb if the only person in is the cleaner.'

'Fingers crossed, then.'

Paterson stepped inside the imposing doors of the ancient building and was immediately struck by a sense of calm. Not a religious man by any means, he nevertheless always felt this calmness whenever he entered these grand monuments to religion and was struck by a sense of awe. As much as these places were, for the faithful, a testament to the power and grace of God, to him they were a testament to the sheer genius of man's inventiveness and abilities.

He was conscious of his footsteps echoing around the church and made an effort to step lightly. Clocks just walked normally, oblivious to the noise he was making with his feet. Minimising Paterson's embarrassment was the fact that it was early and they were, in fact, the first two visitors of the day.

'Ray. Over there, mate. It's only the cleaner, innit? What are the odds? I'll ask 'im where the boss is.'

Before Paterson could say anything, Clocks whistled loudly. The noise echoed around the building like a gunshot. Paterson cringed and the cleaner lifted his head, a look of both surprise and disgust on his face.

''Old up, fellah.' Clocks marched off. Paterson followed.

The elderly man looked directly at Clocks as he approached him, his disdain evident.

'Alright, mate? We're the Old Bill. We're lookin' for the boss of this place. Dunno 'is name. The Pope or somethin'.'

The old man eyed him now with a mixture of curiosity and incredulity. 'Excuse me?'

'The boss. The big cheese. Probably wears a robe an' a big 'at on Sundays. Is 'e about, by any chance?'

'You say you're the police?'

'Yeah.' Clocks fished out his warrant card from inside his jacket pocket and held it up for the man to see.

'We're looking for the vicar,' said Paterson. 'Is it the vicar? I'm sorry. I'm not that au fait with the hierarchy of the church. Do you happen to know if he's in today by any chance?'

The man nodded. 'Yeah. He's in. He gets in early when he comes. If you wait here, gents, I'll let him know you're here.'

'S'alright mate. Just point us in the direction of 'is 'idey 'ole and we'll surprise 'im. Everyone likes surprises, don't they? God pulled a few stunts 'imself, didn't 'e? An' 'is boy too. Walkin' on water an' stuff. Bet that was a surprise.'

'Reverend Codd is not a fan of surprises, no,' said the cleaner. 'Wait here and I'll tell him.' The cleaner gently rested his broom against a well-worn piano and walked off to leave the two policemen standing in the quiet.

'Did 'e say the boss's name was Codd?'

Paterson rolled his eyes. 'Yep.'

'Sounds a bit fishy to me.'

'Yep. Another cracker, Clocksy. Straight off the bat. Dunno how you do it.'

Clocks pulled a face at the cleaner as he watched him disappear through a side door. 'I'll bet you can play this, can't you?' he said to Paterson, nodding at the piano.

'What? Yeah, I can actually. Part of my studies. I took it up when I was five.'

'You any good?'

'Well, as I just said, I took it up when I was five, so yes, I can play.'

'Give us a tune, then.'

'What?'

'Give us a tune. You know any good songs?'

Paterson looked at him aghast. 'What d'you mean *give us a tune*? You're not down the old — what d'you call it — the *rub-a-dub* now. You're in a bloody church. A place of worship.'

Clocks leaned across and opened the lid.

'John! No! Put it down.'

'What?'

'Don't. That's an order.'

'Is it?' Clocks raised an eyebrow. He hit one of the keys, sending a high-pitched note echoing around the building.

Paterson sighed. 'John. Come on. Show some respect.'

Clocks smiled and closed the lid quietly. 'Alright. Sorry.'

Paterson eyed him suspiciously. Contrition wasn't like Clocks at all.

Both men looked up at the sound of footsteps that marked the return of the cleaner, accompanied by the vicar, a smartly dressed man with a Roman nose, a crooked smile and an air of calm authority. He held his hand out in greeting.

'Gentlemen. Good morning. Laurence Codd. I'm the vicar. Matthew here tells me you're looking for "the boss". That would be me.' He shook Paterson's hand. 'So, you're policemen. What can I do for you?'

Paterson took out his warrant card for inspection. 'Good morning, sir. I'm Detective Superintendent Paterson and this is Detective Inspector Johnny Clocks. I wonder if we might have a word with you in private. It's rather a delicate matter.' He glanced across at Matthew, a look that was picked up by Codd.

'Of course. Please, follow me. It's okay, Matthew. Nothing to be concerned about.'

Clocks looked at Matthew. 'What? Did you think we were a couple of wrong'uns, then?'

'Can't be too careful. Even in a house of God.' Matthew picked up his broom and went back to work.

'No,' said Clocks. 'No, you can't.' He trotted off to catch up with Paterson and Codd.

'Can I get you some tea, gents?'

'Please,' said Paterson. 'Had an early start, so haven't had time for a drink yet.'

'I see,' said Codd. He stood to one side and ushered them both into his vestry. 'Would chamomile suit?'

'Lovely,' said Paterson.

'What's that? Chamomile? Nah, you're alright, mate . . . Sorry. *Sir*. I'll 'ave builder's if you've got any. Otherwise, scrub it.'

'Builder's?'

'Yeah. Builder's. Brown. Can't see the bottom of it.'

'Oh, I see,' said Codd. 'Yes, yes, of course. I'll get some sent in.' He picked up the phone on his desk and asked that tea be brought.

'Please take a seat, gentlemen, and we can talk while we wait.'

'Thank you,' said Paterson. He made himself comfortable in the leather chair and crossed his legs. 'I'm about to tell you something that hasn't yet made its way onto the news channels, but my guess is, it'll be out by about ten a.m.'

Codd sat back in his chair and listened.

'Earlier this morning, a woman was savagely murdered in her own home along with her two children — two boys. One was aged five and the other was under a year old.'

Codd flinched. 'My God . . .'

'The man responsible also killed two police officers, making good his escape. The manner of the family's death was brutal in the extreme, and unfortunately a pair of crucifixes were used to end the lives of the mother and elder boy. Judging by the pictures on the wall, we believe the mother was a churchgoer. My forensic team are reporting that they are finding more and more religious objects in the flat.

'So, I wondered if you might possibly know of her or if you could tell us if she went to church and, if so, which one that might be. I know it's a long shot but we're just trying to get ahead of the game.'

Codd looked visibly shaken. 'I . . . don't know, Mr Paterson. I . . . I . . . I'll try. What was her name?'

'Lacey Heaton,' said Clocks. 'Ring any bells?'

Codd shook his head. 'No. No it doesn't. I'm sorry.'

Paterson nodded. 'Okay. Do you think you could look into that for us, please? I know you're busy and it's an ask, but it would help us out tremendously.'

'Yes, of course. I'll get onto it right—' There was a gentle tap on the door.

'Ah, that'll be the tea. Come in!'

An elderly woman pushed the door open and wheeled in a small trolley containing two cups of chamomile and a large mug of English breakfast tea.'

'Thank you, Linda. Gentlemen, this is Linda. She's one of our most respected parishioners and has been involved with the church for, what is it now, Linda? Forty years?'

'Fifty,' she said, her voice quiet. 'Fifty years this year.'

Codd held out his hand, almost presenting her for a round of applause. It didn't come.

'That's remarkable, Linda,' said Paterson. 'May I call you Linda?'

'Yes, of course you can!' She glanced at him. 'A handsome young man like you can call me whatever you wish.'

Clocks wrinkled his nose. 'Steady on, luv. You dunno what you're up against 'ere. This one'll 'ave yer bloomers off before you know what's 'it yer.'

Paterson smiled.

'I think I'd be alright with that.' She threw Paterson a wink. He felt the colour rise to his cheeks.

'Ooh, you're a lively one ain'tcha?' said Clocks. 'I thought you churchy lot were s'posed to be above all that sort of malarkey.'

She looked at Clocks. 'Oh, it's just an old lady having a bit of fun. I'm far too old for him. More's the pity.'

'Well . . .' Clocks picked up his mug. 'That's not gonna bother 'im. Ol' Ray 'ere's not too fussy. If you've still got a pulse, he'll try 'is luck. *'Ave you still got a pulse, Linda?* If you 'ave, then give 'im yer number an' 'e'll give you a bell later on. What's a good time? When d'you go to bed? About half six, seven?'

'Linda,' said Codd, 'I think that's quite enough of that. These officers are very busy men.'

'Nah, you're alright,' said Clocks. 'Never too busy for a bit of fun, are we, guv?'

'Linda,' said Paterson. 'I'm flattered but I'm afraid we do have a lot of work to do.'

Clocks shook his head. It had just been a bit of fun.

'Yes, vicar. I'm sorry,' Linda said. 'I'm sorry, Mr Paterson.'

'Don't be,' Paterson said. 'It's fine. Look . . . before you go, I wonder if you may have heard of a parishioner by the name of Lacey Heaton, by any chance? Had two small children. Boys.'

She stood for a second, and to Paterson it seemed as if she was running a name file through her memory banks.

After a moment or two she said, 'I do know of a couple of Laceys. Not many though. It's an unusual name. Where does she live?'

'Over on the Arnold's Estate, just off Jamaica Road,' said Paterson. 'You know it?'

She nodded. 'If it's the one I'm thinking of, yes. Pretty girl. No husband, of course. Few of them do these days.'

'Do you know if she went to church locally?'

'I believe so but I can't remember which one it would have been. I think there's a few close to where she lives. Why? Has something happened to her?'

'Yep,' said Clocks. 'She's turned 'er toes up, I'm afraid. Kids too.'

'Oh my. Oh dear, oh dear. Er, what does that mean?'

'Dead. Murdered.'

Linda immediately pressed her hand to her chest and swayed backward slightly.

'Here,' said Paterson, standing quickly. 'Take my seat.' He guided her down into the chair then threw Clocks a look that said, *what's the matter with you?*

'That's so awful. That poor family. What happened to them?'

'Well, it's like this . . .' said Clocks.

'John! No.'

Clocks smiled and nodded.

'As my colleague said, I'm afraid that they were murdered in their home. We're investigating their deaths and we were hoping we might find some answers in the church.'

She looked up at Paterson, her eyes brimming with tears. 'Yes, yes. Of course. God will be with you. The answers will be here. In the church.'

Clocks shrugged. *Yeah. Right.*

'Officer,' said Codd. 'I'll get you a list of all the churches within walking distance of Miss Heaton. Would that help?'

'Yes,' Paterson said. 'It would. Thank you. Can you get that for me now, before we leave?'

'Of course.' The vicar picked up the phone and punched in a few numbers. 'Shouldn't be too many.'

Paterson turned back to Linda. 'Do you know anyone who might have wanted to hurt them? Anyone? An ex, perhaps?'

Linda stiffened.

'What?' said Paterson. 'An ex? D'you think an ex-boy-friend might be behind this?'

She shook her head.

'Who, then? You have some idea? You need to tell me if you suspect anyone, Linda. Whoever's doing this could strike again. Time is important and we don't have much of it. So, if you know or suspect someone, now's the time to tell me.'

'Well, there was the father of her children. He was a nasty man.'

Codd finished his telephone call and hung up. He listened in to the conversation in front of him.

'Do you know his name?'

'No. Sorry. It might come back to me later but, the shock . . . I'm sorry.'

Paterson put his hand on her shoulder. 'That's okay. No worries.' He turned to Reverend Codd. 'Any luck?'

Codd handed him a scrap of paper. 'There are only two churches within walking distance of her home and I think it might be wise to start with St Michael's.'

Paterson looked at the scrap. 'Why's that?'

'They have a crèche, so—'

'Good thinking. Okay. We're going to leave you be now, but —' he took out a business card and handed it to Codd — 'if either of you think of anything else. And Linda, if you remember his name, give me a call. Day or night.'

Paterson thanked them both for their time and he and Clocks took their leave.

The church had a few more visitors milling about than when they came in. One or two of them looked at Paterson and Clocks curiously as they crossed the floor and headed out into the sunlight.

'Thoughts?' said Paterson.

'Yep. I was wonderin' if you fancy takin' that ol' bird on a double date with me an' Lyndsey?'

'Fuck you, Clocksy.'

'Amen, Father Paterson.'

CHAPTER FIFTEEN

The Stable Table café was a relative newcomer in the area and was nearly always full, despite its somewhat loose adherence to hygiene laws. If it wasn't for the fact that they did such a good fry-up, Clocks wouldn't have bothered with the place. They squeezed themselves into the plastic seats that were bolted into the floor. The large pale-green table still had a few crumbs and discernible splodges of tomato sauce that was beginning to form a hard ring at the edges.

Paterson grabbed some napkins from the half-empty container and set about wiping the table himself. This had become a new haunt for the pair of them, and he'd become used to the fact that if he didn't wipe the table, it was unlikely it would be done even when Karen, the owner's sister, took their orders.

Clocks went for his usual full English breakfast while Paterson ordered a round of toast. He figured that not too much hygiene damage could be done to two bits of toast.

'Right. So, run it by me again, what you said in the car,' said Paterson. 'You think she's a liar because of what?'

'Because of 'er behaviour. 'Er 'ole demeanour changed when you asked if she 'ad any idea of 'o might 'ave done it.'

'Yeah, I know. I saw that. What do you think she knows?'

Clocks dipped a piece of double-fried bread into his runny egg and then shrugged. 'Dunno. But she's got summin' on 'er mind. Shoulda leaned on 'er a bit.'

'She's an old lady, John. Got to be in her eighties if she's a day.'

Clocks swallowed his fried bread. 'And? You think ol' ladies don't know things? Look, she's been tucked up in bed with God an' the church for nearly a century, right?'

'Fifty years.'

'Whatever. Potato, potahto an' all that. Point is, these crucifix-wagglin' fuckers are up to all sorts of shit, an' they got more skeletons in their closet than a double-sized closet jam-packed *full* of skeletons. I'm tellin' yer, she knows more than she's lettin' on. It's probably 'er. It's always the butler or the old lady who did it.'

'Except we chased a young, fit man from the scene.'

'Could 'ave been a cunnin' disguise.'

'I'm not saying you're wrong—'

'Good. I'm not.'

'I'm not saying you're wrong, John, but unless we bring her in for questioning—'

'We're not gonna get anywhere with 'er.'

'Will you stop interrupting me?'

'Doubt it.'

'Why won't we get anywhere?'

'She don't know anything.'

'*What?* You just said—'

'I know what I said, but even as I was sayin' it an' the more I think about it, it sounds like bollocks. Don't take no notice of me. Besides. You're overthinkin' it again.'

'What'd you mean, *overthinking it*?'

'Your little brain's runnin' off on one. I can see it. Your eyes do this —' Clocks waved his knife in a circular pattern in the air — 'funny shit. Always 'ave done. It looks painful.'

'What? What's wrong with my eyes? I don't do that.'

'Yeah, y'do. I noticed it when I first met yer.'

'Why didn't you say something?'

'Like what? *Oi, guv. What's goin' on with yer marbles? They're rollin' about in yer nut like a seasick sea lion. Look like a fuckin' pinball machine, mate.*'

Paterson chuckled. 'Prick! Eat your . . . whatever that mess is and let's go. We need to go and see the boss at this St Michael's church. See if he can enlighten us.'

'Should be able to. If not, 'e's shit at 'is job.'

CHAPTER SIXTEEN

'Thank you for seeing us at such short notice,' said Paterson as he and Clocks greeted the Reverend Richard Wakker.

'Not at all. Please make yourselves comfortable.' He ushered them into a tiny room that doubled as his office and a storage cupboard, judging by the amount of unrelated objects stacked and leaning against the walls. 'I'm sorry. It's a bit cramped.'

'No worries,' said Paterson. He lifted a pile of dusty bibles off a chair and handed them to Clocks. 'Put these somewhere for me, John. Thanks.'

Clocks looked as though he'd been asked to hold a pile of broken glass. 'What?'

'These . . .' He held the stack out to him. 'Go on. You won't burst into flame.'

Clocks took the bibles and quickly found a home for them by balancing them precariously on top of a stack of old magazines.

'Not a believer then, Mr Clocks?' said Reverend Wakker.

'Nope.' Clocks wiped his hands on his legs.

'Oh. May I ask why? You don't have to answer, of course. I'm just curious.'

Clocks eyed up the man. He put him in his late twenties, bumping close to thirty. He was of medium height, a bit on the overweight side with a flushed face and had tufts of dark hair growing out of his ears.

'No, mate. I'm more than 'appy to tell yer. It's 'cos I'm all grown up.'

Paterson rolled his eyes and sighed. *Here we go.*

'I'm sorry?'

'I said that I'm a grown up. You're what? Thirty maybe? You've still got some way to go yet before you wake up an' see this world for what it really is. Look, son, I don't need to believe in fairy stories anymore. All this walkin' on water and feedin' a million people with a tiger loaf an' a coupla 'ot cross buns. Partin' the seas with a wave of 'is 'and an' burnin' bushes.' Clocks cocked his head to one side. 'I knew a girl 'ad a burnin' bush once. I think that was the clap though. She used to scratch 'er fanny a lot. At least, I *think* she was scratchin' it.'

Paterson shook his head and waited for this little rant to die down. He thought about putting a stop to it, but past experience told him that Clocks wouldn't close the lid on this can of worms until he'd got it out of his system. *Thank you, Vicar.*

'So, no. I don't believe. Plus, I've seen too much shit in my time to think there's such a thing as a benevolent God.'

'Ah,' said Wakker. 'The old "Why does God let children and innocents suffer and die?" argument, eh?'

'I'm not arguin' with yer, but yeah. An' you lot just trot out the old "God works in mysterious ways" bollocks as a way of convincin' yerselves 'e 'as some sort of reason behind all the murderin' an' killin' an' wars an' shit. Well, it don't fool anyone capable of a bit of thought. It's not an answer at all, is it? No.'

Reverend Wakker nodded. 'You're right. It isn't an answer. So, what d'you think the answer is?'

'Oh, no, no, no, no. I'm not fallin' for that one. I'm not playin' this silly game with yer. Leave it.'

'Bloody good idea!' said Paterson. 'We came here to make enquiries into a multiple homicide, not debate Sunday school matters. Can we get back to the matter in hand, please?'

Wakker looked a bit taken aback. 'Yes. Yes, of course. I'm sorry.'

'It's okay. Didn't mean to come across as rude, it's just that we're pushed for time. I'm sure you understand.'

'Of course.'

'Your name,' said Paterson. 'It's unusual.'

'Yes, yes. I suppose it is. My great-grandparents were originally from the Netherlands. Used to be popular there, I'm told. Not so much these days.' Wakker sat back in his chair.

'Just curious.'

'Of course. I understand that your visit is something to do with a number of dreadful murders involving one of my parishioners, Lacey Heaton. I've already had a call from the vicar at St James's. He told me to expect a visit.'

'Did he?' said Paterson. 'That was good of him. Yes. Lacey Heaton and her children. Wondered if you could tell us a bit about her.'

'Hmm. Up until last year, she used to attend Sunday service quite regularly. I understand that she used to come here from a young age. Parents were regulars. I knew her reasonably well. She'd stop and chat when she could, but the children could be a bit of a handful, as I recall. The older child was, shall we say, a rascal, and the baby . . . well, the baby cried a lot, as they do.'

'Was she on her own? I mean, did she have a partner of some kind with her?'

'I don't recall ever seeing anyone with her, no.'

'She ever talk about 'avin' a partner?' said Clocks.

'Not that I recall. Sorry.'

'You said that she used to attend quite regularly. Any idea why that stopped?'

Wakker shook his head. 'No.'

'Did her attendance stop abruptly or did she just fade away?'

He shook his head. 'Just stopped for some reason.'

'Did you do a follow-up of some kind to see if she was alright?'

'No. Why would I?'

'Well,' said Paterson. 'She was a parishioner of yours. I'd have thought you'd have been a bit concerned, perhaps. No?'

Clocks was watching Wakker.

'I suppose. In hindsight, yes, but I had no reason to think she was in danger.'

'I didn't say she was. I just thought it was the sort of thing people in your profession did. Keep an eye on the flock, as it were.' Paterson picked at a fibre on his trousers.

'Anyone in yer church 'avin' a little sniff about?' said Clocks.

'I'm sorry. What?'

'Anyone creepin' about. Y'know. Tryin' it on with 'er. See if 'e can get 'is leg over with a lonely single mum. Might 'ave been a woman even. Dunno, do yer? She might have decided on a bit of rug munchin' fer a change. See 'ow that went.'

Wakker looked at Clocks. 'I'm sorry. I didn't really understand too much of that.'

'He means, were you aware of anyone taking a romantic interest in her?' said Paterson. 'Might be why she stopped coming.'

'Not that I recall.'

Paterson nodded a few times. 'Okay. Can I ask, how long have you been here?'

'Oooh, er, about three years, I think. Yes, must be.'

'Was Lacey a parishioner when you arrived?'

'She was, yes. Why?'

'Nothing,' said Paterson. 'Just thinking. Who was here before you? Perhaps he may be able to tell us a bit more about her.'

Paterson caught the slight but sharp movement of Wakker's head. He glanced at Clocks and could tell from the look he gave back that he'd seen it too.

'Er, yes, maybe.'

'What was his name?'

Wakker sighed deeply. 'Er, let me think . . . David, yes.'

'Surname?'

'Ooh. I can't remember.'

'Well, try 'arder,' said Clocks. 'I'm sure you'll get it in the end.'

Wakker licked his lips.

'Any luck?' Paterson asked.

'Hmm, hmm. Steers. Yes, that was it. David Steers. Nice man. Young, like myself.'

'What 'appened to 'im?'

Wakker shrugged. 'I don't really know. Before my time, I'm afraid.'

'Don't be afraid,' said Clocks. 'Not yet.'

Wakker looked alarmed.

'What?' said Clocks. 'We all know you've slipped into lyin' mode. Fuck me, Andy Botulism could see that.'

'You mean Andrea Bocelli, don't you? Opera singer,' said Paterson.

Clocks tapped his nose then pointed at Paterson. 'That's the very fellah, yep.'

'Lying? I'm not lying,' said Wakker.

'There you go, makin' it worse. Now you're lyin' about lyin'. Ol' Mr Jesus won't be too chuffed with you, will 'e? Tch, tch, tch.'

'Want to tell us something, Mr Wakker, before you go too deep down a rabbit hole you can't get out of?' said Paterson.

Wakker sighed. 'Look. I don't know much. I swear. All I know is that my superiors in the church became . . . worried about him, shall we say?'

'We can say that if yer like,' said Clocks, 'but now you're gonna tell us why they were worried about 'im, so you might as well spit it out an' be done with it.'

Wakker sighed again. 'All I know is that he became something of a liability, an embarrassment.'

'What'd 'e do, then?'

'I'm not comfortable with this . . . Please—'

'You'll be a lot less comfortable with my foot up yer arse, vicar. Out with it. Now.'

He nodded. 'I was told that David had been a bit too . . . er, hands-on with some of the parishioners.'

'That include Lacey?' said Paterson.

'I don't know. I wasn't told names and she never mentioned it.'

'Don't s'pose she would, eh?' said Clocks. 'Not like she could complain to the church, is it? Not with your lot's 'istory of coverin' stuff up. Why, who'd believe a young girls' story about the vicar that stuck 'is 'ands down her drawers an' 'ad a little rummage about in the undergrowth? Not me, fer sure. You, Ray?'

Paterson shook his head. 'I'm surprised it was girls. Normally little boys with your lot, isn't it?'

'Okay, okay. We don't have the best reputation, I accept that. And as for David . . .'

'Go on,' said Paterson.

'Well . . .' Wakker squirmed uncomfortably in his seat. 'This wasn't his first parish.'

'Why's that, then? Naughty boy, eh?'

'Indeed. It seems he had a particular penchant for both boys and girls. Under the age of ten.'

Paterson shook his head. He'd heard this sort of shit too many times in his working life.

'It seems that a few parents made some bitter complaints about him. He was dragged before a council of senior churchmen and questioned at length. He didn't deny the allegations. In fact, he seemed proud of them.'

'Proud of 'em? I can't wait to meet this little sweet'eart.'

'So what happened to him?' said Paterson. 'What was his defence? Did he offer one up?' He was aware that Clocks was showing signs of irritability. He knew where this could go and, after hearing what Steers had done, was of the same opinion as his friend. Justice needed to be served.

'Sort of. He claimed he was doing God's work and helping these poor children prepare themselves for a world made of sin. He also claimed that it was his job to "cleanse" them of evil thoughts and deeds.'

'By diddlin' 'em? 'Ow the fuck's that work, then?' said Clocks.

'It seemed to satisfy the council. He was shipped out of his old parish and sent here to start afresh.'

'And?' said Clocks.

Wakker shrugged slightly. 'And he was severely admonished and warned that any repeat would see him defrocked.'

'And that was that?'

'Yes. It was . . . swept under the carpet, unfortunately.'

'Was it? Well, unfortunately,' said Paterson, 'it's about to be lifted up again. Big time.'

'Wait a minute, 'old up,' said Clocks. 'You're tellin' me 'e diddled a bunch of kiddies an' all 'e gets is a bollockin' from a bunch of older perverts an' a move down the road to start diddlin' all over again, yes?'

'I'm afraid so. For the record, I don't agree with the way the church deals with such matters.'

'No?' said Paterson. 'Then why didn't you say something? Clearly you knew about it, having been told by someone at . . . what, your interview? Your posting? And yet you kept quiet. Hmm. So much for doing the right thing, eh?'

'Please. I'm ashamed of myself. I have put myself through purgatory for keeping my silence.'

'Seems you fuckin' managed it though,' said Clocks. 'What're the chances if we dig into you, you'll 'ave 'ad yer way with a few kiddies yerself? Is sexually abusing children on the curriculum at vicar school, then? I think it must be, judgin' by the amount of you all at it. Bunch of two-faced, hypocritical cocksuckers, the lot of yer.'

'No. No. That isn't true. I would never, *never* do such a thing.'

'Course you wouldn't. But that's what they all say, innit? I can see it now. You're all sittin' be'ind yer desks at church school, big photo of Jesus on the wall and it's Week One. Teacher stands at the front of the class and says, "Right, Rule

One . . . deny everything. Rule Two . . . lie like shit but always deny it too. Rule Three . . . if you're caught bang to rights, say God made me do it."'

'Why'd he leave here?' said Paterson. 'What happened?'

Wakker looked down at his shoes and waggled his feet. 'Er . . . You won't like this . . .'

Paterson glared at him. 'I've not liked any of it so far. Spit it!'

'He sexually assaulted a nun.'

Paterson's mouth dropped slightly. 'A nun?'

'A nun.'

'A fuckin' penguin? He fiddled with a penguin's feathers? Jesus! What the fuck is wrong with you lot? How'd that come about? No. Don't tell me. Christmas party, yes? Probably all off yer nuts on booze an' funny fags an' he chanced 'is arm with the designated driver.'

'What happened next?' said Paterson.

'He was brought before a panel again and this time they were as good as their word and defrocked him.'

'What? No? They took 'is frock off? Wow! You boys don't muck about, do yer? Probably liked that, the sick fucker. Right, Ray. I've 'eld me tongue long enough . . .'

'What? You haven't stopped talking.'

'Yeah, well . . . Look. What I wanna know is, what'd the police do about it? What nick was he taken to, Wakker?'

'Police?' Wakker looked confused.

'Yeah,' said Clocks. 'Police. Oh, 'old up, 'old up. You better not tell me that nobody bothered to call the police. Do *not* tell me that, Wakker. If you do, things will not go well for you.'

'Er . . .'

'Fuck me sideways with a baseball bat! Crimes mate. Crimes. Serious fuckin' crimes, an' you 'ad, what, a panel discussion an' decided to take 'is frock off 'im?' Who the fuck do you lot think you are? You think you can just ignore the rape of children and penguins and that's the end of it? Well, it's not. Right. Get up!'

'What?' Wakker's face was one of confusion.

Clocks moved closer to him. 'I said *get . . . up*. Do it!'

Wakker stood up. Paterson could see that he was shaking. 'John, what are you doing?'

'Well, I was thinkin' of 'urtin' 'im. You got any objections?'

'What? Why?' said Wakker now deeply alarmed. 'What have I done?'

'Fucked me off by keepin' yer trap shut when you shoulda been bumpin' yer gums to the Old Bill about what you knew. You're an accessory to the crimes of kiddie diddlin' and nun 'umpin'. An' given that your lot seem to be fond of decidin' what justice gets 'anded out, I thought I might 'and out a bit meself. Good with that, Ray?'

Paterson sighed and stood up. He looked at Clocks and smiled. He whirled around and with both hands grabbed Wakker by the collar of his shirt and threw him sideways. Wakker crashed onto a little photocopier pushed close to the wall. He grunted as the air was knocked out of him. Paterson still had him. He pulled him up and whirled him around before shoving him into the opposite wall. Wakker grunted again. Paterson let him go and watched the man struggle to stand.

'Where is this man now?' said Paterson, his voice cold, hard-edged.

'I . . . I . . .' Wakker held up one hand, defeated before he had begun. 'Please . . .'

'Where?' Paterson stepped forward again.

'He works at . . . he works at . . . er . . . St Margaret's Academy for Girls.'

Paterson stopped. 'What? Tell me that's a fucking joke.'

Clocks rubbed at his face. 'Christ . . .'

'No . . . It's the truth. He went to work there as a general handyman. The church found him the position. They thought it would help him to get a fresh start.'

'I'm . . . *sorry*? D'you know, for a second there, I thought you said summin' about the church got a deranged rapist a job in a girl's school. I mis'eard that, didn't I?' Wakker shook his head. Paterson watched Clock's face turn to pure stone. He'd

· 82 ·

roughed Wakker up, but judging by the look on his friend's face, it was obvious to him he was about to lose his shit altogether. 'A fuckin' *rapist*. In a girl's school. You lot are out of your minds ain'tcha? What fuckin' doom-brain twat of a prick came up with that bright idea? That's like lettin' a porn star loose in a dildo factory! Jesus fuckin' wept. I can't believe this.'

'Listen to me now,' said Paterson. 'If this David Steers is the man we're after, you need to tell me now if there's anything else we need to know. If I think you're holding back on anything then my colleague here, Mr Clocks, will start up Mr Clocks's naughty Clock, and believe me, you do *not* want that to happen. Understand me?'

'Yes. No. I don't know what that means but I'll help you. I'll tell you whatever you want to know.'

'Okay, then. What else do I need to know?'

Paterson saw the tears in Wakker's eyes. He had him right where he wanted. Isolated, on the back foot and afraid that these two policemen might actually inflict serious harm on him.

'Before the attacks became widely known and investigated, the council had heard rumours that David was taking it upon himself to visit female parishioners who'd stopped coming to church for whatever reason. It seems he was intimidating them quite severely. He turned up at one home with two dogs and began to berate some poor woman who'd missed a few services. Claimed that God was disappointed in her and that she would suffer his wrath if she did not return to the flock.'

'Did he now?' said Paterson. 'I've met those two dogs. I killed them both.'

Wakker's eyes widened.

'Go on.'

'Things degenerated after that. He began to visit as many people as he could and threatened them all.'

'How'd your lot find out about it?' said Clocks.

'Anonymous complaints were made. People were too frightened to come forward in person. They were terrified of him.'

'And how do you know so much about the council's decisions?' said Paterson.

Wakker dropped his gaze. 'I . . .'

The penny dropped quickly. 'Fuck me! You were an investigator, weren't you?'

'I'm sorry. Yes . . .'

'You knew *everything* and did *nothing*. How the fuck could you? You're supposed to be a man of honour. Integrity. You're just as guilty. You're a fucking coward!'

'I'm sorry. I'm sorry, I'm sorry, I'm sorry.'

'Right, let's 'ave another go, shall we? So, let's 'ave a quick recap. You know Steers is doing the nasty with kids an' threatenin' the Sunday school absentees with God's wrath and two fuck-off big dogs — now deceased — an' you reported back to the church, who promptly did fuck all about it until 'e jumped a nun an' 'ad 'is way with 'er?

'An' then, after findin' 'im guilty, they thought they'd cover it up an' get 'im a job in a school for little girls, an' then they thought: Right, job done. That's that sorted. We've got a spare five minutes. Let's see what the archbishop's been up to, shall we? Oh, look . . . got a complaint 'ere that he stuck 'is dick into a sausage roll in the middle of Greggs the Bakers with 'is arse 'angin' out of a pinny an' wearin' suspenders. Any takers for this one? Anyone? No? Ah, fuck it. Let's put it in the "too difficult" pile.'

'Alright,' said Paterson. 'We're done here. Richard Wakker, you're under arrest.'

Wakker's jaw hit the floor. 'What? You can't . . . I did my best. I did—'

'Nothing,' said Paterson. 'You did nothing except let this *thing* out onto the street, and now he's butchered a young woman and her two kids. A baby! If there is a hell, there's a fucking special place reserved for you and your pals. John, get on to the nick. Get a couple of the team down here ASAP to bring him in and start the paperwork off.'

Clocks pulled out his mobile phone. 'Now we're talkin'.'

Paterson cautioned Wakker and explained it in terms he'd understand. From inside his jacket pocket, he pulled out a pair of plasticuffs and secured Wakker to a radiator.

'What are you doing? Please . . . It's all a mistake.'

Paterson backhanded him, knocking his head against the radiator.

'We're leaving now, Wakker. In a few minutes my colleagues are coming to take you to the police station, where you'll be interviewed about your knowledge and involvement in the covering up of the crimes of rape against women and children. Also, your willingness to collude in covering up those crimes has directly resulted in the deaths of a woman and her kids. Far as I'm concerned, you're responsible for that too, so I'm going to have to think of something to charge you with that will see you go to prison for a long time.

'And, if I find out that anyone, *anyone* having anything to do with the church has been tipped off, then be under no illusion that myself and Mr Clocks here will come and visit you in the night. And, honestly, when we come looking for you, you'll have to rewrite the church's idea of the Devil and hell. *If* you're still able to. Clear?'

'Yes. Yes, sir.'

Paterson gave his cheek a couple of quick, admonishing slaps. 'Good. We'll see you later, no doubt.'

Paterson and Clocks walked out of the tiny office, leaving the door wide open. Linda from St James's was just taking off her coat.

'Linda!' Clocks called out. 'What you doin' 'ere?'

Linda shuffled into view. 'Oh. You're here.'

'What are you doin' 'ere?'

'Vicar Codd sent me over to see if there was anything I could do to help.'

Clocks shook his head. 'Did 'e now?'

'Yes. Thought I could be of use. Are you leaving now?'

'Yes, love. Places to go, people to see. Just to let you know, Wakker's in there handcuffed to a radiator. Me mates'll be 'ere soon to drag 'im off to the nick. Be a love an' don't try an' free 'im and definitely don't call anyone to tell 'em about this. If you do, I'll phone Boots the chemist an' get 'em to cut off yer medicine. Nobody wants that, do they?'

Linda looked aghast at him. 'No. I won't. What have you done to him?'

'That's my girl. Not done anythin' to 'im. He fell over a couple of times, that's all. We've just explained to him the rights and wrongs of his coverin' up criminal offences an' now we're 'avin' 'im nicked.'

'What has he done?'

'What 'asn't 'e done, love?'

She shook her head. 'I'm not surprised. He was always a dick!'

Clocks suddenly burst out laughing.

'What's so funny?' said Paterson.

''Is name. Richard Wakker. Dick Wakker. Must 'ave been 'is destiny all along. Can't fight fate.'

Paterson creased up as the pair of them walked out.

CHAPTER SEVENTEEN

'What's the plan, Stan?' Clocks said, fastening his seat belt.

'We nip over to this girl's academy and see if our murderer's in work today. If he is, we nick him. Nice and simple. Bish, bash, bosh, as you would say.'

'Right. That sounds like a plan to end all plans. We tellin' the troops?'

'Yep. Get on the phone and get them to meet us outside. Let them know we're not a hundred percent sure he's in work today but it's worth a spin.'

'Okay. Okay. Question . . .'

'Go on.'

'Why don't we phone 'em an' find out if 'e's in?'

Paterson pulled the car away from the road and out into the traffic. 'Nope. They might give him the nod.'

'Why would they do that?'

'They might not, but better to be safe than sorry.'

Clocks shrugged. 'I'm just thinkin' we're gonna look like a bunch of mugs if we go in mob 'anded an' 'e's not there. I thought maybe a quick call to the headmaster might save us all a trip.'

Paterson nodded. It made sense. 'Do that, then. But we'll head that way just in case he is in.'

'That's a better plan.'

'Will you be alright in there?'

Clocks turned slightly to look at him.

'What'd you mean?'

'I'm just thinking. This place is loaded up with teenage girls in short skirts. You know what you're like.'

Clocks tried to feign indignation. 'What're you talkin' about? I'm a married man. I'm not into teenagers!'

'No?'

'No.'

'My mistake. Sorry.'

Clocks turned back around and looked out of the window. 'S'alright. It's you they should be worried about.'

'Me? Why me?'

'Well, an' it pains me to say this, you've not exactly fell out of the ugly tree 'ave yer? *An'* you've got one of those Calvin Klein underpants bodies. *An'* you've got a few quid tucked away. So, all up, you're a bit of a snog ain'tcha?'

'John. I never knew you felt that way.'

'Fuck off, bender. You know what I mean. I should think you're a bit of a teenage girl's fantasy. Probably a few of their mum's too. Well, we can chuck their grans in there too, judging by ol' Linda's display.'

'You think?'

'Not often, but enough to avoid a headache. Yes, I do think that.'

'Cheers, mate.'

'Welcome. 'Ere . . . Just thinkin' . . .'

'I figured you would. Let's have it.'

'So, I was thinking . . . This mum-and-daughter business . . .'

'What mum-and-daughter business?'

'You know. Where a mum an' 'er daughter jump on the same man. Usually at the same time . . .'

Paterson wrinkled his nose. 'Where are you going with this?'

'I dunno. I just got to thinkin'. That's a bit weird that ain't it?'

'Very weird, yes.'

'I mean, what's that all about?'

'No idea. You been up at night watching Pornhub again?'

'Oh, yeah.'

'Thought as much.' Paterson tooted his horn at the car in front. The driver's head bobbed quickly and then they stuck up their index finger.

Paterson grinned. 'You need to stop watching that. Gives you bad dreams.'

'I know. But seriously. I can't imagine that.'

'Really? I would have thought you'd have no trouble imagining that at all.'

'Har-de-har. Nah. Nasty ol' business, that.'

'Well, they say it's the ultimate male fantasy.'

'Do they?'

'Hmm, hmm.'

'Well, it ain't mine.'

'Don't think Lyndsey'll go for any of that?'

'No I don't and, fuck me, you saw Lyndsey's mum at the weddin' didn't yer?'

'I did. Lovely lady. I'd imagine she was very striking in her day.'

'What? Is that your way of sayin' she's an uggo now?'

'An uggo? No. Not at all. I just meant she's probably not quite as pretty now as she was when she was younger. None of us are.'

'Not pretty? That's the fuckin' understatement of the century. The woman's got a face like a bag of minced minges an' teeth like a witch doctor's necklace!'

Paterson let out a loud raspberry sound in lieu of a laugh.

'An' I'll tell you summin' else about 'er mum. Lyndsey don't know I know this, an' don't you tell 'er I said it, but she's been rogered more times than a police radio.'

Paterson snorted and pulled the car to a sudden halt. 'You fucker, John.'

'What? I'm just sayin'. Truth's truth.' He started laughing too.

'Stop it! Fucking behave yourself. Now. I nearly crashed.'

'Yeah. You need to be a bit more careful. D'you know what 'er nickname was at school?'

Paterson had tears in his eyes. He shook his head and bit his tongue.

'Red cord.'

'What? Red cord? Why?'

''Cos she was summin' you only pulled in an emergency.'

The two men erupted into laughter and for the next three minutes sat in the car trying to get their act together. Paterson was incapable of driving.

'You bastard, Clocksy. I'm sweating.'

'Yeah? I'm sweatin' Lyndsey'll turn into 'er mother when she gets older. They do that don't they? Fuckin' 'ell. Summin' to look forward to, that is.'

'Just stop, alright? You're hurting me now.'

'Am I? Sorry.'

Paterson sniffed a couple of times. 'It's alright. Thank you.'

'Fer what?'

'For makin' me laugh. I needed it. Badly. Things get a bit much sometimes, y'know?'

'I know, mate. You're welcome.'

'I'm serious.'

Clocks looked into his friend's face. 'Is this the bit where you get all serious an' try an' kiss me? I know what you're like. Any 'ole's a goal, eh?'

'Fuck off,' said Paterson. He looked over his shoulder and pulled back out into the traffic. 'And get on that bloody phone and call the team.'

'Will do.'

'Go on, then.'

'An' what about 'er sister, eh? She was at the weddin', remember?'

Paterson immediately pulled over again. 'Don't.'

'Ooh. Big ol' unit, she is. Like a double wardrobe, 'onestly. We were out shoppin' at Ikea with 'er once. I remember she stopped to look at a bed an' this nice young couple ordered two of 'er for their bedroom.'

'Don't! Just don't!'

'What? I'm just tellin' yer somethin' about me family. I'm sharin'. That's what they told me to do on all these cuddle courses you send me on to try an' make me a new man. A *woke* man. I 'ave to share so's I can get better. It's your fault, mate. Anyway, she used to work in a library, she did. Y'know what they used to call 'er?'

Paterson shook his head. 'Don't, John. Please.'

'Conan the Librarian.'

'I fucking hate you,' said Paterson before he started laughing again.

CHAPTER EIGHTEEN

Police Constable Steve Hudson could see light at the end of the tunnel. He was nearing the end of his two-year probationary period and everything so far had been going great guns. He'd not had a day off sick and had one of the best arrest records for a probationer that Southwark had seen for a long time. His workaday colleagues considered him to be a good, solid, stand-up, no-nonsense copper who had your back when things went south. If there was a fight to be had, Steve Hudson was the man you'd want beside you.

He'd seen and done a lot in his short time and never shied from any task or situation he was presented with. He oozed confidence. If he had a weak spot, it was the sight of the dead.

It was irrational. He knew that. After all, the dead couldn't hurt you. But seeing his first body — a thirty-one-year-old man, who, to all intents and purposes, was as fit as a fiddle but who had just dropped dead from a heart attack — seemed to trigger something in his brain. This man wasn't that much older than him. It may have been the fact that the man's wide-open eyes seemed to have registered surprise at the second his heart gave up on him. It may have been the waxy look of his skin. It may have been the pool of urine he lay in. It may have been all of those things or none of them. He just hated the sight of them.

If he'd have looked a little deeper inside himself, chances are he would have understood that it wasn't really the sight of a dead person that unnerved him, it was the not knowing what lay behind the door. The anticipation was the problem; all the way to the call, his imagination ran riot.

All he knew was that a woman had reported her neighbour's door being open, claimed it was most unlike her and had gone to see what had happened. She found her neighbour dead, had a screaming fit, and her husband called the police.

PC Hudson, on foot and close to the scene, was the first to arrive.

The street door was ajar and there were one or two neighbours milling around looking distraught. He made his way along the path that led to the front door and spoke to one of the neighbours, a woman by the name of June.

'What's happened?'

June stared at him.

'Madam. Are you okay?'

She shook her head. 'It's . . . it's . . . she's . . . she's . . . oh, God!'

His stomach tightened and his head became slightly cloudy. If this was going to be anywhere near as bad as he imagined, he hoped that he could hold it together. 'Have you been in there?'

She nodded.

He shook his head and made a mental note. She would have to be checked by forensics, now she'd contaminated the scene.

'Stay here, please. I'll come back in a minute.'

She turned her back on him and began to sob.

'Do we know if anyone's still in there?' he asked one of the male neighbours.

'No idea,' said a fit-looking man in his fifties. 'I don't think so, but be careful, mate. Want me to come with you?'

Hudson shook his head. 'No, mate. It's alright. Thanks though. Stay here.'

He drew in a deep breath, pulled out his canister of pepper spray and, stepping to one side, gave the door a gentle push. It swung open. 'Police!' He stepped inside the hallway. 'Police! Anybody here?' he called.

In the distance, the wail of a siren gave him a small measure of comfort. His colleagues would be here very soon and, with a bit of luck, would find this dead body before he did. He pushed on. Coming to the first door, the living room, he raised the pepper spray. 'Police! I'm coming in.' He kicked the door open and rushed in the moment the door flew back. Empty. He took a deep breath at the sight of bloody footprints on the cream-coloured carpet. Blood smears ran along both sides of the hallway, pictures had been knocked on the wonk.

His mind shifted into overdrive. *The victim staggered along the hallway, no doubt screaming for her life. Maybe pleading? Probably both. May have been the killer leaving the flat and rubbing his hands along the walls as he went.*

He was wary as he approached the kitchen — the scene, he knew, of most domestic murders. In his bones, though, he recognised this wasn't a domestic argument gone wrong. The kitchen was empty too. That left the dining and bedrooms. Buoyed by the louder sound of the siren, he pressed on. He figured them for the end of the road.

'Police!' He stepped nearer. And that's when the first real flutter of fear hit him in the stomach. Somehow, he sensed that someone waited for him behind the door ahead of him. It was easy enough to work out.

His mind ran in different directions now. *How come nobody heard anything? Did they? Why didn't they call us? What was waiting for him behind the door? A victim? A killer? Both? Would his colleagues make it in time?*

His breathing sped up and grew deeper as he stepped up to the door. He holstered his pepper spray and drew his

Taser. Better to be safe than sorry. He kicked the door and it swung open. He stepped inside and stopped.

Slowly, he lowered his arms then dropped the Taser. It bounced around on the blood-soaked carpet until it settled into a congealed pool of blood. PC Hudson fainted.

CHAPTER NINETEEN

Paterson and Clocks scoped out the grounds of St Margaret's Academy as they waited for the rest of the squad to arrive. The building itself looked to have been built in the early part of the twentieth century: red brick and ornamental stone masonry above the doorways. It was set back from the road and surrounded by playing fields. At the back was a small hut, out of which, Paterson guessed, the groundsman-cum-caretaker worked.

Monkey Harris's BMW came tearing around the corner, followed by Jackie Hartnett in her Toyota SUV. Paterson could see that the vehicles were loaded up with his troops. He waved them down and they pulled over.

Clocks signalled at them: 'Keep it quiet.'

Dusty was the first to reach the two detectives. 'What we got?'

'Not much,' said Paterson. 'Just got here ourselves. We're looking for the school caretaker, David Steers. I'll fill you all in later, but for now he's our main suspect and I want him brought in with the minimum of fuss and bother.'

'Got a picture of him?' said Dusty.

'Nope. Nothing.'

'Do we know where to find him?'

Paterson nodded toward the building. 'Somewhere in there.'

Dusty sighed. 'I don't think we're just gonna wander in, guv. Schools are all secured these days.'

'I know. Me and Jackie will go in first. Make out we're mum and dad coming up to see the head about little Adele. Should get us through the front door. We'll wing it once we're in.'

'What d'you want us to do?'

'Skirt the perimeter and keep an eye out. If you see him, give me a call.'

'How will we know it's him?'

'Take a guess, Dusty.' Clocks interrupted. 'He'll be the one leggin' it with the guv and Jackie runnin' be'ind 'im shoutin', "Stop! In the name of the law!"'

Dusty smiled. 'You make a good point, guv.'

'I know. But listen up all of yer: this fucker is as dangerous as 'e is mad. Take extreme care if you confront 'im. Do not engage if 'e's armed. Understood?'

'Guv,' said Yorkshire. 'We got movement.'

Paterson looked to where Yorkshire was pointing. A young man, wearing a baseball cap pulled down low over his eyes, was just coming out of the little hut.

'Is that him?' said Paterson.

Clocks squinted. 'Dunno. Could be.'

'Jackie, let's go,' said Paterson.

The rest of the squad broke up and went their separate ways.

Paterson and Jackie pressed the intercom buzzer and waited. A metallic-sounding female voice answered. *'Hello. How can I help you?'*

'Good morning,' said Jackie in her posh voice. 'We're here to see Mr Merritt with regards to our daughter, Adele.'

Clocks watched the caretaker pick up his broom, attach it to the side of his cart and begin to walk toward the school.

'Do you have an appointment?'

'I'm sorry, no. But he wanted to discuss her university pick with us and this is the only time we've both been able to get together. Work commitments, I'm afraid. My husband travels a lot. All we need is five minutes.'

There was silence for a moment or two. *'Mr Merritt isn't here yet, but he shouldn't be too much longer. Come in and we'll sort something out when he arrives.'* There was a loud buzz and the door clicked open.

'Thank you so much,' said Jackie.

'How'd you know the headmaster's name?' said Paterson.

'It's on the board outside, underneath the name of the school.'

'Told yer she was good detective,' said Clocks, who started to follow them in.

'Where are you going?' said Paterson.

'With you two.'

'What? No. He sees three of us, he's gonna run. We're supposed to look like a mum and dad. Let me and Jackie get close and then we'll take him. Wait outside in the car just in case he gets past us.'

Clocks wrinkled his nose. 'It'll be fine. I'll 'ang back a bit.' He looked past Paterson. 'Better 'urry up. Geezers' comin' our way.'

'Fuck!' Paterson grabbed Jackie's hand and they began to walk casually toward the main entrance. Clocks waited by the gate, his foot holding it open.

Paterson and Jackie slowed just enough to time the caretaker's arrival at the main entrance a few seconds after them. Paterson couldn't make out for certain if it was the same man he'd chased over the rooftops. He could feel Jackie's fingers tighten up. She was ready to pounce. He squeezed her hand to transmit a silent message. *Not yet.*

Paterson pushed the button. The metallic lady's voice answered them again. *'Come in.'*

The caretaker parked his cart against the wall.

'You coming in, fellah?' Paterson sounded as casual as he could.

'Thanks,' said the young man and he quickened his pace to get through the door Paterson held open for him. Jackie was already inside. She partly blocked his way and they did the little side-to-side dance.

'Can you tell us where the office is please, David?' said Paterson.

'Sure. It's . . .' The man turned. He glared at Paterson, spun and pushed Jackie over as he ran. Paterson took off after him, leaving Jackie on the ground.

She pulled herself up, ran to the door and called out: 'Guv! Guv!'

Clocks broke into a run.

'Ray's after him!' she shouted.

Clocks ran straight past her and skidded to a halt at the end of a very short corridor. 'Which way?'

'Left! Left!'

'What's happening? Who are you people?' The receptionist, behind her desk, was in a state of panic. 'Get out! I'll call the police!'

'We're already here, love,' said Jackie. 'But do it anyway. Tell them we need urgent assistance. Do it!'

The woman reached for the phone. Jackie was running.

Paterson was finding it difficult to get much purchase on the polished floor in his Louboutin's. He skidded once or twice and bounced off the wall. A terrified girl jumped out of the way as the two men came hurtling toward her. She screamed as they ran past. The doors to two classrooms suddenly opened and the teachers poked their heads out.

'Move it!' Clocks yelled as he ran at the crowd of girls that were now blocking his way, barrelling his way into the throng. 'Move, move, move! Outta the way! C'mon. Move yerselves!' He barged his way through as the girls began to back away against the walls.

Clocks took off again.

The caretaker rounded a corner and ran full tilt toward a packed assembly hall. Paterson was closing the gap.

More screams erupted as the two men tore into the hall. Paterson dropped into a slide and connected with the caretaker's foot. The caretaker shot sideways and crashed hard to the ground. Paterson was half up and launched himself at him. The caretaker lashed out, catching Paterson on the side of the face. The two men struggled for a few seconds before Paterson punched the caretaker square on the nose, stunning the man. He flipped him over, face down, and knelt on his back while he fumbled in his jacket for some plasticuffs. His pocket was empty.

The teachers, visibly alarmed, were unsure of what to do. They weren't trained for this. 'Girls! Girls!' one of them called out. 'Stay calm!'

Clocks was next into the hall. He skidded to a sudden halt and fell over onto his front. 'Fuck!'

The only male teacher jumped down from the small stage and made his way over to Paterson. 'What the hell's going on?' he demanded.

'Who are you?' said Paterson.

'Who are you, more like it? What do you think you're doing?'

'I'm holding this man down until I can get him cuffed up. What are you doing?'

'I . . .'

'Apart from nothing, I mean.'

'What? How dare you? I'm the deputy head.'

'Well, deputy head. Be a pal and go wait over there out of the way, please. I'm a tad busy just now.'

Clocks pushed though the group of girls that surrounded them. 'You alright, guv?'

'All tickety-boo here, John. Got any cuffs on you?'

'Yeah. Sure.' He handed Paterson a set and, within seconds, the caretaker was secured. Paterson stood him up and began to march him out of the hall.

'Look,' said the deputy head, 'who are you people? The police?'

'Yep,' said Clocks.

'Let me see your warrant.'

'Ain't got one. Don't need it.'

'Yes, you do. I demand to see it.'

'Do yer? Oh, well. If you're demanding, that's different. I'll 'ave a look for it.' He exaggerated patting himself down, felt around inside his jacket and trouser pockets and finally shook his head. 'Nope. I can't seem to find it. I don't know what's happened. I normally keep it with me bag of fucks, but I can't find any of them either. See yer.' He gestured to the girls to move aside.

'*Are* you the police?' one of the girls asked.

Clocks looked at her.

'What?'

'I want to join the police.'

'What? What the fu— What the 'ell for? I thought you're all s'posed to be intelligent at this school? You don't wanna do that.'

The girl's face fell.

'Nah. No job for women, this. You need to learn 'ow to cook an' clean. Proper woman stuff.'

Now the girl looked horrified.

Clocks grinned and decided to address the group. 'Listen up, ladies. Some advice for yer all. Be good gels. Keep yer 'and on yer 'appennies, stay in school, don't do drugs, don't do porn, an' if yer boyfriend ever asks for a nudie picture, "just for 'im", don't do it. Trust yer uncle Johnny. It'll be all over the internet before you know it an' tucked away in some ol' pervs wank bank. Alright? Goddit? Good. Right, ta-ta, ladies.' He pushed his way through the crowd, leaving them all looking bewildered.

CHAPTER TWENTY

PC Hudson snapped awake the instant the sharp smell of ammonia tore into his brain. It took him just a couple of seconds to realise what was going on. Two paramedics were peering down at him with concerned expressions on their faces.

'You alright, son?' the elder of the two said.

Hudson's eyes followed the small brown bottle as the paramedic quickly moved the smelling salts away from him. 'Yeah. Yeah. What happened?' He sat himself upright with the help of one of the paramedics.

'It don't matter . . .'

It hit him then and his eyes widened. He panicked.

'Here we go,' said the elder. He held up a hand in front of Hudson's face. 'Just take a deep breath. You've had a shock. A bloody nasty one, too.'

Hudson became aware of movement from others in the room. He tried to look past the kneeling paramedic but the man blocked his view. 'Best not expose yourself to a double dose, mate. Let's just get you up and out of here.' The two men took an arm each and hoisted him to his feet.

'Wait!' Hudson said. 'My mates. I heard them come in behind me. They okay?'

'Yes, son,' said the younger paramedic. 'They're good. Shaken, but they'll all be fine. So will you.'

Hudson nodded. 'Where we going to?'

'We'll run you into Guy's casualty for a once-over. I'm sure your colleagues in the CID will want to have a chat with you as soon as possible, but this little trip will give you a bit of time to get your head together.'

Hudson nodded again. 'Thanks, gents.'

As the two paramedics guided him toward the door, Hudson glanced sideways and saw what had caused him to faint. He felt his stomach tighten and tasted bile in his throat. He jerked to a halt. Well versed in the signs of people about to throw up, the paramedics jumped to one side while still holding onto his arms. Hudson spewed up and wobbled. His legs collapsed again and the paramedics struggled to support his weight.

Once he'd finished puking, they helped him to sit down gently.

'It's alright, son. I know it's rough.'

Hudson, eyes streaked with tears, face pale and clammy, unable to uncomprehend what he had just seen, looked up at the man. He began to retch again.

'Let's just give him a minute, Kev,' said the older one. 'I get the impression he's not seen this sort of thing before.'

'Neither have I,' said Kev. 'Not like that.'

CHAPTER TWENTY-ONE

Paterson pushed the caretaker in front him, herding him toward the car. The boy looked back at him every so often, his face red.

'Problem with me, son?' said Paterson.

'Fuck off, bully boy. Fucking hard when the cuffs are on, ain't you?'

Paterson laughed. 'I'm fucking hard when they're off, son.'

The boy stopped and planted his feet. 'Well, take 'em off then, copper. We'll see what you got. Do it!'

'Son,' said Monkey, opening the car door. 'You really don't want that to happen. Seriously. You don't.'

The caretaker looked at him. 'Fuck off, fat boy. Not talking to you. Talking to this prick. Take 'em off of me!' His face was now a bright red and he strained to break the plasticuffs that held his hands behind his back. 'Take . . . them . . . off! I'll fucking kill you all.'

Paterson grabbed him by the shoulder and pushed him forward slightly. 'Your wish is my command. Monkey. Knife.'

Monkey Harris grinned and pulled out a small pocket knife. He handed it to Paterson.

He cut the plastic. 'Me and you it is then, fellah.'

The caretaker immediately spun around, his right arm flailing. The heel of Paterson's palm hit him straight on the chin, knocking him backward into Monkey. He pushed him back to Paterson.

Dazed, the caretaker swung wildly. Paterson dodged the swinging punch with ease and dropped a right hander onto the boy's chin, hard enough for him to feel it but not hard enough to do damage. He staggered back, eyes glazed.

'I'm curious, mate,' said Paterson. 'When exactly are you going to kill us all? I'm asking because, so far, you're making a shitty job of it.'

The young man threw another wild punch. Paterson blocked it, stepped aside, dropped low and punched him hard in the stomach. The force of air that exited the body told Paterson his job was done. There would be no fight left in this man.

'Can *I* give 'im a dig, Ray?' said Clocks.

'No. Not yet.'

The sound of a car roaring into the car park got everyone's attention.

'Aye, aye,' said Monkey. 'What do we have here?'

An angry-looking man dressed in a lightweight mac jumped out of the car. 'What's going on here! Who the hell are you people? I demand to know.'

Clocks grinned. 'Who are you, then?'

'I'm the headmaster. What have you done to this boy?'

'Gave him a slap,' said Paterson. 'He wanted to fight so I thought it'd be a good time to educate him not to pick fights with strangers. I think he's cottoned on.'

'Who are you?' the man demanded.

'Detective Superintendent Paterson. I'm a murder squad officer. This man is my suspect and is under arrest for the murder of a woman, her two children and two of my officers. So you're Merritt, are you?'

The headmaster nodded. 'Yes.'

'Well, you're late for school.'

Merritt frowned. 'What?'

'Nothing.'

The caretaker coughed and struggled to get his breath. 'I . . . I . . . Not me. Not me . . . Please.'

'Cuff him back up and put him in the car, Monkey,' said Paterson.

'There must be some mistake,' said Merritt.

'Possibly, but I don't think so. FYI, he'll be taken to Tower Bridge police station if anyone asks.'

Paterson and Clocks walked away and jumped in the car. Monkey squeezed himself into the back with the boy.

'Jackie!' Paterson called. 'Do me a favour, please. Spend a bit of time squaring up Merritt here, and you and Dusty start taking statements for me. I want to know as much as I can about him.'

'Sure, boss. See you later.'

Paterson gave Mr Merritt a quick nod and drove away.

'So,' said Clocks. 'Gotcha, didn't we? You crazy little shit.'

The boy was getting his breath back. 'I didn't do nothing.'

'No? So why 'ave it on yer toes, then? Innocent people don't run.'

'I didn't do what you're accusing me of.'

'What've you done, then?'

'Nothing!'

'Of course not,' said Paterson. 'As he said, why run if you've done nothing? I called you by your name and you panicked. Then you ran, didn't you? Why do that?'

'You had Old Bill written all over you. I thought you'd come to nick me.'

'We' ad come to nick yer,' said Clocks.

'Yeah, sounds like you got your facts all fucked up though. I thought you'd come to nick me for an outstanding warrant.'

Paterson frowned. 'For what?'

'Look . . . I got into an argument with my bird. Nothing serious. We was both a bit high. She said something — can't

106

even remember what it was — and I lost my temper. I slapped her about a bit. That's all. I got my collar felt and got bailed. I didn't go back to answer bail, so I think there's a warrant out for me.'

'Oh, that's all, is it?' said Clocks without bothering to turn around. 'That's alright then, innit? A big 'ard lad like you slappin' yer bird around. That's nothin', that is. We'll just let you go an' forget about it, shall we?'

'No need to be sarky, copper.'

Clocks whirled around, unclipped his seat belt and started climbing between the seats. The boy threw himself back and raised his feet.

'Fuckin' talk to me like that, you cop-killing, child-murderin' prick!'

'John!' Paterson yelled. 'Sit the fuck down!' Clocks caught the steering wheel with his arm, causing Paterson to swerve.

Clocks desperately tried to punch the boy and the boy was doing his best to fend him off. Monkey quickly put him into a headlock and pulled him down onto the seat. 'Stay down, son!' he said. 'Stay down!'

'Sit the fuck down, John. I mean it! Sit. Down!'

Fuming, Clocks did as he was told.

'What's the matter with you? You could've killed us.'

Clocks shrugged his jacket back into place. 'Nah. You're too good a driver to let that 'appen. I'm not takin' any mouth off this little bastard. Not 'appenin'. If 'e mouths off to me again, I'll beat the fuckin' granny out of the snot-gobblin' little prick, I swear to God I will.'

'What's your name, son?' said Paterson.

'David. David Kember.'

Paterson gripped the steering wheel a little bit tighter.

CHAPTER TWENTY-TWO

'Where do you live, David?' said Paterson.

'I've got a flat on the Aylwin Estate.'

'Anyone live there with you?'

'Not anymore.'

'Anyone staying with you?'

'No. My bird moved out after the . . . argument. Why?'

'Because we're going to spin your address.'

Paterson flicked the indicator stalk and headed toward Druid Street.

'What? Why? You can't do that!' He became agitated again.

'Calm it down, son.' Monkey gave him a death stare. 'Don't start again.'

'I can and I am,' said Paterson. 'Section Eighteen of the Police and Criminal Act empowers me to carry out a search without a warrant if I believe that the property contains information or evidence of a serious crime.'

'I've already told you. I haven't done anything. You've got the wrong man.'

'Maybe. Only, I'm not convinced. Y'see, you look a fair bit like someone I chased across the rooftops a little while ago and—'

David shook his head. 'Rooftops? Not a chance, mate. I'm terrified of heights. Always have been. Not me.'

'Well, we'll see, won't we?'

'Okay, then. Do what you want. Search it, just don't leave it in a mess.'

'Wasn't planning on it. Are we going to find anything?'

'Yep. A bit of puff and a few bags of H. Need to pay the rent. The wages from this job are shit!'

Ten minutes later, David Kember sat handcuffed on his sofa while the three policemen searched the flat. Clocks had turned up at least a quarter pound of heroin and fifty bags of cocaine, and the bathroom had been turned into a miniature cannabis-growing factory.

But nothing relating to the murders.

'Can I 'ave a word, guv?' Clocks pointed to the hallway.

Paterson nodded. 'Keep an eye on him, Monkey.'

They stepped out into the hallway and Clocks closed the door.

'Fuck!' he said in a low voice. 'He's not our man.'

Paterson sighed. 'Maybe not. Could be using a false ID though.'

'Possibly. But every single letter is addressed David Kember. His driving licence is David Kember's. There's not a shred of evidence to link him to the killings. Wrong David. Wrong man.'

'He bloody well looks like him, though.'

'No 'e don't. I mean, for starters, this bloke ain't got white eyes, a Miss Piggy 'ooter and a pair of greasy curtains for a barnet, as 'e? You just *want* 'im to look like 'im the same way as I wanna look like Tom Cruise, but I don't.'

Paterson smiled. 'That's true. The second bit, not the bit about wanting Kember to look like Steers.'

Clocks's phone rang. It was Jackie Hartnett. 'Everything okay there, Jackie?'

'Not really, Clocks. Merritt's doing his bollocks. He's found out about the chase through the school and our man's arrest. He's also pissed off at the advice you gave a group of his girls. What did you say?'

'Nothing. I gave them a bit of sensible advice, that's all.'

'Did you tell them not to be porn stars or take nude pictures of themselves, by any chance?'

Clocks sniffed. 'I mentioned it to them, yeah. I thought that was solid advice. Is it not?'

'Fucking hell, guv. Really? They're just young girls.'

'And?'

'You don't say stuff like that!'

'Why not?'

'Because . . . Oh fuck it! Never mind. You'll never understand anyway.'

'Why bring it up, then?'

'I just thought—'

'Movin' swiftly on. Any other news?'

'Hmm, hmm. Merritt says that our man's name is David Kember.'

'That's what we've got.'

'He's a temp. Been with them for just over a week. Seems that Steers did work there but left abruptly. No notice, nothing. The school have tried contacting him. Again, nothing.'

'Bollocks! They got an address for 'im?'

'Yeah. It's on the Arnolds Estate. Merritt said they sent someone to the address to see if he was sick or something. Neighbours said he moved out. Lock, stock and barrel. Said he was a weird fucker and were glad to see him go.'

Clocks sighed deeply. 'Can you arrange for a couple to double check the addy for me? Y'never know.'

'Yeah, of course. Laters.' She hung up.

'School confirmed. David Kember. Steers left on the 'urry-up. Jackie's sending a couple to check his last known address.'

Paterson dropped his back onto the wall and looked up at the ceiling. 'Okay. He's still going into the nick, though. I want this place swept for forensics and, yes, I know, we've been stamping around. They'll have to work around that. We might get something.'

'We won't, Ray. It's not 'im.'

'Fuck!' His phone rang. 'Paterson.' He listened intently for a full minute. 'We're on our way.'

Paterson pushed himself off the wall.

'Don't tell me . . .'

'Yep. Another one. This one's a doozy.' He opened the door to the living room. 'Monkey. Stay with him. Mr Kember . . . your lucky day.'

'What's going on?' said Kember. 'I'm going to sue the arse off of you lot. Wrongful arrest.'

'Yeah, okay. Good luck with that. Monkey, get the drug squad here.'

He winked at Kember. 'When I said lucky day, I was lying.' He looked at the drugs they'd found, now laid out on a coffee table. 'Seems you had a bit more stuff than you first told us. I reckon seven years for this little lot, and I also reckon when they get here with sniffer dogs, there's a good chance they'll find at least another three years' worth of prison time for you. Mind how you go, trappy.'

CHAPTER TWENTY-THREE

'Get suited up before you go in, gents.' Tony Kent, the senior forensics officer in charge of the scene held out two sealed packets, each containing a white paper suit. Paterson and Clocks had dealt with him before. He was a no-nonsense, highly professional man with zero sense of humour and couldn't stand either of them. His biggest mistake had been in letting them know that.

'Mr Kunt. How lovely to see you again,' said Clocks, his smile genuine.

Kent peered at him. 'Who are you?' he said, downplaying Clocks's arrival.

'It's me. Yer ol' mate, Clocksy. You must recognise me? I look exactly the same as when I last took the piss out of yer. Not that long ago, was it?'

'Ah yes. I do remember you now. The ignorant man with the attitude.'

'That's it! That's me! So, 'ow's it 'angin', then?'

'What?'

'I said, 'ow's it 'angin'?'

Kent shrugged. 'No idea what you're talking about, Clocks.'

'Me neither most of the time.'

'Just put it on.'

'You got any other colours? This one makes me look like a walkin' tampon.'

'Not sure you need a suit for that,' said Kent. He allowed himself a little smile.

Clocks chuckled. 'Ooh. Nice one, Tone. Nice one. Not expected, but I'll give yer that.'

Paterson unpacked his paper suit. 'Kent, what've we got in there?'

'A serious mess. Victim is female. Age to be determined but I would say . . . early twenties. Late twenties at a push. She's naked, staked out with crucifixes in each wrist. She's been decapitated. The head has been placed face down between her legs in what I can only suppose is some sort of symbolic gesture and it looks like a crucifix has been inserted into her anus, although I'm not completely sure yet as we haven't moved the body.

'Oh, lovely,' said Paterson. 'That sounds pleasant.'

'Photographer can't get a clean picture. Once I'm ready, we'll move the head and confirm.'

Paterson hopped about on one leg as he pulled the paper shoes on over his own. 'Who's in there now?'

'Photographer and my assistant.'

'Charlie?' said Clocks. 'I like 'im. Nice chap.'

'Yes, that's him. Of course. You've met him too, haven't you? Hmm. I seem to recall he couldn't stop talking about you two when last we met.'

Clocks smiled. '*When last we met?* Is that Shakespeare? It sounded a bit Shakespeary.'

Kent ignored him. 'Thought you were both extremely good policemen.'

'Well, 'e thought right, matey. We are. The best of the best of the best. If we flew planes, we'd be Top Guns. I know *you're* not a fan, but I checked earlier and my big bag of fucks is already empty so I can't let you 'ave one of 'em. I used 'em up early today. Y'know 'ow it is in this job, don'tcha?'

'Ready, John?' said Paterson.

'Leave off. Gimme a minute or two. I'm swappin' banter with Mr Kunt 'ere. Takes up a bit of time.'

'I heard. Great fun.'

'Don't forget the hat,' said Kent.

'What?'

'Hat.'

'Oh, come on. That bleedin' thing makes me look like I work in a bloody bakery.'

'I don't want your hair contaminating the scene, Clocks. Put it on.'

'I'm going in,' said Paterson.

'Wait a minute. One minute. Not like the 'eadless corpse is goin' anywhere, is it?'

'Hurry up, then.'

Clocks hopped on one leg as he slipped the cover on over his shoe. 'I preferred the old days when we used to just bowl into a crime scene large as life. None of this suit shit.'

'I hear you two still do that,' said Kent. 'But you don't do that at my crime scene. Never.'

Clocks gave him a grin. 'Whatever you say, Mr Kunt. You're the man in charge.'

'My name, Clocks, is Kent. Kent. Can you stop being a bloody child and pronounce it correctly?'

'I could. But I won't. This is way more fun. You comin' back in with us or you just gonna strut about outside makin' out you're someone important?'

Kent bristled. 'I'll come with you, Clocks. I need to make sure you don't fuck anything up.'

Clocks stretched out the white paper hat, placed it over his head and let it snap into place. 'There we go. Now I'm a tampon, and you're a cunt. Bend over.'

CHAPTER TWENTY-FOUR

Dressed head to toe in black, David Steers climbed over the chain-link fence that surrounded St Margaret's Academy for Girls. He'd picked his spot well: no CCTV coverage and, being at the back of the grounds, it was dark and close to the caretaker's hut that he used to work in.

In his hand he carried a pair of bolt cutters and over his shoulder was a small black bag. He set about the small padlock that secured the hut. He grunted as he squeezed the bolt cutters and cursed as the little lock held fast. He tried again. And failed again. Frustrated, he resorted to the time-honoured method of delivering several infuriated kicks until the hinges gave out and the door flew inward.

Walking with the conviction of a man who knew his way around, he dropped the bag on top of a small fridge and rummaged around for a few seconds before pulling out a small Maglite. He pushed the door to and switched on the torch.

He looked around the small building until he found what he'd come for. Piled up next to the toilet was a large number of cardboard boxes. He smiled to himself and turned off the torch. When his eyes had adjusted to the gloom, he picked up two boxes, tested their weight and went back to the door.

He gently toed it open and peeked outside. It was all quiet. He walked out and headed for the school's eighteen-seater minibus. Putting the boxes down, he rummaged around in his pocket and fished out the spare keys to the minibus, stolen when he left the job.

He walked the two boxes to the back of the bus and placed them on the floor. He smiled again as he walked back down the aisle of the bus to fetch the rest of the boxes.

Two at a time, he brought his cargo onto the bus and, once he had them all on board, set about opening them.

Ten minutes later he had 540 eleven-inch canisters of compressed LPG, liquefied petroleum gas, intended for school camping trips, neatly stacked inside the storage compartment underneath one of the bench seats and close to the petrol tank.

When he'd finished lining up the canisters, he attached a small detonator and flicked a switch. He smiled as a tiny red light glowed in the dark.

'Oh, Father in heaven. Thy will be done,' he said as he closed the seat down.

He locked the bus back up, flattened and threw all the empty boxes into a large skip, and let out a chilling screech as he climbed back over the fence.

CHAPTER TWENTY-FIVE

The dead woman was in the living room. Tony Kent had done a good job of describing the scene accurately using as few words as possible. No more were needed. The photographer was dancing around the place taking photographs of the entire room, and kneeling down by the body was Charlie Kennedy, Kent's assistant. He looked up at Paterson and Clocks's arrival.

'Hello, gents. Good to see you again.'

'Whatcha, Charlie,' said Clocks. 'Been a while.'

'Charlie,' said Paterson. 'How's things?'

'Y'know. Grim, most of the time.'

Clocks chuckled. 'Don't s'pose it 'elp's workin' with Mr Chuckles either, does it?'

Kent glared at Clocks. Charlie put his head down and went back to work.

'Fuckin' 'ell, Ray. I've seen some things in me time but never someone who took personal hygiene this seriously. She's sniffin 'er own fanny, this one.' He pointed to the head placed between the victim's legs.

'Jesus, John,' said Paterson. 'Steady on, mate.'

'What the hell is wrong with you, Clocks?' said Kent. 'Show some respect. Give her some dignity.'

'Bit late for dignity when you've got yer nose shoved up yer own chuff, innit? I'd say that ship's well an' truly sailed, mate.'

'John,' said Paterson. 'Give it a rest. That's enough.'

Clocks shrugged. 'Yeah alright. Sorry, Ray. I'm out of order on that one.'

'Anything you can add for me, Charlie?' said Paterson. 'Can I come nearer? Take a look?'

'Yeah, by all means.'

'Don't touch anything, Paterson,' said Kent. 'I don't want anything contaminated.'

'Mr Kent. I think we need to get something straight.' Paterson stepped closer to the man. 'We've met a couple of times now and I get the impression that you seem to think that I'm your subordinate and that you can talk to me like a piece of shit. I think it only fair of me to advise you otherwise.

'Now, I know you don't like us, and I can live with that quite happily. The feeling is mutual, to be honest. Up until now, I've cut you a lot of slack with your manner toward us but today it stops. You understand me?'

Kent's body language changed completely and he looked confused.

'Because if you don't sort out your God complex and start showing us some bloody respect, I *promise* you I will make your life a fucking misery and you'll end up wearing this fucking paper suit at your new job as a tampon model for Kotex. Do I make myself clear?'

Clocks grinned at the scene unfolding in front of him.

Kent cleared his throat and pulled himself straight.

'I . . . don't appreciate your tone, Paterson.'

Paterson stepped in closer, inches from Kent's face. '*Superintendent* Paterson to you. And I don't care *what* you appreciate, Kent. You *will* show some respect for the rank and for those people around you or we will fall out big time. Now, this is the only time I will tell you this. Ignore me and you'll be sorry.'

Kent cleared his throat again. 'I don't appreciate threats, *Superintendent* Paterson.'

Paterson shrugged. 'But there it is. Deal with it but don't forget it.'

'I've a good mind to make a report about you.'

'Do that, then. But do it later. For now, we have a killer to find.' Paterson turned away from him. 'Charlie? Anything we don't already know?'

'Maybe. How much do you know?'

'Only what yer boss told us an' what we can see for ourselves,' said Clocks. 'So, any idea 'ow 'e sawed 'er nut off, then? Any blood-soaked saws lyin' around by any chance?'

'I don't think it was sawn off.'

'Come again?'

'Look at the neck, the stump. It's too clean — no rough edges. It wasn't hacked off for those same reasons. Clean.'

'So, what then?'

'Just a guess at this point but I'd say wire. Very strong, very thin wire. Our man pulled it tight and just kept on pulling until it dug in and then he kept going.'

'Fuck off!' said Clocks. 'You sayin' 'e lopped off 'er turnip with a bit of cheese wire?'

'I'm saying it's possible, John. Yes.'

'I don't see how he could have,' said Paterson. 'Not all the way off, surely? Wouldn't he have met some resistance at the end of the pull both from the spine and the proximity of his own body to hers? Not sure he'd get the leverage.'

'Could be. As I said, I don't know yet. Going to need some more work both here and on the table back at the morgue.'

'He moved the body,' said Kent.

'Who did?' said Paterson.

'Whoever did this.'

'Go on.'

'Look at how much blood is in here.'

'A small lake,' said Clocks.

Kent shook his head. 'Leakage. Nothing more.'

'Where then?'

'Dining room.'

'Why didn't you mention this before?'

Kent sighed. 'We were all too busy pissing on each other, and I figured you'd want to see the body first.'

Clocks frowned. 'Pissing on each other?' he mumbled. 'I don't remember any of that ol' caper,' he said out loud. 'Pretty sure I would 'ave noticed if we were pissin' on each other.'

Kent ignored him. 'This way . . .' He led them into the dining room.

As they stepped in behind Kent, Paterson took in the room. A large dining table was set in the centre. It was smothered in blood and a much larger quantity lay in a messy pool on the thick fawn-coloured carpet. Arterial spray decorated three of the walls in wild streaks that left congealed drips down the wallpaper. Paterson looked up and saw several streaks on the ceiling.

'He killed her in here,' said Kent.

Paterson looked at the pool of blood. Something about it looked off to him. It was smeared at the edges. There were also smeared shapes that he guessed were handprints. 'Do you have any theories?'

Kent shook his head. 'Not as yet, no. What do you think?'

Paterson looked all around him. 'This is pure speculation but I'm thinking he came up behind her and looped the wire around her neck. She struggled but the wire was already digging in. No way she could have got her fingers in, and even if she had, they'd have been sliced through. They weren't. Once it cut into the artery she started spraying the room. Thrashing about decorated the walls and ceiling.'

He looked at the table. 'I think he threw her on here, on her back, pulled her head over the edge and then sat down. Then he pulled again.' He pointed to the smears on the edge of the table. 'She's been dragged. Not much. Maybe a foot. He wanted her head over the table. See the puddle on the carpet? It's not even. I think he twisted himself around and then sat down heavily, dropped down if you like, pulled hard and the wire went right through.

'I'm guessing she'd have been either dead or half dead by the time he did that. No struggle left in her. Her head popped off and bounced around on the carpet. I think he sat there for a while savouring what he'd done and maybe . . . maybe lying under her neck while she bled out. Look at the blood. There's more on one side than the other. I think it suggests he sat there, and there's what looks like handprints. Can't be sure.'

Clocks sniffed. 'Fuck me, Ray. You been watchin' that Sherlock 'olmes DVD I got yer fer Christmas? I mean, wowsers! That's good.'

'Just a theory, Clocksy. Don't take it as gospel. And, what's a DVD?'

Clocks shook his head.

Kent nodded. 'Interesting theory. Sounds very plausible, I have to admit. We'll certainly consider it and we'll let you know what we find.'

'Wonder why 'e moved 'er?' said Clocks.

Paterson shrugged. 'Who knows? He's mad, isn't he? I take it she's the only body? We weren't told otherwise.'

'We haven't found any extra's. So, yes. She's the only vic.'

'Have your boys found anything to identify her?'

'Lesley!' Kent called.

A young woman came out of the kitchen. 'Sir?'

'Do we have any ID for our woman?'

'I believe so.' She opened her clipboard and took out a sealed and signed plastic envelope containing a driving licence. 'We think this is her, sir. But until we see her face properly, we can't make a visual confirmation. The photos in the house match the picture on the licence, so . . .'

Paterson took the envelope from her. He moved it around to lose the reflections from the halogen lamps. 'Hmm.'

'What is it?' said Clocks.

'What was Lacey Heaton's date of birth?'

'Er . . .'

'Ninth of September, nineteen ninety-nine, wasn't it?'

'Yeah. It was. Why's that?'

He handed Clocks the licence.

'Two for two,' he said.

CHAPTER TWENTY-SIX

'So, what d'you think's the significance of the birth dates bein' the same, Ray? Any ideas?'

'Not a clue.'

'Can't be coincidence, can it?'

Paterson climbed out of his paper suit and bagged it up.

Clocks, already out of his, took off the hat and dumped it in a bag. 'I mean, it's possible alright, but the odds must be what . . . a bazillion to one?'

'Probably a gazillion.'

'D'yer think? What's bigger, then? Is a gazillion bigger than a bazillion?'

'Oh, yeah.' Paterson signed himself out of the crime scene. Clocks did likewise. 'Much bigger. About ten times bigger, I think.'

'Fuck! That's huge.'

'Right. Anyway, we now need to figure out what the birth date is for, *if* it's got any real significance at all. Might just be a red herring. Something he's done to confuse us.'

'Maybe. Got a plan?'

'Round up the troops, get back to the nick and put our heads together.'

'Okay, then. Let's do that. Don't tell our victim we're doing that, will yer? On account of she an' 'er 'ead 'ave parted company. She'd be right upset.'

* * *

Paterson took a quick glance at his watch then pulled open the bottom drawer of his desk. He figured it was vodka o'clock. He poured himself a small glass and drained it quickly. There was a tap on the door, followed immediately by Clocks's stern-looking face.

'Where's mine, then?'

'Hold on. I've just this second poured this. Thought you were talking to Monkey.'

'I was but 'e's borin'. I'll 'ave a large one.'

Paterson poured him a drink. 'Small it is. We have a briefing to give.' He handed the glass to Clocks. 'Ready?'

'Born ready, mate.'

'Let's go, then.'

Paterson rose from his desk and headed for the door. 'Alright everyone . . .' He walked into the main office. 'Briefing.'

After a few minutes of dragging chairs, grabbing note-books and finishing half-drunk cups of coffee, Paterson's troops were settled.

'Okay. We all know what we've got. A second body showed up today. Badly damaged. We're still working up a theory for this one in terms of method of death, but until we get a full forensics report, we stay with the one we have. This young woman's name was Andrea Glass.'

'By all accounts, she was a smashing lady,' said Clocks.

A few of the team chuckled, most groaned.

'Again, from what we can make of it so far, she appears to have been religious in her outlook. Forensics have turned up the usual paraphernalia: bibles, religious knickknacks, reading material and so on. We'll need to establish if she was a churchgoer and, if so, where and how often. Also, we need to find out about any partners. One good thing is, from what we know so far, she didn't have any kids. Before I go on, take a look at the scene video.'

Paterson pressed a button on a remote control and the large screen that hung on the wall flashed into life.

For the next few minutes, the team sat in silence, following the cameraman as he walked through the house and showed them scenes of depraved carnage. The killer had gone through the house smearing blood everywhere: the kitchen, the hallway, the bathroom.

Everyone except Paterson and Clocks winced when they got to see Andrea's carcass. Jackie closed her eyes as the cameraman ran the camera along the woman's torso. Then it was over.

'Neighbours see or hear anything, guv?' said Dusty.

Paterson shook his head. 'It seems not. Well, nothing over the top.'

'Seems a bit odd given the state of the scene. Looks like she put up a good fight.'

'Hmm. Not good enough though.'

'What's with the head between the legs, boss?' said Monkey.

'No idea,' said Paterson. 'It may be symbolic or it may be nothing. We'll need an expert or something to look at the photos and clue us in to that aspect.'

Clocks looked horrified. 'An expert? In what?'

'I don't know yet. We'll figure that out later.'

Clocks shook his head. 'You know my feelings on experts. They can do more bleedin' 'arm than good.'

'I know. But we need to see if this is just a random thing or not. Agreed?'

Clocks shrugged. 'No. Not agreed. Too early to call in an outsider. Let's see what we can find out ourselves first, can we?'

'I'll think about it,' said Paterson.

'How old was she, sir?' said Jackie.

'And this is where it gets interesting,' said Paterson. She was the same age as Lacey. Not only that, but her birthday was exactly the same. Ninth of September, nineteen ninety-nine.'

'Well, that's not a coincidence, is it?' Jackie said.

'If it is, it's a fuckin' big one,' said Clocks. 'I'd say it's about a gazillion to one.'

'At least,' said Paterson, a wry smile on his lips. 'So, we also need to find out the significance of the date, too. Must be somethin' there.'

At the back of the room, Colin Yorkshire sat with his arms crossed and his eyes closed. Clocks spotted him.

'Oi! Tetley. Wake the fuck up!'

Yorkshire stayed in the same position: eyes still closed. 'I'm not asleep, sir. I'm thinking. Give me a minute, please.'

'What? Open yer eyes now an' pay attention.'

'I have paid attention, sir. Now I'm thinking.'

Clocks bunched his fists and moved toward him. 'I said—'

Paterson blocked his path. 'Leave him, John.'

Clocks stopped but his body language left no doubt he was pissed.

'What is it, Tetley?' said Paterson.

DC Yorkshire opened his eyes. 'Okay. It's just a theory. The first victim was religious to some extent. I think we'll find victim number two was also a churchgoer. So, it's not a huge leap to suspect that these two murders are closely linked in some way. But it's the dates of birth that bothers me.'

'In what way?' said Paterson.

'The year, nineteen ninety-nine. Take off the one and you're left with nine, nine, nine.'

'Someone call the police!' said Clocks.

Paterson dismissed him with a wave of his hand. 'Go on,' he said to Yorkshire.

'I thought that might have significance but then I thought, what do you get if you turn the numbers upside down?'

The penny dropped. 'Six, six, six,' said Paterson. 'The number of the beast.'

'Beast? What beast?' said Clocks. 'There's a beast?'

'Book of Revelations, John.'

'Book of what?'

'Revelations. It's the final book in the Christian Bible.'

'Is it? I always assumed it was just one big book of bollocks. I didn't know there was a series.'

Paterson gave a little nod. '*This calls for wisdom. Let the person who has insight calculate the number of the beast, for it is the number of a man. That number is six, six, six.* It's been written a number of ways depending which version you read, but the essence is the same.'

'I thought you said you weren't religious. 'Ow come you can recite that lot?'

'I'm not religious. Some things stick though. There's a lot more to that passage but, if I recall rightly, scholars say that seven, seven, seven is a perfect number, a divine number, the number of the heavens, but six, six, six is the number of mankind. Man can never be as God.'

'Nope. You fuckin' lost me. Try again.'

'Alright. Bear in mind this is open to interpretation like all written things, particularly in the realm of biblical or other religious writings. In the Bible, the number seven figures prominently. God worked for six days and rested on the seventh. God set apart the seventh day as holy. There are seven statements in the Lord's prayer, and Jesus allegedly made seven statements in agony while on the cross.'

'I'll bet 'e did. What'd 'e say? "Fuck, fuck, fuck, fuckety, bollocks, fuck! That 'urts!"?'

'That's eight, John.'

Clocks looked to one side and nodded a few times to himself. 'Oh, yeah. Take out a fuck, then.'

'Anyway, then a prophet directed a leper to bathe in the Jordan River seven times to be healed and Jesus healed seven people on the seventh day, okay? I think there's something like seven hundred references to the number seven in the Bible.'

'And the number six,' said Yorkshire, 'refers to man.'

Clocks wrinkled his nose. 'What?'

'Look, seven deals with heavenly things: healing . . . God . . . Jesus . . . but the number six deals with mankind. Six being lower than seven.'

'You two God rockers are doin' me 'ead in. What're you rattlin' on about now?'

'Some Bible scholars believe that the number seven indicates completion or perfection, especially of God. The number six, not being the perfect number that seven is, signifies imperfection. Adam ate the apple and allowed sin into the world, and from man's weakness, six became called the "number" of man. Lower than God.

'As the guv said earlier, Revelations 13:18 states the number of man is six, six, six. God is referred to as the Holy Trinity. The Father, the Son, the Holy Spirit. It is a holy perfection. Three sixes, though, denotes Satan, a perfect unholy evil. Some scholars say it means "Not God, Not God, Not God".'

'You're all off yer nuts.' Clocks shook his head. 'I mean, seriously, what a load of ol' bollocks! These fuckers must've all been off their tits when they came up with all that claptrap. Sixes an' sevens. Load of ol' shit.'

'Maybe,' said Yorkshire. 'But what six, six, six really means is—'

Paterson stole his thunder. 'Our boy's saying these people have turned away from God. In doing so, they join the beast, Satan, and become enemies of God. They have become the beast and he will fight to restore God's kingdom here on earth.'

'Oh, 'ave a listen to yerselves,' said Clocks. 'Whatcha sayin' don't even make sense. You're both goin' on about the year but what about the rest of the date then? That's the ninth of September, nineteen ninety-nine, so what about the other two nines or sixes or whatever? That's five nines. . . *or* sixes, in total. Six, six, six, six, six? What's that then, you ask? Thank you. I'll tell you. That's the number of my arse'ole.

That's what that is. Look it up in yer Bibles. It's in the book of Johnny Clocks, chapter seventeen, verse eight. Amen.'

Paterson chuckled.

'Look. You two are givin' me a bleedin' 'eadache tryin' to keep track of all these soddin' numbers. Let's just keep it nice an' simple an' go with the theory that our killer's just off 'is fuckin' nut. No more. No less. That's it. Nothing else. Job done. Mad as a box of frogs. If he thinks he's doin' God's work, that's because he's mental, nothing else. So, instead of wastin' time fannyin' about 'ere talkin' about bloody angels an' demons and perfect numbers and religious shit, I'm off to go find this fucker and kick 'is mental 'ead in. Anyone with me?' He started for the door.

'John!' Paterson called. Clocks looked up as he slipped his jacket on. 'I know you don't believe in all this. Neither do I, but it may be his motive.'

'So what? That don't 'elp us stop 'im, does it? All it gives us is a peep be'ind the mad curtain. Don't 'elp us at all.'

'Well, it could do.'

'Go on, then. Tell me 'ow.'

'We can contact churches in the local area and see if any other recorded parishioners share the same birthdate. Might give us a jump start on the next victim. We can plot up and wait for him.'

Clocks stopped straightening his jacket and sniffed. 'Yeah, alright then. Sold to the man with a bad temper and no time for religion.'

Paterson smiled.

'Jackie,' Clocks said. 'Be a love an' put the kettle on. Two sugars in me tea. Good gel.'

CHAPTER TWENTY-SEVEN

Bob the minibus driver was a stickler for time. An old army habit that had stuck with him since leaving almost twenty years ago, he was serious about his schedule. If anyone was late, Bob wasn't hanging around for them. The school supported him. Discipline was important, and so, every Tuesday and Thursday morning at 8.25 a.m. precisely, a group of eighteen girls from St Margaret's Academy would board the school's minibus. At 8.30 a.m. it would leave the grounds and drive through Bermondsey on its way to the Crystal Palace National Sports Centre. Weaving its way through the streets of South East London during the rush hour could be tricky, but they would somehow always arrive before 9.45 a.m.

St Margaret's had a long association with sport, and these girls were considered to be elite swimmers. Each and every one of them had a shot at being entered for the Olympics, but only six were thought to be serious contenders and St Margaret's did everything it could to ensure their future success.

Today would see a different plan unfold.

At 8.28 a.m. David Steers stepped onto the bus. One or two of the girls looked up from their phones. Bob, startled, recognised him.

'Mr Steers! What are you doing h—'

Steers grabbed him by the hair and jammed a knife into his throat. He twisted it once before wrenching it out. The bus erupted into screams as Steers dragged Bob out of his seat and threw him out onto the concrete. He held up his black canvas bag. 'Phones!' he screamed at them. 'Phones!'

Steers walked slowly along the aisle. The girls, all hysterical, dropped their phones into the bag. Having collected them all, he sat himself down in the driver's seat. 'If you move, I will *kill* every one of you. If you try to alert anyone, I will *kill* every one of you.'

At 8.30 a.m. Steers started the bus and drove out of the school. Fifteen-year-old Zara Morgan was the only one who looked back at Bob's body and wept for him.

At 8.58 a.m. they arrived at Steers's destination. Tower Bridge.

CHAPTER TWENTY-EIGHT

Steers stopped the bus on the northern approach, one of the busiest routes into Central London. It took less than ten seconds for the first impatient driver to sound their horn. Fifteen seconds later another one joined in, and within forty-five seconds, there was a cacophony of beeping and tooting as annoyed drivers demanded he get out of the way.

David Steers smiled. Satan's soldiers would come for him soon.

He reached into the bag of phones, pulled one out and held it up. 'Whose is this?'

Fifteen-year-old Monica Abbott let out a loud sob and slowly put her hand up. 'It's . . . mine . . .'

'Come and get it. Hurry!'

The frightened girl slowly pulled herself up from her seat, grizzling as she did so. 'Pleeeaasseee . . .'

'I said *come and get it*! Now! Come here! Move, whore!'

Her friends tried to offer her comfort as she made her way out into the aisle. She was shaking. Her grizzling grew louder the nearer she got to the front.

'There's a good little whore.' He handed her the phone. She looked at it, her hands shaking violently. 'Call the police. Tell them what's happened and where we are. Then, go onto social media. Tweet it, TikTok it, Facebook it. Do whatever you need to do to tell the world what's happening here.'

Standing in front of Steers, Monica lost control of her bladder. He looked down at the pool of urine as it flowed around her feet.

'You filthy bitch! You show your fear in the face of God's warrior as I knew you would. Coward bitch!' He snarled at her.

A sudden thump on the door of the bus made all of the girls scream at once. Steers pushed a button and opened the door to an angry-looking man.

'Oi! What you playing at, mate? Move the fucking bus! Traffic's a mile long now 'cos of you.'

Steers glared at him. 'Begone, filth!'

'The man looked shocked. 'What'd you say to me? You just call me filth?'

'Filth!'

The man jumped on the bus and reached out for Steers. As soon as his hand touched him, Steers shrieked, startling the man long enough for him to plunge a knife into his stomach. The girls all screamed out again, intensifying their weeping and wailing. Monica Abbott dropped to her knees.

The man staggered backward. He looked down at his stomach as a bright red patch bloomed out onto his shirt. Steers rose from his seat and kicked the man in the chest, sending him crashing backwards onto the pavement.

He closed the door.

'Whore of Satan . . . Get up and do as I did command thee.'

CHAPTER TWENTY-NINE

Clocks poked his head out of the office window. 'Jesus, Ray. Traffic's a bastard out there today.'

Head buried in a report, Paterson didn't bother to look up. 'Hmm, I can hear the horns honking. Shut the window, John. Bad enough I can hear all that racket with the window closed.'

Clocks ignored him and kept looking out, craning his neck forward. 'Something's kicked off, I reckon. Probably a coupla motorists 'ad 'emselves a prang. That'll cheer everyone up. Fuckin' glad I ain't gotta sit in that lot every day.'

'Hmm.' Paterson carried on reading. 'Can you *please* shut the window, John? This is important. I need to think.'

Clocks pulled his head back in a little.

'There could be some fisticuffs goin' on. I might get a good view of it from 'ere.'

Paterson shook his head.

'Oi! Oi! 'Old up! Coupla 'elmets 'ave just legged it out of the nick. They're givin' it some welly.'

Paterson looked up.

'Fuck me! Looks like the entire nick's bailin' out now. Summin' big's goin' on, Ray. Can we go?'

Paterson stood up, intending to join Clocks at the window. His mobile rang.

'Paterson.'

Clocks strained to hear what was being said at the other end of the line.

'On our way!' said Paterson. He ran for the door.

Clocks was straight behind him. 'Whassamatter?'

Paterson ran through the office. 'Everybody! With me!' The four people still in the room dropped everything they were doing and scrambled to get out from behind their desks. 'Station officer called. Hostage situation! On the bridge. One dead!' He charged down the stairs and ran out into the station yard. He kept running and hit the fob on his keys to open the back gates.

A quick left into Queen Elizabeth Street and he saw two uniformed police running along Tower Bridge Road onto the bridge itself. He followed them. Ahead, he saw the bus parked up. A large crowd of people were gathered around it but not close to it. He spotted more uniformed police. None of them were near it. He thought it strange and kept running.

As he got closer, he saw the heads of a group of girls. They looked to be standing in a loosely formed line. He got to the back of the crowd and started forcing his way through. 'Police! Move! Move!'

Behind him, he heard Clocks. 'Out the way! Move yerselves!'

And then he saw.

Seventeen terrified, crying girls, stood lined up in a row secured to each other by collars attached to chains. On the ground, he spotted a man lying on his back, bleeding profusely. His heart sank.

Behind the line, Steers pressed himself close into the last girl . . . his shield.

Without taking his eyes from Steers, he shouted. 'Get everyone back! Off this bridge!' The uniforms, until that moment, had been standing by helplessly, paralysed by indecision and fear. They snapped into obedience and started to push the crowd back.

'Get 'em off the fuckin' bridge!' Clocks started pushing people himself. 'Off! Get off!' Jackie and Yorkshire grabbed a couple of the uniforms and instructed them to stop any traffic coming from the north side of the bridge.

Monkey and Dusty busied themselves telling drivers in no uncertain terms to get out of their cars and move back. Those that protested were dragged out and sent on their way.

Paterson heard the distinct *clack-clack-clack* of a helicopter in the distance. He sighed.

Within a few minutes, the crowd was back at the junction with Queen Elizabeth Street and no further traffic came south. There was a clear zone of at least a hundred yards in either direction, taped off with plastic ribbon.

Clocks joined Paterson. 'This don't look too clever, does it?'

'No. It doesn't.'

From the distance came the sound of sirens. Paterson hoped at least one was an ambulance. 'Steers!' he shouted. 'Let me help that man!'

'The Devil's emissary will die!'

'Fuckin' Devil's emissary!' yelled Clocks. 'You prick! Bloke's goin' to work.'

'Don't goad him, John. We need to know what his game is.'

'I don't think it's goin' to have a good endin', whatever it is.'

'What do you want, Steers?' Paterson said.

The man shrieked. 'I want . . .'

'What? What d'you want?'

'To purge . . . them.'

'Oh, shit,' Paterson said under his breath. Then he shouted, 'Of what? They're just kids!'

'Whores!' he screeched. 'Satan's whores!'

'That's a bit 'arsh, innit?' said Clocks.

Paterson could see his friend becoming more agitated, gearing up for a fight that they couldn't win.

'John. Not now.'

'Fuck 'im! Oi! Fucknut! You wanna purge someone? Let 'er go an' get over 'ere. You can try an' purge me if you like. See 'ow that goes.'

Paterson closed his eyes for a second. 'I'm serious, John. Shut . . . the fuck . . . up.'

Clocks looked at him, unimpressed by the tone.

Two paramedics broke through the plastic tape that had been strung across the road and ran toward Paterson. He held up his hand to them and they slowed to a trot.

'Paramedics are here!' Paterson shouted. 'Let them help this man. Please.'

Steers's tongue flicked out. 'No!' he gasped. 'If they come, she will die!'

The girl Steers held in front of him moaned as Steers pulled her tighter against his body and breathed on her cheek.

Paterson turned to Clocks. 'Our vics with the same date of birth . . .'

'What? What about 'em?'

'Six, six, six.'

'And?'

'It was a message.'

'You goin' on about all that number bollocks again?'

'You counted the girls?'

'What? No.'

'Eighteen. You can break that down into three groups of six. Six, six, six. He's going to kill them all.'

CHAPTER THIRTY

'*We have some breaking news.*' Julia Beko, the BBC's senior news presenter wore her stern face, the one she reserved for bad news and bad news only. '*Police are responding to an incident on London's Tower Bridge. Earlier today a man was stabbed and a number of schoolgirls were taken captive and are now being held hostage. We have live images from our eye in the sky but I must warn you that these are likely to cause distress.*'

* * *

Paterson looked up at the news helicopter. 'John. Grab a couple of radios and get that prick out of the sky. The girls' parents are gonna see this, for Chrissakes.'

'On it.'

'And try and get some sort of update.'

Clocks took off toward the cordon.

'You know this will only end badly for you, Steers!' he called.

'Say nothing, Satan.' He moved up and down the line of girls still holding one of them close.

Paterson realised that whatever had screwed this man's brain up, it hadn't made him a fool. The chances of a sniper getting a clean shot without killing the girl were next to zero. He stood straight and walked toward Steers.

'Let them go. Your fight is with me, is it not? Am I not Satan, the great destroyer? Is your fight not with me, Son of God?'

Steers's head twitched and his tongue darted in and out. 'We will meet when God commands me. And, with the light of Him who is all powerful, I will smite thee. I will cleanse God's good earth of your wicked ways.'

Paterson's chuckle turned into a laugh. The smile vanished and he walked toward Steers.

'Get back, Satan! I command thee!'

Paterson stopped. 'Let them go. Now.' He kept his voice devoid of emotion, his meaning crystal clear. 'If you do not, I will destroy you, Son of God. I will send you straight to hell, where you will burn for eternity. There will be no light for you save the light of my flames.'

Steers held up his hand. Paterson saw the remote. *Shit! Bomb!* Time to drop the act.

'Come to me then, Satan!' taunted Steers. 'We will end this!'

Paterson glared at him, turned and walked back to where he was previously. No longer posing a threat.

* * *

Clocks returned a couple of minutes later with two radios. 'There you go. The Yard are gettin' onto the news choppers now. India 99 is on its way. They'll make life difficult for 'em.'

'Problem just got way worse, John.'

'Why? What's 'appened?'

'Fucker's holding a remote. Bus is rigged.'

'Shit!' Clocks rubbed his forehead. 'We're gonna need the bomb squad. I'll give 'em a bell.'

Paterson nodded. 'Yeah. Do that for me. Thing is, don't think they'll make it in time.'

'Plan?'

'Really don't know yet. I just tried to goad him into a fight but that flopped, big time. Let's hold on until a hostage negotiator gets here.'

'A what?'

'Hostage negotiator.'

'Seriously? This bloke's fell out the nutty tree and whacked his 'ead on every branch on the way down. You can't negotiate with someone like him.'

'Protocol.'

'Oh, yeah. I forgot. Protocol. Bit late for that, ain't it?'

Paterson nodded.

Clocks looked over at Steers. 'Oi, you fuckin' doom brain! Let 'em all go now, safe 'n' sound and I'll kill you quickly. Deal?'

Steers shrieked.

'Oh, give it a rest, mate! You're not impressin' anyone with all that girlie screamin'. All you're doin' is givin' me a fuckin' 'eadache.

Steers started walking up and down the line.

'SCO19 on the way, John?'

'Yep, but they won't get 'im. Tucked 'is nut right down, ain't 'e?'

* * *

'*From what we can see,*' said the news presenter, '*it would appear to be a lone man holding a large group of girls hostage. We have no idea at this stage what this is about. Our reporter, Jonathan Summers, has arrived on scene. We'll go live to him now. Jonathan, what are you able to tell us?*'

The TV screen showed a head-and-shoulders shot of a man holding a microphone with one hand and holding his ear with the other. There was always a five-second delay in live broadcasts. Standard with cases like this. If the situation turned bad and the hostage taker killed someone, the news editor could cut it from the broadcast.

'Thank you, Danielle. As you rightly said, we've only just arrived, so the information we're getting is sketchy at the moment. The police have cordoned off a section of Tower Bridge and appear to have the situation contained. What I can tell you for certain is that a man has been stabbed and may be dead and that a lone man is holding a number of schoolgirls hostage. Tower Bridge police station is just the other side of the road. Police were on scene very quickly and it looks as though two plain clothes officers are trying to negotiate with the man.'

* * *

'Steers!' Paterson called. 'What are we doing here? What's the endgame?'

'You know, Satan. You know . . .'

'Well, I don't, otherwise I wouldn't have asked, would I?'

'These are the whores of Satan. Your whores. Do you not recognise them?'

'What's this thing he's got with whores?' said Clocks.

'Don't know. Seems to think every girl in town is a whore.'

Clocks shrugged. 'Well, we are in Bermondsey, so . . .'

In the sky, the Met Police helicopter, India 99, headed toward the news crew. It pleased Paterson. One less thing to think about if this all went sideways.

'I will purge this earth of them and then I will destroy you, Satan, and your ugly demon!' Steers pointed toward them.

Clocks looked around. 'What ugly demon, Ray?'

'Well, I'm Satan so . . .'

'Cheeky fucker! Oi! You better not be callin' *me* ugly, you fuckin' nutter!'

'Satan's spawn!' Steers called back.

'Spawn! That's summin' to do with frogs jizz, innit?'

'Don't worry about it.'

'Don't worry about it? Bastard just called me frogs jizz. I'm not 'avin' that. That's right out of order.'

Paterson ignored him. 'You've nowhere to go!' he called. 'Just give it up, Steers, before we come for you!'

'Come for me then, Satan! Come for me! But you cannot!' He held up the detonator. 'I will rid the earth of your evil. You will kneel before the Lord God almighty. Ugly demon! You must kneel before him!'

'Whassat?' said Clocks. 'That a phone or summin'?'

'That's the detonator.'

'Oh, fuck me sideways with a baseball bat.'

'Would it help?'

'Might take me mind off the shit we've got 'ere.'

Paterson smiled. 'I'm ready to try anything at the moment.'

Clocks called across. 'Oi! Wank stain. If you call me ugly one more time, I'll kick the livin' granny outta yer!'

'You will kneel!'

'No I won't! N.O. spells fuck off!'

Steers head bobbed up and into view a couple of times, his anger palpable. Paterson knew that even if a sniper was on scene, he wouldn't risk a shot. But Steers was getting angry, and angry men made mistakes. Usually.

CHAPTER THIRTY-ONE

Dusty's voice crackled over the radio. '*Hostage team are here, guv.*'

Paterson lifted the radio to his mouth. 'Tell them to stand by. I think our man's about to do something.'

'*They say you're to stand down, guv. They're taking over and they want you both out.*'

'Tell them to fuck off.' He switched the radio off.

Clocks nodded his approval.

'This is it, Steers! There's just us, now. You have nowhere to run to. Even if you get past us, there's snipers waiting for you. They'll pick you off even if you are jumping around everywhere. Clocks can't shoot for shit, but these boys? All that jumping about won't help you. They love a moving target. It's a challenge to them.

'We both know you can't hurt all of these girls before we get to you, so whatever your game is, you didn't think it through, did you?'

Steers shrieked again and swayed from side to side. The girl he held in front of him trembled violently. Still, he kept his head low, kept her close to him. He leaned forward and whispered something in her ear.

Her voice trembling, she spoke to the other girls. 'Everyone . . . back. Step backwards. Two . . . two steps.'

The line of girls, all visibly shaken, did as they were told and took two steps backward. Steers and the girl he held backed up too, until his back pressed into the metal of the bus.

Paterson frowned.

'Fuck's 'e doin', Ray?'

'I don't know, John.'

Steers ducked low. Still holding the girl by the neck, he pulled her into a crouch and made his way along the line of girls. Paterson craned his neck to see what was going on.

Steers shrieked again. The girl's legs finally gave out and she dropped to her knees, crying. He jerked her to her feet. 'Up, bitch!' The tone of his voice acted as a trigger for the girls to begin crying and snivelling louder. All of them seemed to know what his plan was and that time had started to run out.

'Fucker's up to summin',' Clocks said.

Paterson took a couple of steps forward. Steers stood up straight and pulled hard on the chain of the two girls nearest him. They screamed as they were jerked violently backward and began to fall. The rest of the girls screamed too as the tension on their chains increased. Like a row of dominoes, the whole line of them began to tumble. As they staggered backward, Steers pulled the girl he shielded behind to the ground. 'Roll!' he screamed at her. 'Roll!' She understood and rolled herself under the bus, and Steers followed her.

Paterson watched the line of girls stumble backward and fall to the ground. Their screams were now more urgent — panicked. He realised what he was witnessing. 'Oh, fuck! No!'

Paterson ran toward the girls. Clocks went with him. No more than five steps in, the bus erupted into a ball of flame and shattered glass. Both men were thrown back by the blast and dumped onto their backs.

Seven girls died instantly, blown apart by the shattered metal and concussion from the blast. They were the lucky ones. The remaining ten were peppered with shrapnel and thousands of tiny fragments of glass, shotgunned into them with tremendous force. Several of them lost limbs. All were engulfed in flames and writhed screaming on the ground as their skin, charred black, hung in lumps from their skeletons.

* * *

'Oh, God!' Johnathan Summers, the reporter, ducked at the moment the bus exploded. Everybody did. The pilot of India 99 pulled the helicopter up in panic. Several nearby office alarms emitted high-pitched whistles. A number of cars lost their windows.

'A bomb's gone off!' Summers shouted into his microphone. 'Oh, God!'

The broadcast editor immediately cut the feed, saving viewers from witnessing the blast, and cut back to a visibly shaken Julia Beko in the newsroom.

* * *

'Er . . . er, it would appear that there's been some kind of explosion down there on the ground at Tower Bridge. We're not going to show you what I can only imagine is a horrific scene. We obviously don't know yet what the extent of the damage is or how many have been injured. We'll bring you more as this terrible, terrible tragedy unfolds.'

CHAPTER THIRTY-TWO

Ray Paterson slowly opened his eyes. He lay there on the ground and looked up at the sky. Two helicopters circled above him but he had no idea why. He couldn't make sense of it. Wisps of smoke floated gently on the breeze above him. He turned his head to one side, aware now of a high-pitched ringing in his ears.

Next to him, Johnny Clocks groaned. Paterson watched as Clocks's right arm moved and one knee bent into a crook. Somehow, they were still alive.

He rolled his head back and looked up at the sky again. Where were the helicopters? He looked around for them. Nowhere. Didn't matter. His head pounded. The whistle in his ears intensified and he shook his head, hoping that that action would stop the noise. It didn't.

He moved his own arms slowly, then his legs. They felt heavy to him. His chest hurt. He took a few deep breaths and scrunched his face up each time. Pain. Then it hit him.

Clocks! Bomb!

'John!'

Paterson rolled onto one side, ignoring the intense pain in his head. He became aware of the sound of shrieking. Lots of shrieks. For a second he thought it must be Steers but then he realised there were too many squeals to be one person. The girls! An intense, choking smell of burning assaulted his nostrils as his senses switched back on. He coughed and forced himself to sit up.

'John . . . John!'

Clocks rolled onto his side. Blood streaked his face and his eyes were glazed. Paterson watched as Clocks slowly pulled himself into a sitting position.

Paterson saw a blurry group of people running toward them. Uniformed police, paramedics, Jackie, Monkey, Dusty, Yorkshire. He vomited and spat out stringy residue.

'Ray?' Clocks's voice was weak.

Paterson looked at him. His voice sounded muffled, the sort of sound that could be heard when underwater. Bassy. Inaudible.

'I . . . fuckin' 'ate . . . this bloke.'

Paterson fell back onto the ground.

CHAPTER THIRTY-THREE

Chaos swirled around them. The streets thickened with emergency service crews of all stripes. Within minutes of the explosion, the fire brigade were on scene and busied themselves getting the burning bus under control. The police were shouting at them to back off, frantic to preserve the scene from the damage the foam was causing. Those uniformed police not engaged in a shouting match with the fire fighters were immersed in tending to the injured girls with the paramedics.

Paterson and Clocks were both on their feet, and apart from king-sized headaches, earaches, wobbly legs and chest pains brought on by the blast concussion, they were in reasonable shape. They were both peppered with tiny fragments of glass but the girls had absorbed most of the blast, a fact not unnoticed by Paterson.

Looking toward the bus, he felt a stab of immense sorrow. A couple of the dead girls had already been covered and the screams of pain and distress from the maimed survivors cut through him. He moved toward the bus.

Clocks put a hand on his chest and breathed deeply. 'Where we goin'?'

'Steers. Where is he? I want to see his body.'

Clocks looked around. 'Can't see 'im.'

Paterson made his way over to where a young probationary constable was standing his ground against a senior-looking fireman. Clocks followed him.

'You!' he shouted to the fireman. 'Is there any immediate danger this bus might blow again?'

The fireman shook his head. 'Doubt it.'

'Then shut that hose off. Now! This is my crime scene you're fucking up, you idiot!'

'What?' said the fireman.

'Fucking turn it off! Now!'

The fireman made a gesture with his hand toward his crew and they immediately stopped spraying the bus.

'Now fuck off out of it.' He turned to the young police officer. 'You alright, son?'

The young man looked at him, clearly nervous that so senior an officer had even deigned to talk to him, let alone worry about him, and grateful that the conflict with the fireman had been resolved. 'Yes, sir. Thank you for that.'

'Don't worry about it, kid,' said Clocks. 'Fuckin' smash 'n' squirt brigade think they own the fuckin' place. Wankers!'

'Did you cover these bodies?' said Paterson. The question was irrelevant, but Paterson's head was muzzy.

'No. They were covered when I got here. Are you alright, sir? I saw you lying in the road.'

Paterson nodded. 'Yep.'

'You, sir?' he said to Clocks.

'Yeah, good as gold, mate. Take a lot more than that to take us out. Now, stop being me fuckin' mum fer a minute and tell me summin' . . . D'you know if one of these is a man's body? Tell me one of 'em is.'

'I'm sorry, sir,' the probationer said. 'I don't know. But I heard chatter on the radio.'

'About?' said Clocks.

'Some members of the public reported seeing a man pulling a crying girl as they ran along Shad Thames. Said the girl was screaming and trying to resist but the man was having none of it. He grabbed a fistful of her hair and dragged her along.'

Paterson gave a heavy sigh. 'Fuck him! He's got away.'

'A couple of men tackled him, sir.'

Paterson's face lit up. 'And?'

'And he stabbed one and slashed the other across the chest. Neither men are too badly injured but they lost the will to fight.'

Paterson bunched his fists so tight, his fingernails bit into his flesh.

'Where was 'e last seen?' said Clocks. 'Shad Thames or what?'

'Last seen running into Lafone Street, sir.'

''Ow long ago?'

'Five, six minutes.'

Clocks shook his head. If Steers had a car he could be a couple of miles away by now. And he still had the girl.

'Thanks, mate. Be a good lad an' go get a coupla strong coffees from the nick for us.'

Paterson took off at a clip, heading back to the station.

'Oh, fuck!' said Clocks. 'Where's 'e goin'? Oi! Guv!' He took off after him.

Clocks broke into a trot as he tried to catch up with Paterson. A paramedic came toward him, bag at the ready.

'Fuck off!' said Paterson. He ducked under the tape and headed off into Queen Elizabeth Street, leaving a stunned paramedic behind him.

'Ray! What we doin'?'

Paterson ignored him.

'Ray!'

'Gotta find him.'

'How? How we gonna find him now? 'E's on 'is toes!'

'Not gonna get far dragging a screaming girl around, is he? We take the car and wait for a call. It'll come and then we'll have the bastard.'

Clocks shrugged. 'What if 'e's jumped into a car? Fucker planned this out a treat. Pulled us in, killed the girls and 'ad it away, I can't see 'e's gonna be dumb enough to catch a bus with 'er, can you?'

Paterson tapped his entry card on the door pad, wrenched it open and headed for his car. 'Probably not, but what do you suggest we do? Stick our thumbs up our arses and wait for the next call? We find the girl dead in bits somewhere? No, John, we've got to hunt him down and stop him.'

He jumped into the car and started the engine. 'You with me?'

Clocks pulled the door open. 'Course I am, but I think it's a waste of time, I really do.' He slid into the passenger seat and pulled the seat belt around him.

CHAPTER THIRTY-FOUR

David Steers sat in a darkened room. He repeatedly pressed the button of a TV remote, flicking between various news reports on different channels. He jumped up from his chair, threw the remote against the wall and watched it smash into pieces. He snapped his head back. Crouching low, he screeched at the ceiling.

'Whore of Satan!' he called. In the corner of the darkened room, a naked, broken Zara Morgan tried desperately to make herself smaller as she huddled in a corner. She wrapped her arms tightly around herself to keep out the cold, to hide her nakedness and to self-soothe. She quietly murmured to herself. 'Mummy . . . Please . . . please. Daddy, daddy, daddy . . .'

'Your master and his ugly demon have escaped the wrath of God. They are saved. This cannot be. This *must* not be!' Still crouching, he scampered over to her.

She whimpered quietly and hugged herself tighter.

He panted heavily. 'Perhaps . . . God has other plans . . . for them?'

She buried her face deeper into her arms. 'Please . . . please let me go. I won't tell a soul, I won't.'

'Tell a soul?' Steers chuckled. 'What souls would you tell, hmm, my little *whore child*? You have no souls to tell. I am the only soul here . . . a good soul . . . a cleeeannn soul. And I will not listen to the lies of a child of the Devil himself.'

He sniffed her hair. A trickle of his saliva dropped onto her thigh.

'You and your friends . . . *tempted* me for years with your vile ways . . . your bodies. You raised your skirts . . . thrust out your chests as I went about my work. You *knew* that you did the work of the Devil. You did as your master commanded. You did what he told you. To seduce me, to take me to the dark side with him so that my soul would rot in hell for eternity. But I was . . . strong. So strong. I resisted you, whore child.

'I stood firm against you, against your army of seducers! Not once did I succumb to your bodies. Not once did I fall for the lies and tricks he taught you, for your master *is* a trickster! But I . . . I have the light of God shining through me. It is a pure light, a clean light, and He has commanded me to rid the world of you all.'

He stood up, breathing heavily. 'And I . . . I failed . . . Him. I failed Him who is so pure. But . . .' He unzipped his trousers. Zara whimpered. 'He has commanded me thus . . . *You* can be saved, whore child. I must force the Devil out of you. I must fill you with His light, His goodness, His love, and only then can you be saved. Praise be! Through me, He will save you.'

He dropped his trousers around his ankles.

Zara moaned loudly. She tried to make herself smaller, curled herself tighter. She understood what Steers had in mind for her. 'Noooooooo . . . Pleeeeaaasseeee . . . Noooo!'

'I can smell you, child. You stink of . . . evil. You must be cleansed.'

He grabbed her by the hair and yanked her head back before throwing her onto her back. 'Devil! Begone!'

Zara Morgan, fifteen, cried quietly.

CHAPTER THIRTY-FIVE

Johnny Clocks played the game. He looked out of the window of Paterson's car knowing that the chances of spotting Steers were roughly the same as being struck by lightning at the exact moment his numbers came up on the Euro Millions lottery.

'Ray. I know you're pissed off, mate. Me too, but we're not just gonna stumble over 'im. You know that.'

'I don't and nor do you.'

'So what's the plan, Stan? We just drive around aimlessly for hours on end? We get jumpy every time we see a man draggin' a girl along the street? Oh, 'ang on. Thinkin' about it, we should get jumpy for that, shouldn't we? Still. You know what I mean. That's not a sensible plan, is it? We need to go back to the scene. Help out. Get our wounds seen to, that sort of stuff. I think I've got a shard of glass in me todger. Stings like a bitch.'

'When doesn't it?'

'Ooh, you're a cheeky bugger, ain'tcha?'

Clocks's phone rang. 'Clocks. Whassup?' He nodded a few times. 'Yep. On our way, guv.'

'Who's that?' said Paterson as Clocks hung up.

'Commissioner.'

'Wondered when he'd call. Go on?'

'Say's we've gotta go see 'im a bit lively.'

'Fuck! How lively?'

'Blues an' twos lively.' He reached forward and flicked a couple of switches tucked away under the dashboard.

'Turn it all off, John.'

'What?'

'Turn it off. I'm not ready yet. We have to keep looking.'

'What'd you mean, *not ready*? Sam wants us over there now. A shitstorm's breaking out over this. It's all over the news and social media, and the 'ome Office 'as got a stick up its arse.'

'Why?'

'I dunno. At a guess, I should imagine it's to do with a bunch of kids gettin' blown up. *That's* why we need to get over there. You won't find 'em, Ray. Not now. Not today. So let's just knock it on the 'ead an' go see what Sam wants, okay?'

Paterson nodded. 'I'm not happy.'

'Too right. I know what one you are: Grumpy. Oh no, wait a minute. We've done that one, ain't we? My mistake. Come on. We'll catch 'im. You know we will.'

Paterson turned the car around. 'As long as we do it before he kills that kid.'

'What's the plan for when we do catch up with 'im? Will it involve a bleedin' good 'iding?'

'Yep.'

'Oh, good.'

CHAPTER THIRTY-SIX

The commissioner of the Metropolitan Police, Sam Morne, was sitting behind his desk waiting for them as the two detectives were shown into his office. Paterson clocked the two men either side of him and knew this wasn't going to be just a briefing.

'Take a seat, boys,' Morne said. 'This is Steven Ross from the Home Office and this is Commander David Baker. He's in charge of Hostage Rescue.'

Both of the men he'd introduced sat stoney-faced, glaring at them.

Paterson nodded in their direction as he and Clocks took their seats. 'Gentlemen.' He turned to Morne. 'What can we do for you, sir?'

'First of all. How are you two? I saw what happened on the TV until they blacked it out. The blast caught you both?'

'Yeah,' said Clocks. 'Took us off our feet. Ironed us out for a coupla minutes, but apart from a dozen or so cuts and my stingin' knob, we're peachy.'

'Well, I can see you both have cuts. John, don't even think of talking about your penis.'

Clocks grinned.

'I'm sorry, Inspector,' said Steven Ross. 'Ironed you out? I don't understand.'

Clocks looked at him. 'Yeah. Flattened us out. Like we'd been ironed.' He nodded to reinforce the point.

Ross nodded back.

'Good,' said Commissioner Morne. 'Good to know. I'm going to need a full briefing of the events that took place this morning, gents. Best you can.'

'Fair enough,' said Paterson. 'Got your pens ready, gentlemen?' he said to Ross and Baker. The two men ignored him. Paterson spent the next ten minutes filling them in on how events had unfolded and their subsequent search for Steers and the girl. The two men took copious notes, a fact that didn't go unnoticed by either Paterson or Clocks.

'And that's where we are,' Paterson said.

Morne looked satisfied. 'Well, thank you. Thank you. I'll need your written reports as soon as you can, yes?'

'Of course,' Paterson replied.

'I have questions,' said Baker. He looked at Morne. 'May I?'

'Feel free.'

'Thank you. Mr Paterson. Toward the end of this siege and the subsequent tragic events that took place, you were informed that one of my hostage negotiators had arrived on scene, is that correct?'

'Yep.'

'I think you mean "Yes, sir." I'm sure I don't need to remind you that I'm two ranks above you, do I?'

Paterson gave him a tight-lipped smile. 'No. Sir. You don't.' Paterson read the writing on the wall. He'd been in this position too many times before to not know the way this was going. A pitiful attempt by a desk-bound pencil pusher trying to impress everyone with a big-man act. He was neither impressed nor fazed. And, from the corner of his eye, he saw that Clocks had tensed up.

'Good. So, to the question then, if you please.'

'You're correct. Sir.'

Baker nodded slowly. 'I also understand that you were instructed to stand down. Correct?'

'Correct.'

'But you didn't.'

'Correct.'

Baker took in a deep breath and sat himself straight. 'And why was that?'

'No point.'

'*No point?*'

'No.'

'And why is that?'

'Your boy was late getting there.'

'Excuse me?'

'Where is your team based?'

'What? Why?'

'Just asking.'

'Here at the Yard.' Baker eyed Paterson with suspicion.

'This siege started at what? About nine o'clock. Rush hour. You'd have got the call within ten minutes at the latest of the first officer arriving on scene. Sound about right?'

Baker said nothing.

'With blues and twos, your boy should have been with us within ten minutes. Fifteen tops. I'm being bloody generous if I said twenty minutes, given that the traffic was building. DI Clocks and I were on scene within a few minutes. We'd been talking to the suspect for some time before your man showed up. We had a rapport of sorts. Plus, our boy blew that bus up within minutes of your man's arrival. He'd never have managed to open a dialogue in time and, even if he had, Steers was always going to kill them. That was always his plan.'

As Baker bristled, Paterson turned his plan to blame him and Clocks back on itself. He decided to give the man a dig. 'So, don't blame yourself for what happened, sir. It wasn't your fault.'

'What? *My fault?*'

'Yes, sir.'

'You wilfully disobeyed an order, Paterson!' he blustered. 'And that got people killed and maimed!'

'Oh, just *fuck off*, will yer!' said Clocks.

Commissioner Morne grimaced. 'Clocks!'

'What? No. I'm not 'avin' it, guv. I'm fucked off with every shiny-arsed knob of a senior officer trying to sidestep the blame and shove it onto us.'

Baker shot up out of his chair, his face flushed and his fists bunched.

'Don't you dare talk to me like that, *Inspector*.'

'Tch. Look at you gettin' all lairy in yer old age. Sit yerself down before I put you down, you silly ol' sod.' Clocks waved at him to take his seat again.

'*John!*' Morne's voice carried a warning. He shook his head to emphasise his point.

'What the . . . ?' Baker looked apoplectic. 'Who the . . . who the hell do you think you're talking to?'

Clocks sighed. *Sorry, Sam.* 'I know *who* you are and I know *what* you are and I know you're all bunched up because yer arse is in a sling, but that's not on us an' you're not puttin' it on us. We did our best, but the fact is, like me guv'nor said, this mad fucker was *always* gonna blow the bus. *Always*. An' if you think otherwise, well then, you're just another deluded senior officer thinking he knows how to do the job of policemen.'

'Mr Morne. Are you going to allow this level of insubordination?'

Morne shrugged. 'To be fair. It was obvious to me from the start that you came here with the intention of laying the blame for this incident at these men's feet and, to be fair, from what we saw on the telly and what they've since told us, it seems a somewhat ill-judged attempt on your part. You should know that these two officers are not cowed by rank or authority and are not afraid to say their piece. Granted, Mr Clocks can be somewhat . . . undiplomatic, shall we say, but he does make himself clear, doesn't he?

'Besides, this shouldn't be about laying blame. This meeting was a briefing and we've been briefed — so let's all move on. Do we know yet what caused the blast? Why isn't anyone from the bomb squad here?'

'Still on scene, I suppose,' said Paterson.

Baker nodded. 'One of the survivors says the bus was loaded up with a large amount of LPG gas, large camping-sized bottles, I think. While he was busy offloading the girls, he ordered one of them to puncture each and every tin with a knife. Once the door was closed, the whole bus filled up with LPG. A crude but sizeable bomb that he somehow triggered with a remote. I suspect there was some sort of ignition device inside the bus on or near the petrol tank.'

'So, he has knowledge of bombmaking?' said Ross.

'If he does, then I would suggest it to be at an amateur level,' said Baker. 'If what we've been told is correct, then this probably something he learned from the internet.'

'*Could* he have rigged it to the petrol tank?' said Paterson.

'In theory, yes. But, contrary to what Hollywood tells us, petrol doesn't just go up easily. It's a bit more complex than they'd have you believe, but . . . if the conditions were set up correctly beforehand then it's feasible. Feasible but not likely. That said, we shall have to wait for a full forensic report.'

'Mr Ross, what's the Home Office's take on this?' said Morne.

Ross cleared his throat. 'Well, they're keeping tight-lipped at the moment, but they have authorised you to use any and all resources at your command to find this man and bring him to justice. Basically, whatever you need is yours.

'The prime minister expects you to meet with the relatives of the victims and offer them whatever you can in the way of condolences, but — and I'm sure you already know this — promise them nothing. Our legal department has already indicated that there is likely to be some form of action mounted. No doubt the vampire army that makes up the legal profession have already left their coffins and are descending on the bereaved as we speak. You have a press conference scheduled for noon, commissioner. Mr Paterson . . . Mr Clocks . . . will you be in attendance?'

Both men nodded.

'Ray,' said Morne. 'I hear that you're working on some theory that this is all religiously motivated. Something about dates of birth?'

'Hmm. We have a working theory, but that's all. The first two victims shared the same date of birth. Ninth of the ninth, nineteen ninety-nine. Turned upside down, nine, nine, nine becomes six, six, six. There were eighteen girls on the bus. That divides into three lots of six.'

Morne frowned. 'Are you saying that this is, what, some sort of Devil worship?'

'The opposite. For some reason, he believes that *I* am the Devil incarnate and that he is doing God's work to rid the earth of me and my disciples. Apparently. The first two victims, Heaton and Glass, had recently dropped away from the church, and with those dates of birth we think he took that to be a sign that they had fallen under the spell of the Devil. The numbers were a calling card to come looking for him. We've thrown around a few ideas relating to the Book of Revelations and numbers found in the Bible. So, at the moment, things are pointing toward that.'

Morne nodded. 'Hmm. Interesting. That's a conversation I'd like to have been involved in.'

Barker snorted. 'Bloody stupid theory. Devils and Bibles.'

Paterson glared at him. 'Not devils. *The* Devil. And as your job is nothing to do with policing and everything to do with hostages, it might be best if you spoke only about what you know about. Oh, we already did, didn't we? And I think we determined that you're not that quick off the mark at that either.'

Baker reared up again. 'Do *not* talk to me like that! I am your superior officer!'

Paterson grimaced. He knew from old that Clocks hated that expression with a passion. He also knew he wouldn't let it go. He didn't.

'Oi! Never mind that, mate. You're not superior to any-one in this room an' don't kid yerself you are. You might hold a higher rank, but that don't make you superior in any way, shape or form, so pull yer wrinkly ol' neck in.'

'That's it! I want this officer sanctioned.' Baker pointed at Clocks.

'Hmm. I'm sure you do,' said Morne. 'Not happening.'

'Don't point at me!' Clocks snapped.

'Sir,' said Paterson, shaking his head. 'Don't . . .'

'If I want to point at him, I bloody well will!'

Paterson shrugged. 'Okay. Please yourself. Just so you know, the last senior officer to do that to him got his finger bitten. Badly. Your choice.'

Baker stared at Paterson. 'Are you serious? He *bit* someone? A senior officer?'

Commissioner Morne hung his head and shook it several times before looking back up at the shocked commander. 'Hmm, hmm. To be fair, he did warn him not to do it, just like he's warned you.'

'Commissioner! You surely cannot let this level of unruliness go unchecked. This . . . officer *bit* a colleague and now he's threatening me.'

'No charges or complaints were made, so . . . all in the past, eh? Now, I'd appreciate it if you'd stop puffing yourself up and don't wind him up any further. He's had a bad day. They've *both* had a bad day. *I'm* having a fucking bad day, too.

'I don't have the time or the inclination to watch you swing your dick around with these two men. Believe me, it will not be big enough. But, if you continue to do so, don't come crying to me if they snap it off. Now, what Paterson said is true. Your man never made it on time. Not his fault. Not your fault. I will take responsibility for any balls-ups, so you don't have to worry.

'The most pressing matter now, and one that will receive our full attention, is where the hell this bastard is and what's he done or going to do to this girl . . .' Morne looked down at his notes. 'Zara Morgan. Ray . . . John . . . do what you do. Whatever it takes. Go. And keep me informed.'

Paterson grinned. 'Thank you, sir.'

'Don't I even get an apology?' said Baker.

'The fuck for?' said Clocks. 'Not like I bit yer, is it?'

Both men headed out of the door, leaving behind them a fuming commander, a bemused Home Office representative and a very concerned commissioner of police.

CHAPTER THIRTY-SEVEN

'Every *fuckin'* time,' said Clocks as he watched the floor coun-
ter in the lift work its way through the floors. 'Every time
somethin' goes tits up, we get the blame.' The female inspector who was sharing the ride down with them looked a bit
taken aback by the anger in Clocks's voice.

'Well,' said Paterson. 'You should be used to it by now.'

'I know I should, but I ain't. These wanky little fuck-
sticks — sorry, love — just don't 'ave the bollocks on 'em
these days.'

'I'm sorry,' said the inspector. 'Please don't call me
"love". I'm not your love.'

Clocks sighed. Paterson rolled his eyeballs.

'And you never will be with that bleedin' attitude, *love*.
Lighten up a bit, eh? I didn't mean anythin' by it. Fuck me.
Everyone's so uptight these days. Call me this. Call me that.
Don't call me this. Don't call me that. Don't tell me to do
this. Don't tell me to do that. Don't call me "missus". Call
me This, That, They, Them, Himbo, Shimbo, Dimbo. Gives
me a fuckin' 'eadache, all this dancin' around in case some
little nancy gets offended. Can't be doin' with it.'

'Do you know who I am?' said the woman.

'Nope. D'you know who I am?'

'No, I don't.'

'Both in the dark then, ain't we, love? Lemme guess though. You're some post-modern thinker who's just graduated from lefty college an' you've got the arseache with devastatingly 'andsome middle-aged white men? No? 'Ow about a defender of the little pansies with no ability to take a joke without 'avin' to lay down with teddy and a bottle of mummy's thruppenny-bit milk? Or you're someone who designs the "tired an' emotional rooms" for the whiney, self-important, thinks-they're-entitled-to-special-treatment-'cos-they're-wankers senior management.'

'I'm the head of the Diversity and Cultural Unit.'

'Bingo! There you go. Lefty with an agenda. I knew it. Even worse.'

'How dare you talk to me like that. I'll have you out of a job.'

'Oh, no! Not the sack! Oh, please miss, or whatever you call yerself today. Don't make me leave the job I love. *Seriously*, you're fuckin' welcome to it, love. Sorry. *Babe*. An', just so you know, people a lot higher than you 'ave tried to "get me" an' failed.'

The doors slid open. Clocks backed out and winked at her. 'Anyway, sweetie, I'd love to stay and upset you some more, but I've got a proper job to do. You crack on pushin' out the ideology and today you can tell all the class that mummy was *vewy, vewy* upset by the naughty policeman who was an absolute *beastly* prick to her.' He turned around and breezed off with a big smile on his face.

'You love this, don't you?' said Paterson.

'Ray, me ol' China. As I wander my way through this life, if I get the opportunity to upset just one whiney little crybaby with an attitude and no idea of the real world, even just a little teeny-weeny bit, then I can go to bed knowin' that I've done my bit for common sense an' the workin' man — sorry, *person* — who no longer 'as a voice. A man . . . sorry . . . *person* can do no more.'

Paterson nodded.

'Right, then,' said Clocks. 'No more playin' about. Let's go find this snot-gobblin', Bible-bashin', rat-fuckin' son of an 'airy cunt an' kick the livin' granny out of 'im all the way to the Pope's 'ouse an' back again.'

'Amen to that, Brother Clocks. Amen to that.'

The head of the Diversity and Cultural Unit was already on her phone lodging a complaint.

CHAPTER THIRTY-EIGHT

'Zara . . .' said Steers. 'It's an unusual name.'

Sitting hunched over, Zara Morgan hugged herself tighter and shivered in the cold. He ran his eyes across her young body, noticed the goosebumps and the raised hairs on her arms, the smears of blood on her thighs. He smiled. God would be pleased with his work.

'Please . . . Please, sir. Please let me go. I promise, I *promise* not to tell anyone. I swear to God.'

'What? What did you say?' Steers dropped onto his haunches and stared at the girl. He moved his head from side to side slowly, savouring his prey. 'You would say the name of our Lord God! You who have only just been initiated into His Kingdom. You are not worthy, girl! *You* do not speak His name. *You* do not speak His name until He commands it so.' He reached out and grabbed the arm covering her breast, pulled it away and stared at it. She cried harder under his gaze.

'I'm sorry. I'm sorry. I'm so sorry. Please. Please let me go. I want my mum. Please, sir. I'm sorry.'

Her begging seemed to appease him. He let her arm go and stood up. Zara immediately covered herself the best she could.

'I cannot let you go.'

'Whhhhyyyy . . . ? Pleeeeassseee.'

'I still have work to do.'

Zara sobbed. 'Please . . .'

'The two policemen. One is the Devil himself, sent to destroy all that is good on this earth. The ugly demon protects him. He will die before he allows harm to come to his master. They both must die.'

'No . . . please . . .'

Steers looked down at her.

'No? You question me child?'

She shook her head. 'Please don't kill anyone. No more, please . . .'

For a full ten seconds he stared at her hunched up body before he slowly slipped off his belt.

'I'm disappointed. *God* is disappointed. There is more work to do with you, child.'

She screamed in pain and shock as the first swish of the buckle bit into the flesh on her back.

'They *will* die and *you* will help me to rid the earth of these demons.'

CHAPTER THIRTY-NINE

Paterson leaned forward and cradled his head in his hands. For a couple of seconds, he pressed his fingers into his eye sockets and looked at the kaleidoscope of colours and patterns that formed on the back of his retina. He let go, watched the shapes fade and then sighed.

He and Clocks had stopped off at the nick to catch up with any new developments, but Paterson wasn't surprised to find out there were none. This was the way investigations went, he knew. Sometimes a case was easy to solve, sometimes it wasn't. This should be easy. They knew Steers's name. They knew what he looked like. They knew a fair bit about him. Except where to find him. And, as every second ticked down, he knew hope was fading for the girl.

His desk phone rang.

'Paterson,' he said.

'Satan.'

Paterson sat bolt upright.

'Hear me, Satan, lord of all that is evil. Listen to me now or I will strip the flesh from the child. Do nothing. Call no one or I will destroy her like I destroyed the others.'

Paterson's heart pumped faster, a mixture of rage and adrenalin.

'You, and you alone, will meet me tonight. Midnight. If the demon is with you, she will burn for eternity.'

Paterson fought to keep his voice under control. 'Where?'

'The old Bermondsey swimming baths.'

Paterson searched through his memory bank. 'That place was demolished. Years ago.'

'On the surface, yes.' The phone went dead.

Paterson closed his eyes and ran a map of the local area through his mind until it stopped in Grange Road, SE1. The old public baths used to be there, he was sure of it. The place closed in 1973, long before his time, but he knew of it. Whatever posting he'd been given in the past, he always made a point of finding out some local history. He found it helped him get a feel for the place, for the people. If he'd got it right, the old baths were on or near the junction with Spa Road. He couldn't be sure. Not yet.

Why there? It was an office block now. Had been for years. It made no sense. He tapped his pen on the desk. *On the surface . . . On the surface.* He looked at his watch: 9.47 p.m.

Paterson grabbed his desk phone, then stopped. Clocks had gone to the canteen for a top-up. *You and you alone . . .*

He put the phone down and walked out of his office.

* * *

'Jesus! What're you doin' slummin' it up 'ere?' Clocks pushed a slice of bacon into his mouth without waiting for Paterson to reply.

'You got anything new?' Paterson said.

Clocks shook his head. 'Nah. All quiet on the Western, mate.'

'Go home, then.'

'Come again? *Go 'ome*? I ain't goin' 'ome. We've got a cunt to catch. *Go 'ome*? Yeah, an' the rest, mate.'

'We're both tired, John. Exhausted. We need to rest. The night team will call us if anything crops up.'

Clocks eyed him suspiciously. 'What you up to?'

Paterson shrugged. 'Nothing. Just think we need a rest.'

'Since when? You're a relentless bastard at the best of times and when there's kids involved you're even worse. So, what's up?'

'Nothing! We need some rest.'

Clocks picked up the last sausage on his plate, dipped it in his egg and stood up. 'Bollocks! What's goin' on, Ray? Tell me now.' He bit into the sausage.

'John, there is nothing going on. Can't I be interested in your welfare?'

'You can but you ain't, so tell me what the fuck is goin' on or I'll beat it out of you.'

Paterson smiled. 'Oh, well. If you're going to beat me up . . . Idiot. Why won't you believe me?'

'Simple. You're fuckin' lyin' an' we both know it. I can smell a liar at fifty feet, an' right now you smell like you fell into a big ol' vat of Boris Johnson's lyin' juice and came up covered in lies. You got a call, didn't you?'

Paterson sighed.

'Didn't you?'

'Yep.'

Clocks punched the air. 'Back of the net! I knew it! Who's the best copper you ever met? Go on. Who is it?'

'You, John.'

'Say it.'

'What?'

'Say it.'

'No.'

'Say it.'

'You're the best copper I ever met. Happy?'

'Over the moon, son. I've still got it. Right, where we goin'?'

'You're not. I am.'

Clocks smiled. 'Yeah, right. You only think you are.'

'He said, me only or he'll tear the skin from her flesh.'

Clocks grimaced. 'Ooh. That sounds nasty.'

'Take it from me, it is.'

Clocks's face lit up. 'That's right! You know all about that, don'tcha? The old Childmaker 'ad a go at yer boat race, didn't 'e?'

Paterson touched the scar that ran under his bearded jawline. A constant reminder of the killer who tried to slice his face off.

'So, what's the plan?'

'I do exactly as he says.'

'Do you, bollocks. I'm backin' you up whether you like it or not.'

'I'd like you to, but it's not happening. Not this time.'

'We'll see. Where you goin'?'

'Better you don't know.'

'What? Why?'

'Because you'll turn up all *Die Hard* style and we might lose the girl.'

'S'alright. What's another one?'

Paterson scowled.

'I'm only jokin'. You know I am.'

'Hmm. Not now though, eh? That's not really funny, is it? Got to work out some sort of plan before I leave.' Paterson checked his watch again. 'Gotta meet him at midnight.'

'I've got it!'

'What?'

'A plan.'

'Let's hear it, then.'

'You go on yer own. But not really, 'cos I'll be in the car layin' down between the seats with a Glock. You get out an' go in. I give it five minutes then I creep in. I find out where you are—'

'How will you know where I am?'

Clocks shrugged. 'Dunno. I'll keep me ears open for yer screams.'

'Thanks.'

'Welcome. Anyway, I creep about all quiet, an' when you two are 'avin' a dance-off or whatever, I'll jump up an' shoot 'is fuckin' face off. Hurrah! The kid's saved. Job done.

We go 'ome. Get another medal or some shit off the commissioner and everybody's 'appy.'

Paterson sniffed. 'That's your plan?'

'Yes it is. Copyright J. Clocks, Esquire. Yep. You got a better one?'

'No, actually. I haven't. Yours sounds reasonable enough.'

'What?'

'Sounds reasonable.'

'Does it? I thought you'd say it was shit an' I was a wanker.'

'Oh, it's shit and you are a wanker, but I haven't got time to think of a better one.'

'So where is it, then?'

'The old Bermondsey baths.'

Clocks crinkled his nose. 'Never 'eard of it.'

'It shut down in seventy-two, seventy-three, I think. Somewhere around then.'

'Alright, so where *was* it?'

'If it's where I think it was, Grange Road, junction of Spa Road.'

'That's offices now, innit?'

'Yeah, but I've got a feeling there's a gym with a swimming pool in the basement.'

'So what?'

'I think he has something special planned for me.'

CHAPTER FORTY

Paterson glanced at the clock on the dashboard. It was 11.58 p.m. 'Right, I'm going in,' he said.

'Can you pull yer seat forward?'

'What? Why?'

'I've got meself stuck between your seat an' the back seat.'

'What?'

'You 'eard. There's no room in the back of this bleedin' car. Me fuckin' arm's wedged against me chest. I can't get it out. I can't move.'

'How did you do that?'

'Dunno. I think I dropped down a bit too quick when we pulled into Grange Road. Didn't get me arm out the way in time. It fuckin' 'urts, mate.'

Paterson chuckled. 'You're a dick, you know that?'

'Yes. *Everyone* knows that. But, I'm super cute.'

'Is that right?'

'It is. And sexy. Now get out the bleedin' car and pull yer seat forward. If you don't, I can't get out of 'ere to save yer bony arse, can I?'

'I guess not. John?'

'What?'

'Stay there.'

'What? No.' He began to struggle.

'Stay there, John. This is between me and him. I can't lose one more soul.'

'One more soul. What're you? The fuckin' RNLI? Fuck you, Paterson! Move the fuckin' chair in an' let me up.'

'No.'

'I'll do you if you go in there without me!'

'No you won't. You love me.'

'Do I fuck! Let me up, you poncey knob.'

Paterson pushed his chair further back, locking Clocks down even tighter, and exited the car. 'It's twelve. See you soon, mate.' He slammed the door.

Clocks writhed around the footwell, kicking out at the back door. 'Ha!' he shouted. 'That's two grand's worth of damage, moneybags.' His body slipped lower. 'Balls!'

Paterson found his way in around the back of the building. A door had been left ajar, ready for him. He stepped into the darkness.

* * *

Plotted up two streets away, Paterson's team stood by waiting for word from Johnny Clocks. Monkey Harris was in the driver's seat. Next to him was Jackie Hartnett. Sitting in the back were Yorkshire and Tommy Gunn. Clocks had called them together for a sneaky meet in the station office while Paterson had been getting himself ready.

The plan itself was quick and dirty. As soon as Clocks exited his car, they would exit theirs and take up positions around the building and then wait for his signal. If their suspect came out of the building, they were to use any force necessary to stop him.

Jackie looked at her watch.

'What time you got?' said Monkey.

'Eight minutes past,' she said.

'That's enough time, surely?'

'Don't know. You know those two. Probably changed the plan at the last minute and "forgot" to tell us.'

'I dunno,' said Monkey. 'Something's . . . *off.*'

'That'll be your feet,' said Gunn. Even Yorkshire raised a little smile.

'I'm going.' Monkey opened the door.

Jackie grabbed his arm. 'Monkey! No! The guv's inside by now, I should think. If that mad bastard smells a copper, it's likely to go tits up.'

'I think it might have already.' He stepped out into the night.

* * *

Paterson stood still in the entranceway for a moment or two and allowed his eyes to adjust to the dark. Silence shrouded the foyer. When he felt ready, he crept through a long corridor, stopping every few feet to listen for sounds. He strained his hearing. Nothing. Reaching into his pocket, he pulled out his phone and opened the torch app. His thumb hovered over the on switch for a second before he put it back in his pocket. No point making himself too easy a target for his enemy.

Cautiously, he rounded a corner into a new corridor. At the end of it, a faint, whitish light cocooned a vending machine.

Ten feet away from the end of the corridor he spotted a window to his left. *Sniper? Not this man's style.* Peering around to the right, it became obvious why the machine had been left on. It was softly illuminating the sign to the swimming pool. Paterson smiled to himself.

* * *

Monkey Harris weaved his way along the pavement to Paterson's car, singing softly to himself in a slurred voice. Playing the part of a drunk was no real hardship for him. His thinking was simple: if Steers happened to be watching the car, he'd just think he was some pisshead making his way home.

The car itself was in darkness. Drawing nearer, he saw that it was rocking slightly and he could hear muffled thumps coming from inside.

'Shit!' He dropped the act and ran to it. Cupping his hands around his face he peered in through the back window. He couldn't see anything as the car had tinted windows, but he could clearly hear Clocks's voice raging at someone or something.

'Guv?' he called.

Clocks was too busy ranting to himself to hear Monkey. 'I'll fuckin' do you if anything 'appens to you, Paterson!' He kicked out at the door again.

'Guv?' Monkey raised his voice.

Clocks stopped squirming. 'Monkey? Zat you?'

'Yeah.'

'Gemme out of 'ere. The guv's fucked off an' left me 'ere.'

Monkey pulled on the handle.

'It's locked, guv.'

'I know it's fuckin' locked. Put the window in!'

Monkey stepped back. 'What?'

'Put . . . the . . . fuckin' . . . window . . . in. Do it!'

'It's a Bentley,' said Monkey, very unsure.

'It's a car. A car! Get me outta 'ere, Monkey. I can't breathe. Chest compression an' shit!' C'mon, before I peg out.'

'But—'

'Monkey, you listen to me. The guv's gone off on 'is own, right? So, I need to 'elp 'im. *We* need to 'elp 'im. But I'm fuckin' stuck in this poxy motor. Now, if the guv gets 'urt or killed, that's on you, an' at some point, when I do get outta 'ere, I'll shoot you in your fat bollocks an' sling you in the Thames for lettin' that 'appen. Goddit?'

'Got it.'

'Good. Now break this fuckin' window an' get me outta 'ere!'

Monkey drew his extendable baton, flicked it open and took a full back-handed swing at the window. With a loud bang, it exploded inward, covering Clocks in a shower of glass.

Monkey wrenched the door open. 'Bloody hell, guv! How'd you get down there?'

'Oh, I slipped when I went to pick up me mint imperials that fell out the bag. Get me out!'

Monkey dragged him out, cutting him on the small bits of glass as he did so. Clocks stood up and sucked air into his lungs. 'You alright, guv?'

'Never better, me ol' son.' He swept glass out of his hair. 'Get everyone in position around this buildin'. If Steers comes out, don't talk to 'im. Shoot 'im. Goddit? Shoot 'im an' shoot 'im properly.'

Monkey watched Clocks yank on the front doors of the building to no avail and then set off back to his car as Clocks slipped around the back.

* * *

Paterson crept down the stairs toward the swimming pool. Ahead of him, two swing doors were wide open. The smell of chlorine brought him straight back to memories of being a child. He closed those thoughts down and moved forward in the darkness. Drawing level, he stopped and peered into the room. He could just about make out the shape of the pool: regular . . . rectangular. It seemed empty, but some sixth sense or other was telling him it wasn't. He stepped in and waited for an attack that never came.

A gentle clinking sound snapped his head around to its direction. It sounded to him as if it came from somewhere above and to his left. Slowly, he slipped his hand in his jacket pocket and pulled out his phone. *Now might be a good time to shine a little light on the situation.* He switched it on and held it up.

'Shit!'

Before he could react, a lightning bolt of pain shot through his entire body. All of his limbs stiffened. The pain stayed with him as he fell, like a plank, onto the side of the pool. His head smashed onto the tiles but he felt nothing. The Taser had blocked out all pain but the pain it alone was inflicting. The last thing he saw and heard before he lost consciousness was the screwed-up, hate-filled face of David Steers.

'I have you, Satan.'

CHAPTER FORTY-ONE

'Ray?' Clocks whispered. 'Ray!' No reply. He drew his weapon and held it out in front of him.

Clocks followed a corridor, where a vending machine's glow sent him down toward the swimming pool, until he found himself outside two swing doors, now closed.

In the middle of the doors were circles of reinforced glass. He put his foot against one of the doors to prevent it being slammed into his face and carefully peered through the circular window. The pool room stood in darkness. He wrinkled his nose a few times, a protest against the chlorine smell.

Slowly, he moved away from the glass and gently pushed the door open. The gun went in first. Nobody hit his arms. A good sign. He stepped inside.

'Ray?' he said, his voice a couple of notches above a whisper. 'You in 'ere?'

'John! Get out!' Paterson shouted.

The pool area lit up once Steers threw the power switch.

'Oh, fuck a duck!' Clocks hissed. He lowered the gun at the sight before him.

Chained and dangling over the pool was a naked Zara Morgan and a fully clothed Paterson. The girl looked drained of life. Paterson hung over the deep end. Clocks saw the depth sign underneath Zara: 3.0 metres. Beneath Paterson, it said 4.5 metres. Dangling from the feet of both of them were a number of 20 kg kettlebells and assorted barbells. He counted three weights on Zara and six on Paterson.

Steers walked into view from the double doors at the other end of the pool. Clocks spotted the release control in his hands.

'Ugly demon! Your master will die tonight, as will this child of Satan. It is the will of God that she no longer live. She has been deemed . . . unworthy. You cannot defy the will of God!'

'No?' Clocks raised the gun and pointed it straight at Steers. 'Ain't no fucker in this world or the next that I can't or won't defy, pal.'

Steers let loose a maniacal laugh. 'Go ahead. Shoot me if you will! I long to be sent home to be with Him once again. My master awaits my return. But, if you do, they will drop into the water.'

'What is it you want?'

'To kill them.'

Clocks frowned. 'That's a shitty plan ain't it, doom brain? So, by the sound of it, you're gonna drop 'em anyway, ain'tcha? Fuck it, then. Might just as well shoot yer.'

'John!' Paterson shouted.

Clocks tore his eyes away from Steers.

'Save the girl. You hear me? Save her, John.'

No reply. Clocks's mind had gone into overdrive.

'Ray. I can save you both.'

Paterson looked at the water below him. He noted its depth and felt the weight pulling him down. 'Doubt it. Whatever you do, you get her out first. You hear me?'

Steers laughed. Guttural this time. 'Touching.'

'John?'

'Shuddup, Ray. I'm thinkin'.'

'John. If you have time, just remember. You've got three thirty-seven.'

Clocks furrowed his brow.

180

'You remember? Three thirty-seven.'

Clocks shook his head until a light came on inside. During one of their late-night discussions in which Clocks regularly berated him for being a well-educated rich boy, Paterson once told him he'd been a swimming champion at school and had once held his breath for three minutes, thirty-seven seconds. Clocks opened rapid fire at Steers.

The first two shots missed their mark. The third caught him in the top of his thigh. He screeched in pain and pressed the button.

Clocks looked on in horror as Zara and Paterson dropped, hitting the water at the same time. As they sank like stones, he kept pulling the trigger. Steers took another bullet before he limped off through the doorway. This time, it grazed his shoulder.

Clocks dropped the gun and dived into the pool.

CHAPTER FORTY-TWO

Monkey Harris shouted into his radio. 'Shots fired! Shots fired! Standby!' He pulled his gun, took up a two-handed stance and focused on the back door. It burst open and a figure came running out. He recognised Steers immediately. 'Police!'

Monkey opened fire, and Steers half ducked and kept running. He watched Tommy Gunn burst out of hiding and run toward the fugitive. From the opposite direction, Yorkshire came running too. Monkey lowered his gun. He'd seen Gunn in a fight before and knew he could easily handle himself, and Yorkshire, in a pinch, could and would hold his hands up. *Game over.*

Except . . . except he saw Steers's hand swing across as Gunn laid hands on him. Gunn staggered backward holding his chest. He watched as Steers launched himself into a forward dive, hitting Yorkshire square in the chest with the full weight of his body, and he heard a sickening thud as his head smacked onto the kerb. Yorkshire lay still as Steers limped off into the dark.

Monkey broke into a run. 'Tetley!' He never took his eyes off Yorkshire. This had gone bad. Very bad. Running to his colleagues, he screamed into his radio. 'Urgent assistance! Grange Road. Back of Alaska buildings! Ambulance required!'

Immediately a calm voice repeated his call. '*All units. Urgent assistance required. Rear of Alaska buildings. Grange Road.*'

Monkey never heard the units that piped up in response. His focus was concentrated solely on Yorkshire. Gunn at least was standing. He'd be fine. He reached Yorkshire within seconds. He looked down at him and knew straightaway. Dead.

DC Yorkshire lay face up, his eyes wide and glassy. A dark pool of blood seeped out from beneath his broken skull and mixed with the dirt in the gutter. Monkey Harris let out a deep sigh and pushed his hair back tight against his head. He spun around. 'Fuck! Fuck!'

Tommy Gunn, shocked, trotted over toward Monkey and Yorkshire. 'Aah, no. No, no, no, no, no. No!'

'He's gone, mate,' Monkey said, his voice flat. He saw Gunn's face. 'That's gonna scar.'

Gunn nodded. 'Coulda been a lot worse,' he said, peering down at Yorkshire. Jackie came running around the corner.

'C'mon!' Monkey shouted. 'Paterson and Clocks!'

Jackie diverted and ran toward the open door from where Steers had emerged.

CHAPTER FORTY-THREE

Clocks swam the first ten feet underwater. The blurry shape of Zara was twisting and writhing, struggling to break free. She couldn't. He broke the surface and slapped the water heavily as he swam to her. Two feet from her, he went under again. Planting his feet on the bottom of the pool, he grabbed her around the bottom of her legs and pushed her upward. She lifted up with relative ease, buoyed partly by the water, mostly by the gift of Clocks's adrenaline. They both broke the surface. Zara, over Clocks's shoulder, coughed up a mouthful of water. He strained to keep her out of the water and get her to the side.

Against the edge, he dropped his body slightly and grabbed at the chain around her legs. With both hands and tremendous effort, he boosted her up and shoved her force-fully onto the side of the pool. Her feet, burdened by the weight of the kettlebells, dangled in the water and threatened to drag her back down. Clocks grabbed her feet, and with all his strength, lifted them clear of the water and spun her around. She was safe.

'Ray!' he gasped.

He hauled himself up and out of the pool, rolled onto his side and pulled himself to a standing position. The time went through his mind. He must have spent a minute on saving Zara — 2.37 left. Maybe. He ran, slipped, righted himself and dived back into the water.

Paterson, eyes closed, appeared to be calm. He opened them as Clocks tugged on the chain at his chest. Clocks dropped down and put his arms around Paterson's legs. He pushed off from the bottom. This time, he went nowhere. Paterson was 210 lb of sheer muscle. The combined weight of the kettlebells was 120 lb, making it 330 lb to shift. Almost twenty-four stone. Plus the weights of the chains. Clocks couldn't do it.

Paterson smiled.

Clocks, in a panic and desperate, tried again. He didn't have the strength left in him.

1 minute left.

Paterson understood. He nodded and gave another slight smile. *It's alright.*

Clocks shook his head furiously. He ducked low and put his head between Paterson's legs and grabbed onto his thighs. He strained to stand. Bubbles of air blew out from between his clenched teeth until he ran out of oxygen. He surfaced, gulped a big lungful of air and went straight back down.

He tried exactly the same move once again. He lifted him no more than a foot from the floor. Brainwave. He pushed Paterson backward.

45 seconds.

With Paterson prone, he dragged him by his feet. Better. But it was a long way to go before the water became shallow enough to stand. Suddenly it hit him. The shallow end was about six feet deep. Even if he stood him back up, Paterson still wouldn't break water.

Clocks, lungs burning, looked at his friend. He couldn't save him.

25 seconds.

Paterson gestured with his head. *Get up. Get out of here.*

Clocks, desperate for air, let him go and kicked his way upward. He looked down at his friend. *I'm so sorry, Ray. So, so sorry.*

185

CHAPTER FORTY-FOUR

As Clocks broke the surface and gasped for air, he narrowly avoided being struck by the massive frame of Monkey Harris jumping in. Right behind him came Jackie and Tommy Gunn. They went straight down to Paterson.

15 seconds.

Paterson struggled and started to spasm.

9 seconds.

His three colleagues all did the same as Clocks had done. They went low. Monkey got him on his shoulders and stood. Gunn and Jackie boosted him up.

Paterson's head broke the surface. He sucked in a huge lungful of air and coughed and spluttered desperately. Clocks, still in the water, scrambled out. He turned, grabbed Paterson by the lapels of his jacket and pulled for all he was worth. It wasn't much.

Monkey put his hands under Paterson's feet and pushed upward as hard as he could. Paterson's shoulders broke the surface. Clocks had little left. His arms felt like jelly as he struggled to pull his friend to safety. His feet skidded on the wet tiles. No grip. He was losing him.

He didn't hear the commotion as at least five uniformed police officers came running into the pool area, and he wasn't sure what was happening when Paterson's weight began to shift around and pulling him out wasn't nearly as difficult as it had been. He looked around him, suddenly aware of the voices. Help had arrived.

Monkey, Jackie and Gunn all broke the surface at the same time, gasped for air and splashed around. They looked shocked at what they'd just done.

As they made their way to the side of the pool, Paterson, lying sideways, spluttered and retched up water. When he'd finished, he took a deep, shuddering breath.

'Get these . . . chains . . . offa him,' said Clocks. The uniforms set about freeing him.

Other uniforms were busy freeing Zara. Paramedics were with her and two more waited for Paterson.

Monkey, Jackie and Gunn all sat on the side, legs dangling in the water. They'd done their bit.

It took about five minutes to get Paterson free and the paramedics darted in to do their job.

'I'm okay,' he said in a shaky voice. 'I'm fine.'

The paramedics ignored him and set about their work.

Paterson watched Zara, oxygen mask over her face, get wheeled away to a waiting ambulance outside. A few minutes later, he convinced his paramedics that a trip to hospital wasn't on the cards.

When the fuss had died down, all that could be heard was the echoing sound of breathing and coughing and the odd lapping of water.

'Thank you. Thank you all. I'm so grateful.'

'No bother,' said Monkey.

The other two raised their hands and nodded. *You're welcome.*

'How'd you all know I was here?'

Gunn nodded toward Clocks. Paterson swivelled his head toward his friend. He smiled at him and threw his arms around him. He slapped him on the back a few times. Clocks slapped him in return.

'Yeah, yeah. Alright. Tha's enough, you fuckin' big nancy. Tha's enough. Get offa me.'

Paterson ignored him. The others grinned at Clocks's discomfort at being the recipient of such an open display of affection. Clocks would never live it down and none of the team would let him. Paterson slapped him on the back a few more times and let him go. He looked into his face. Clocks's eyes were red rimmed. If anyone said anything, he'd blame it on the chlorine. But Paterson knew different.

'Thanks, buddy.'

'Don't thank me, Ray. I didn't do it for you. I just wanted me overtime signed. An' if you'da drowned, I'd been bollocksed, wouldn't I?'

Paterson took a deep breath and sniffed a few times. 'How did you get out of the car?'

'What?' said Clocks.

'The car. How'd you get out of it? You were wedged in.'

Monkey Harris started to walk away.

'Er . . .'

'What did you do, John?'

'Me? Nothin'.'

'*John?*'

'What?'

'What did you do?'

'Tch. Look. It wasn't me. It was Monkey. Monkey smashed yer window.'

Monkey spun around at the same time as Paterson's eyes widened. 'What?'

'You fuckin . . .'

Clocks held his finger up. 'Monkey. Shh. We both know what you did. Ray, I was dyin', mate. Chest compression. You left me to die, but luckily Monkey disobeyed my orders an' came lookin' for me. Good job 'e did otherwise I'da been deaded, mate. Deaded. 'E saved you from being me murderer.'

'D'you know how much one of those windows cost?'

Clocks shrugged. 'Dunno. 'Undred grand? Two 'undred?'

'That's the cost of the car, John, not the window.'

'Ah, you'll be alright. Kwik Fit'll bang one in fer yer.'

Paterson started to laugh. 'It's alright, mate. You saved my life. You all saved my life. What's a window between friends? Monkey. Good job, mate. I wouldn't want to be the one to have killed Clocksy.'

Monkey looked at Clocks and spoke through gritted teeth. 'Wasn't quite like that, guv, and I'd be happy to kill him.'

Paterson smiled. 'I don't doubt it for a second. Thanks anyway.' He nodded and looked around him. 'Where's Tetley?'

Nobody answered.

'Oh, yeah. I forgot about 'im,' said Clocks. 'Where's that fucker at?'

Paterson caught Monkey's wince. 'What? Where is he? What's happened to him? Is he hurt?'

'Yeah, guv,' said Jackie.

'Whassamatter with 'im?'

Jackie shook her head as Monkey looked into the distance.

'Oh, fuck! No!' said Paterson.

'What 'appened to 'im?' said Clocks.

'Steers drop-kicked him,' said Monkey. 'I saw his head hit the kerb. Instant.'

Clocks bunched his fists. 'Motherfucker!' he shouted. His voice echoed around the near-empty room. 'I swear to 'is fuckin' God I'm goin' to kill this fucker when I get 'old of 'im. You 'ear me? I'll fuckin' cut 'is dirty bastard throat an' pull 'is gizzards out the 'ole!'

Everybody nodded. It sounded like a plan they were all happy to get behind at that moment.

'I take it nobody has a problem with this?' said Paterson.

The group stayed quiet. Monkey and Gunn shook their heads.

'Good. Let's go to work.'

CHAPTER FORTY-FIVE

Paterson shouted his orders to the new batch of uniformed officers that had arrived. 'He can't have gotten too far. DI Clocks shot him in the leg. Get some more officers here and get searching!' He pulled the blanket tighter against his body.

'What's he look like, sir?' one of them asked.

'Like he's got a hole in his leg. Can't really miss him. He'll be the one limping away from you at some sort of speed.'

'Sir,' said the PC, suitably embarrassed.

'Go in pairs. This man has just killed a police officer and injured another. Consider him armed and dangerous. If you spot him, do not challenge him. You call me. Understood?'

All the officers nodded.

He clapped his hands a few times. 'Okay! Let's go. Let's go, go, go!'

Clocks was busy stamping around and raging to himself. Paterson took his turn at being concerned for his friend's state of mind.

'John . . .'

Clocks ignored him.

'John!'

Clocks stopped. 'What?'

'Calm down, eh?'

'Calm down? Are you takin' the piss? He's just done Tetley and nearly did for you an' the kid. Calm down!'

'We will find him, John. We will.'

'You've changed yer tune. Last I remember, *you* were doin' *your* bollocks.' He shook his head. 'Bastard's more slippery than a fishing net full of fish all covered in extra slippery fish oil an' grease. Bastard's escaped us more times than Houdini got out of locked microwaves.'

'Microwaves? Pretty sure that's not right.'

'You know what I mean. Fridges, then. Some sort of 'ouse'old appliance anyway.'

'Maybe a blender?'

'Yeah. One of them. I shoulda took my time an' shot 'im in the nut.'

Paterson shrugged. 'Hmm. I dunno. You're not exactly the best shot in the world, are you? You'd have probably still missed him.'

'Don't need to be the best in the world, Ray. Just needed to be good enough to pop one into 'is nut. I'da been well 'appy with that.'

'Well, you got two into him.'

'Outta seventeen bullets!'

'What can I say? Two's not bad.'

'Hmm.'

'Are you okay, mate?'

'No, Ray. Not really. I've done a few people in my time, cracked more than my share of bad 'eads, but this one? This one I want so fuckin' much. I can't understand 'ow 'e keeps gettin' away from us. It's embarrassin', fer fuck's sake. We've got a bloody reputation to up'old.'

Paterson nodded. 'What you said back there, at the pool . . .'

'What about it?'

'Not sure it was the best time to vent like that. Shouting the odds about killing him. Not the cleverest thing to do.'

'I was angry. Still am.'

'I know, but can we trust them?'

'In what way?'

'Not to dob you in.'

'Dob me in? Dob me in? Oh, fuck. I forgot you're private school, ain'tcha? I take it you mean they'll all keep their mouths shut an' not grass me up for threatenin' to kill 'im?'

'That's it.'

'Yeah. Don't matter anyway. I'd just say I was ragin'. Blood squirtin' around inside from me 'eroic save of you and the kid, shootin' me trap off. That's all it was. They'll swallow that.'

'And when we find him?'

'Then I'll kill 'im.'

'And if we do that, can we be a hundred-per-cent sure one of 'em won't crack?'

Clocks shrugged. 'I think they're solid.'

'All of them?'

'Hmm. I think so.'

'Gunn's pretty new to the team.'

'That's a point. Shall we go talk to 'em?'

'Think it's a good idea.'

'I think he's sound though, Ray. Besides, the bastard slashed 'is face, didn't 'e? Can't see 'im bein' a fan of 'im now.'

'Come on. Let's feel it out.'

Clocks nodded and they both wandered over to where the squad was. All of them were shivering against the cold; all were wrapped in blankets.

'Listen, what I said back there. At the pool. You do know it's me just 'ollerin' an' 'ootin', don'tcha?'

They all nodded.

'Sure, guv,' said Monkey.

'Yeah, course,' said Jackie. 'You're pissed. We all are.'

'Tommy?' said Paterson.

Gunn stared off into the distance.

'Tommy!' said Paterson.

Gunn started. 'Guv. What? Sorry. I was miles away.'

'We good? Clocksy here was just venting, yes?'

'Yeah, course. Course.'

'Good stuff.'

Clocks breathed out slowly.

'Listen,' said Paterson. 'Get yourself to the hospital, Tommy. That cut'll need stitches.'

Gunn nodded.

'Go now. Go on.'

'What happened back there?' Dusty, the only officer to have missed out on the shout, turned up at the same time as the team came staggering out of the office block. 'What'd I miss?'

'Nothin'. Don't worry about it.' Clocks reached into his back pocket and, from his wallet, pulled out a sopping-wet twenty-pound note. He held it up and let a few drops of water fall from the corner. He flicked it to get the last drops off and held it out to Dusty.

'Dusty. Be a love an' nip over to the petrol garage down the road for me. Pick up 'alf a dozen full-fat Cokes and as many Mars bars as yer can. We need a bit of sugar. Good man.'

'What?' Dusty looked miffed.

''Alf a dozen Cokes an' some Mars bars. We're all in shock. Need a good ol' dose of the white death. Sugar! Off you pop.'

'I'm not a fucking errand—' He saw the look on Clocks's face. Message received.

'Do *not* be gettin' any of that diet shit. Full-fat Cokes. Or Fanta. Anything loaded with sugar'll do.'

'Lucozade?' Dusty said. 'They still do that?'

'Yeah.'

'We'll 'ave that, then. Ooh! An' some crisps, too. I fancy some crisps. Anyone else?'

They all nodded.

'Get a mix, will yer? Just don't get Marmite flavour. Fuckin' 'orrible, that is.'

'I like Marmite,' said Jackie.

Clocks sniffed. 'Do yer? One packet of Marmite for the bird, then.'

Dusty sneered at the twenty.

'What? Tha's enough, innit?'

Dusty shrugged. 'Hope so.'

'Take it out yer overtime, then. Treat yer mates, yer tight bastard.'

Clocks watched Dusty trot off toward the garage.

CHAPTER FORTY-SIX

The search of the surrounding area turned up nothing. Frustrated, Paterson and Clocks returned to their office and got themselves dried and changed. Having done the same, the rest of the team drifted in behind them and sat themselves behind their desks. Business as usual.

'Vodka?' Paterson said to Clocks.

'Don't mind if I do. Large would be good.'

Paterson nodded. 'Done.' He took the bottle and two tumblers out of the bottom drawer of his desk and began to pour them both a good measure. 'Say when.'

Clocks watched him but said nothing.

Paterson stopped pouring two inches from the top of the glass. 'You not hear me?'

'Yep. You hear me say stop?'

'No.'

'Keep pouring, then. When you get to the brim, I'll go an' get meself a straw so I don't spill any.'

'What we going to do with all these Cokes and Mars bars?'

Clocks shrugged. 'Dunno. I thought everyone would've mullered 'em. They'll keep for a while in a drawer.'

'Look, we need a new strategy.'

'New? Didn't know we 'ad an old one.'

'Well, I don't suppose we did. But we need to move fast on tracking him down. C'mon.'

'What? Where we goin'?'

'Office. Meeting.'

Clocks slugged back a big mouthful of vodka and followed Paterson into the main office.

'Listen up, folks. First off, I never thanked you all properly for your help tonight. I genuinely thought that was me gone. John, you didn't give up. I deeply appreciate it. You others, I can't ever repay you. Thank you.'

'Guv, you gonna do all this poncey cuddlin' stuff again?' said Clocks. 'Only, there's no need. It's what we do for each other. Brothers.'

'And sisters,' said Jackie.

Clocks raised his glass. 'Yep. And sisters. Oh, by the way, Jack. Nice set of nips on yer.'

'*'Scuse me?*' she said. 'What'd you say?'

'Nice nips. Couldn't 'elp noticin' 'em when you got out the pool.'

For a second, Jackie looked a bit embarrassed, but she'd dealt with Clocks before and she knew what he was like for teasing. It wouldn't pay to bite. Play him at his own game.

'I thought that's what you said. Cheers, guv. I appreciate that. Wish I could say the same about your knob, but it's so small I didn't notice.

'No, no. It's the—'

'And don't go on about the water being cold either. The pool was heated, so it's just down to what Mother Nature dished out to you. And being honest, she clearly gave you a swerve in the cock department, didn't she?'

'Oi, 'old up.' Clocks looked confused.

'You know the expression "It's not what you've got, it's what you do with it"? Well, we girls say that to keep you blokes happy, but it helps us a bit if you've got enough for us to notice it's actually in, and then we can make up all the noises you less-endowed chaps like to hear.'

'Hmm,' said Clocks, chastened.

'It's nothing to be embarrassed about though, guv. It's one of those things. I'm sure you're a half-reasonable kisser.'

'You two finished?' said Paterson.

'Yes, guv,' said Jackie.

'Good. Okay. To business, then. Obviously, we lost him again. We know John shot him in the leg and possibly somewhere else. There's a chance he'll have to go to hospital, but in all likelihood it won't be local. I want all hospitals within a ten-mile radius put on alert. Send them this man's picture. Tell them he's of the highest priority. If he walks in, I wanna know. Immediately.'

Dusty nodded. 'If he goes in anywhere, the hospital is duty bound to report a gunshot wound anyway.'

'I am aware, Dusty. But if he goes in anywhere outside the Met, we may not get to hear about it quick enough. I want to. Unless, he's dying, he won't be staying there long. A patch up and he'll be on his toes.'

'Yep. Good point.'

'Underground quacks . . . struck-off doctors . . . surgeons that make a few quid on the side treating the scum buckets . . . I know there's a few on our manor. Put the squeeze on them. Offer them good money if you need to. Come down hard on informants. Anything they know, I want to know. Understand?'

Heads nodded.

'Tommy still at the hospital?'

'Yes, guv,' said Monkey. 'He called a while ago. Seven stitches. Hopefully he won't have too big a scar.'

'Good. Listen, this is what I'm thinking. John and I are going to the Yard. I want a meeting with the commissioner and all commanders from the surrounding boroughs, Kent and Surrey. We're going to hunt this fucker down with everything we have at our disposal, and I want to make sure everyone's on board and up to date.

'I want all forces through the UK informed — airports, ferries, harbour masters, anyone who controls a way off of this island of ours. If he tries to skip out, we need to be on him. This is a shit ton of work, I know, but it has to be done. Any questions?'

'Manpower?' said Jackie.

'Get it from wherever you can for now. Use the commissioner and the Home Office as the authorising powers if you bump up against any resistance from a stroppy senior. Do not take no for an answer. When we meet the commissioner later, I'll make sure you get all the help you want, but for now, bluff it. We'll also need a liaison team to pull all the information together. Jack, can I leave that to you to get the ball rolling?'

'Yep. On it.'

'Good. Alright, everybody, let's get to work.'

Paterson walked back into his office. Clocks followed behind.

'What's happening with Tetley, John?'

Clocks sat down. 'Message has been sent to the locals where his folks live back in Yorkshire. They'll do the necessary. Tell 'em what 'appened.'

Paterson dropped down into his chair. 'Jesus. I can't believe he's gone.'

Clocks shook his head and took another swig from his glass. 'Me neither. Don't make sense. I mean, I wasn't 'is biggest fan, but . . .'

'I know. He could be obnoxious, but he was bloody thorough. He was good. A good copper and a good man.'

'Truth be told, 'e will be missed. I weren't 'appy when 'e said 'e was leavin' us. I should'nta rode him so 'ard all the time.'

'Well, doesn't matter now, does it? What's done is done.'

'I feel like I should go visit 'is folks though.'

'Yeah. We will. When this is over, we'll take a trip up there. Pay our respects.' Paterson raised his glass. 'To Tetley. A good man gone far too soon.'

Clocks raised his. 'Tetley. Rest in peace. Revenge is coming, mate. For you and for them all.'

CHAPTER FORTY-SEVEN

At 11 a.m. Paterson and Clocks strode into the meeting room on the eleventh floor of New Scotland Yard. The commissioner, Sam Morne, had cleared his diary and summoned together his commanders and those of the surrounding rural forces. Paterson brought them all up to speed on the night's events and explained what he wanted in terms of manpower and co-operation. To a man, he got it.

'One other thing, sir,' he said to Morne.

'What is it?'

'I want a press conference. Full coverage. I want as many eyes and ears looking for this man as we can muster.'

Morne baulked. Paterson caught it.

'What? Why not? We've used the public before for this. The Thames burials case. They got behind us then. Now we're looking for the man that murdered nine schoolgirls, maimed several others for life and killed a baby and a young boy. Not to mention two God-fearing mums and three coppers. I think they'll get on board with it.'

Morne nodded. 'Okay. Okay. Leave it with me. I'll make the arrangements and call you when we're ready.'

'We are ready, sir.'

'Sorry?'

'I anticipated your agreement. Press has been called and were gathering outside when we came in. All the main players and a number of locals too.'

'Ray! You can't—'

'Waste time, sir? You're right. Do you want to come with us or are you happy to leave it to us?'

Morne looked flabbergasted. 'I'm not . . . I'm not ready. I need to think about what I'm going to say.'

'Nah, yer don't,' said Clocks. 'Just tell 'em we need their 'elp to find this mad bastard and then let Ray do the talkin'.'

Morne stood up and sighed. 'I'll just follow you then, shall I? Seem to have it all worked out.'

Clocks gave him a thumbs up.

'Ladies and gents,' Morne said. 'Thank you all for coming in at such short notice and for your assistance in this matter. Tell your officers to stay safe and keep me up to speed with any developments in real time.' The room stood as Morne turned to Paterson and Clocks. 'Lead on, boys.'

CHAPTER FORTY-EIGHT

The reporters had gathered in their dozens. Since the bus incident on Tower Bridge, they'd been waiting for someone to talk to them. It was now common knowledge that Paterson and Clocks were on the case and they were excited. These two had proved themselves to be newsworthy on many an occasion and they expected an interesting conference.

Paterson had decided that the steps outside New Scotland Yard, rather than an airless conference room, was a better place to say what he wanted to say. It just seemed more real to him. The reporters were held back by tape and a number of uniformed officers.

Sam Morne made his way to his position. Paterson and Clocks flanked him either side. Morne held up his hand and the crowd quickly settled. He cleared his throat.

'Good morning. As you know, we are currently investigating the murder and attempted murder of a number of schoolgirls that occurred yesterday on Tower Bridge. These girls were murdered by a man we now know to be David Steers. During the confusion that followed this incident, Steers unfortunately made good his escape, taking one girl as a hostage. Her name is Zara Morgan. She is fifteen years old.

'During the early hours of this morning, an operation was put into motion to track and apprehend Mr Steers and recover Ms Morgan. During this operation Mr Paterson was almost killed in his initial attempt to rescue her. Inspector Clocks risked his own life to save them both, and I am pleased to tell you that Ms Morgan is now safe and well and has been reunited with her parents.

'However, it is with great sadness that I must report to you that during this operation another police officer was brutally murdered by Steers during his escape. Detective Inspector Clocks shot and injured him. We don't know for sure the extent of those injuries, but it was clearly not enough to prevent his escape. Rest assured, we will find him.

'I will now hand you over to Detective Superintendent Paterson, who would like to address the public and answer some of your questions.'

Morne backed away and the crowd of reporters fired themselves up when Paterson replaced him at the top of the stairs. Paterson, however, walked down to them. He wanted to be eye level to the cameras.

'What is the name of the officer who died?'

'How did Steers escape?'

'What had he done to Zara?'

'Was she raped?'

'Has she been tortured?'

'Where was she being kept?'

'Why is he doing this?'

Paterson watched them machine-gunning questions at him and baying like a pack of hungry dogs for answers. He took a deep breath and held up his hand.

'I'll take questions in a moment. For now, I'd like us all to take a minute's silence as a mark of respect for all of the victims of David Steers.' He looked at his watch, held his hands in front of his body and bowed his head.

The reporters looked confused. This wasn't normal. No one ever did this sort of thing. The TV and radio crews panicked. One minute of unexpected dead air was never a good thing in their profession.

Paterson knew exactly what he was doing. A minute's silence for fallen victims was deeply ingrained in much of the British psyche and he was subtly triggering his audience here and at home to view this manhunt with all the seriousness it deserved.

One minute later, he cleared his throat, startling the now subdued reporters.

'First of all, I would like to offer my deepest sympathies and condolences to the victims of this . . . man. I don't intend to waste your time giving you details of what he has done. These you already know. He has destroyed the lives of not only his victims but also those of their families and friends. It is of deep personal regret to me that he has somehow continued to evade capture, but last night's events took a different turn.

'As the commissioner said, DI Clocks managed to shoot and wound him, and as he also stated, his injuries were not sufficient to stop him getting away. *But* we do believe they are severe enough for him to seek medical attention somewhere, and if he does, then we want to be there. This time there will be no escape for him. We need your help. *I* need your help.'

Again, the crowd looked confused.

'You may recall that I asked for the public's support before and the response was overwhelming. Today, I'm asking for that support again. Now, as then, I am offering one million pounds from my family trust for any information leading to the arrest and conviction of this man.'

The reporters completely lost control. Commissioner Morne closed his eyes and sighed deeply. Paterson stood silent and waited until the clamour died down.

'To be clear, I do not want bounty hunters or mercenaries to hunt him down, and I certainly do not want anybody taking the law into their own hands. No reward will be paid in the event that harm befalls him.

'David Steers is a very sick individual. He believes he is the avenging angel of God here on earth and is doing all that he can to "cleanse" London of its wickedness. We all clearly know what he is capable of and that he will do anything necessary to avoid capture in order to continue with his mission. If you see him, do *not* approach him. He will not hesitate to kill any man, woman or child to escape. Call it in. That's all you have to do. Thank you.'

The reporters erupted.

'Mr Paterson! Mr Paterson! Steven Holiday, Sky News. Who's the officer who died?'

'I'm sorry. No names as yet. The officer's family has only just been informed and I would like their privacy respected.'

'Do you know if he's killed anyone else since? Has he taken anyone else as a hostage?'

'At this moment, we don't believe he's killed anybody else and we have no reason to believe otherwise. Nor do we believe he has a hostage.'

'How is Zara Morgan? What did he do to you both?'

'Zara received a number of injuries during her incarceration but fortunately they are not life threatening. I suspect she will need help coming to terms with her experiences. Thankfully, she is now back home with her family and we are offering all the support that she needs. What happened to both of us is irrelevant for now. Details will be released when the time is right.'

'DI Clocks! Lynn Shanks.'

Clocks looked startled. It was unusual for the press to speak to him. His relationship with them was shaky at best.

'Why did you feel it necessary to shoot Steers?'

Clocks baulked at the question. ''Scuse me?'

'Why did you shoot him? Was it your intention to kill him?'

Clocks glared at her.

'That's a ridiculous question, Miss Shanks,' Paterson said before Clocks could snap back at her. This was neither the time nor the place.

'No, no, Ray. Lemme answer 'er.' He walked down the steps to join Paterson.

'John . . . don't.'

Clocks ignored him.

'Right, love. I shot 'im because there was no other way for me to stop 'im. He was goin' to kill Mr Paterson and Zara. Shootin' 'im was my only option or I wouldn't 'ave done it, would I?'

'You have a reputation — you *both* have a reputation — for violence, do you not?'

'Yep. We do. And?'

'Well, it may not be too much of a stretch to assume that your intention was to kill him rather than arrest him.'

Clocks sniffed. 'Listen, love. I'm old enough to remember the days when reporters were 'alf decent and reported the facts, not assumptions. You standin' there an' accusin' me of tryin' to kill a man 'cos you've got a bleedin'-'eart liberal stick jammed up yer arse without knowin' any of the facts is a disgrace. Should be ashamed of yerself.' He turned his back and walked up the first two steps. He stopped and whirled around to face her again. He jabbed his finger at her. 'An' I'll betcha if you were in the same position as Zara and the guv, you'da *begged* me to shoot 'im. *Begged me.* Guarantee it.' He turned away again and re-joined a suitably embarrassed commissioner.

'That alright, guv?' he said.

Morne kept a poker face just in case the cameras were zooming in for a reaction. 'No. None of it. But at least you didn't swear. That was impressive.'

Paterson was holding up both hands now, trying to calm the crowd down. They were barraging him with questions, pushing and jostling to get pictures. His control was beginning to slip and now was a good time to end the conference. But something pushed a button in him.

'Quiet please! Can we all settle down now? Thank you. Please!'

The clamouring continued.

'Shut up!' he shouted. 'Just. Shut. Up. And. Listen.'

The shouting dissipated to a low grumbling.

'The Metropolitan Police . . . we don't get to say much on the ground floor. People like the commissioner get wheeled out to speak on important matters and the odd superintendent like myself from time to time, but we have to be very mindful of what we say. You all know that. That's the game. But, like DI Clocks, I've had enough of it. So, listen up, as I'm about to get on my long-overdue soap box.

'What we do, my team and I, brings us into contact with the worst, the *very* worst that society has to offer. During those encounters, we have been stabbed, shot, beaten, almost set on fire and nearly drowned to name but a few instances. In every case, we have done everything we needed to do to survive and to bring those perpetrators to justice.

'Do we fight hard? Yes, we do. We have to if we are to protect London and catch the bastards that do these things. If we don't, they will continue to do what they do and you or your loved ones could be next. Do I regret some of the things we've had to do? No. Not for one second. I wish violence wasn't necessary, but very often with *these* types of criminal, it is.

'I know that very few of you here today are staunch supporters of the police, less so of our methods. I know you don't like it, but I don't really care, to be honest. I've given up trying to please people, much less reporters with an agenda.

'You'd do well to remember that police officers are the only thing that stands between you and the burglars, robbers, rapists and murderers that would happily prey on you if we didn't go out and head them off for you. Uniforms, CID, admin, pencil pushers, everyone. We do what we do so you can rest just that bit easier in your beds at night. Do we get it wrong sometimes? Oh, yeah. I'm the first to admit it. But out here on the streets, in the thick of it, normal rules of polite society do not apply. They do not. Nor do we get to mull over the consequences of our immediate actions in the comfort of an office sitting behind a computer all day. That's a luxury for others.' He turned his gaze at the reporter. 'A luxury for *you*, Miss Shanks.

'It's simple. If you don't like the police and our methods, then don't call us when the shit hits the fan for you. It would make you less of a hypocrite too. And while I'm thinking about it, instead of slagging us off and sticking the boot in when we're down, it would be better if you got behind us, imagined we were Americans and bloody well thanked us for our service. That's it. I'm done.' He turned and walked away to see the shocked face of Commissioner Morne.

'Sorry, sir. I know that was bit off the cuff, but they needed pulling in line.'

'And you thought this was the time and place to do it?' said Morne.

Paterson shrugged. 'Well, nobody else was gonna do it, were they?'

Clocks's phone rang. 'Clocksy.'

He nodded and *huh-huh*'d a few times before hanging up. 'Guv. A word.'

Paterson looked at him. He guessed what was coming by the look on Clocks's face.

'Inside,' he said.

The three policemen hurried through the doors of Scotland Yard and stopped in the foyer.

'Go on,' said Paterson.

'That was Jackie. She's just saved you a million quid. We've got a bite already. She took a call from the Royal Surrey County 'ospital. Bloke with a gunshot wound to the leg limped in a few minutes ago. She clocked him from the TV on Tower Bridge. 'E tried palming it off as some sort of work accident.'

'Where's the hospital?'

'Guildford. Thirty odd miles away. Take about an hour if we proper step on it.'

Paterson turned to Morne. 'Sir?'

'What? Yes, yes. Go. Be careful. I'll inform the locals you're on your way.'

Clocks jabbed furiously at the lift button to take them to the underground car park. 'Come on! Come on, you cowson!'

'Sir,' Paterson said to Morne, 'he's ours. They are not to apprehend him. Don't tell them who he is or why we're there.'

'They'll work it out, Ray.'

Paterson trotted over to the lift. Now inside, Clocks jabbed away at another button, cursing again.

'As long as they back off when we come for him.'

And then they were gone.

CHAPTER FORTY-NINE

Paterson's car, blues and twos in full swing, shot out of the car park and screeched into a hard left. Clocks had the wheel.

'I take it you know where we're going?' said Paterson.

'Nope! You?'

'Not really.'

'Best you bung it in the GPS then, a bit lively!'

Paterson pressed the large screen on his on-board GPS, and as the software worked out their destination, he sat back in his seat before putting on his seat belt. He'd been privy to Clocks's driving style on more than a few occasions. This had all the hallmarks of being a dangerous trip.

London traffic at almost any time of the day could be a nightmare, and today things were no different. Queues and queues of cars, vans and motorbikes fought to get through the tangled mess in a frantic effort to be somewhere as quickly as humanly possible.

Drivers panicked when Clocks came roaring up behind them, screaming at them to get out of his way. He jabbed the brakes, the accelerator, wove in and out of the traffic and did everything he could to get them swiftly out of London. A couple of cyclists lost their balance and one tumbled into the road.

'I'll call Monkey,' said Paterson. 'Get them all to join us.'

'Good idea.'

'John, I think you might've knocked a cyclist down.'

'What? Oh, no! I didn't, did I?' Clocks glanced in his rear-view mirror. 'I'm 'eartbroken. Boo-hoo.'

Paterson nodded. 'I *thought* you'd be upset.'

'I'm not *upset*, mate. As I said, I'm 'eartbroken.' He glanced in his mirror again. 'You think he's 'urt?'

Paterson turned and looked out of the rear window. 'No. He's up. Probably shaken.'

''Ad a result then, ain't 'e? Ain't got time to go back and run 'im over properly. Must be 'is lucky day.'

'Careful!' A car pulled out of a side turning, narrowly missing them. Clocks jerked the wheel.

'What? I saw 'im!'

'Did you?'

'Did I 'it 'im?'

'No.'

'That's cause I saw 'im. Now shut yer bunny an' lemme drive.'

Paterson inhaled sharply.

'Now what?'

'Nothing. Carry on. Just do me a favour and look at the road once in a blue moon.'

Clocks swerved around a line of cars waiting at a red light and shot through the junction. 'Look, Mr Perfect. If you're gonna be'ave like a little Mary Anne all the way over to Guildford, get the fuck out an' I'll go on me own.'

'Alright. No need to get your knickers in a bunch, is there? It's just that you put me a bit on edge, that's all.'

'And that's because you're a fuckin' little Mary Anne. You need to stop liftin' yer nightie up every time you get into a car with me. I'm a bloody good driver.'

'Like you're a bloody good shot?'

'Oi! Don't start about that! I slipped on some water round the edge of the pool.'

'You slip on a lot of things.'

'Oh, you bitch! Is this about France again? You know I slipped on a snail. Place is runnin' alive with 'em. Can't 'elp that.'

Paterson smiled. 'No, mate. You're right. Not your fault. Just get us there alive, eh? I don't want this fucker going for another run.'

'Yes, sir!' Clocks stamped on the accelerator.

CHAPTER FIFTY

David Steers sat atop a steel trolley in a little side room. A patterned curtain was pulled across the entrance to give him some measure of privacy. His thigh burned where the ugly demon's bullet had punched through the muscle and exited the other side, leaving a messy hole. The graze on his shoulder was nothing. He looked over to where his bloody trousers lay haphazardly on a bright green plastic chair. A woman with a badge that said *Dr Sue Young* was busy typing into her computer, showing no interest in him at all.

While he waited for her to be done, his mind took him back to the pool. Satan's helper had proved himself to be more formidable than he'd imagined. The sense of crushing pain he'd felt when he watched the morning news overwhelmed him. *Satan and his child live. Once more I have proved that I am unworthy in the face of you, my Father. But, perhaps, you have other plans for them? For me? What's that, oh Lord? Yes, yes. Thank you, Father. Your will shall be done. Just show me the way, Lord. Please.*

'Won't be a moment, sir. Just have to finish this and I'll be with you. We're up to our eyeballs. Sorry. I'll be as quick as I can.'

What? The woman. This . . . doctor. She is one of Satan's followers? She plots to destroy me? To betray me to her master? Yes, of course, Father. I understand. Your will be done.

He glared at her. 'Doctor?'

* * *

Sue Young held her finger up and then, with a flourish, hit the *Enter* key and swivelled around on her chair to face Steers. She gave him a big smile.

'Sorry about that. Paperwork. Now, let's have a look at you.' She peered at the hole in his leg. Definitely a bullet. She'd already been briefed that police were on their way. She just had to keep him there without arousing his suspicion. She'd had plenty of experience keeping drunks and druggies waiting for the police to arrive, but this one? Nothing like this. The news said he was a vicious killer and here he was. In *her* cubicle.

She knew she should have stood her ground and refused the job when her senior told her who he was and that she was to treat him but slow everything down. Life could be a bitch. As could her senior.

'Ouch!' she said. 'That looks painful. How did that happen?' She rolled her chair toward him and moved in for a closer look. There were no obvious signs of infection. It looked like an in and out job. Straight and clean. 'Can you stand up, please? Are you able to?'

Steers nodded and did as he was asked. He grimaced the moment his foot touched the floor. It must have been some time since he'd caught the bullet, and now, with the adrenaline out of his system, the pain was coming through.

The doctor peered at it and then looked around the back of the leg. Bigger hole here where the bullet had bunched up all the meat inside before punching its way out.

'Can you walk? Obviously, you can,' she said, embarrassed. 'Otherwise, you wouldn't be here, right? I meant, can

213

you just walk over there for me, please? I want to see *how* you walk.'

Steers took a deep breath and walked over to the back of the cubicle, turned and made his way back to the trolley. There was a definite limp.

'So, go on, then. Tell me what happened.'

'I fell.'

'You fell? Onto what?'

'Does it matter?'

'Depends if you want me to treat it properly. I need to know what caused it because it might have given you an infection. I can take away the pain and stitch you up after you've had a scan, but it would help if I could give you the right medication.'

'Scan? I don't need a scan.'

She sat back in her seat. 'Er, you do. Particularly if you're thinking of walking again.'

Steers frowned. 'Explain.'

Doctor Young sighed. 'OK. I'll be honest with you. That looks to me like you've been shot. I don't know by whom or why, nor do I care. What I *am* concerned about is that the bullet may have hit a bone and done some serious damage. Your walk would indicate that the whatever-it-was-that-did-this has missed the bone, but I can't be sure. Hence, the scan.

'If it *has* hit the bone, we need to know how much damage has been caused and where that damage is, *exactly*. I can't and won't guess at it, so there are two ways we can go. Either we scan and look or we'll have to open your leg up and take a look around the old-fashioned way.' She shrugged. 'To be honest, that can do more harm than good. So, if I were you, I'd go for the scan in the first instance. If you choose neither option, then that's up to you and you take the chance of a bone infection, muscle weakness and possibly a wheelchair later in life. As I said, your choice.'

'I was not shot.'

She shrugged. 'Okay. So, what caused the hole?'

'I fell onto a spike. A large nail.'

'A spike?'

'Yes. I was doing some gardening. I removed a fence and I fell onto a nail.'

'Oh, right. I see. Yeah, okay, that would do it, I guess.' She didn't believe a word of it. 'Okay. I'll need to give you an injection and some antibiotics at the very least and then I'll have to make arrangements for the holes to be cleaned and closed. I'd still prefer it if you went for that scan though. I can't make you, but—'

'I don't like injections.'

She chuckled. 'Me neither.'

'I just want it cleaned and stitched. Can you do that?'

Doctor Young shook her head. 'I can't, I'm afraid. I have to see other patients, but I'll get you seen to as quickly as I can. Make yourself comfortable and let me make a call.'

She swivelled around on her chair, picked up the phone and tapped in three numbers.

Steers watched her.

'Hi, it's Sue. I'm fine thank you. You? Good. Listen. I've got a patient with me now who needs some stitches in the front and back of his leg. Holes in the back and front. Something has passed through. He's refused a scan. I'm up to my eyeballs, so can you get someone to give me a hand please? I'll prep the wound.

'So, he'll need an anaesthetic and some strong antibiotics. Blood loss? Yeah, some. Seems okay in himself and he's only showing minimal signs of bleeding at the moment. Hmm, hmm. Patient had it securely bandaged when he came in and it's looking clotted at the outside. Okay. Thanks. See you soon.'

She swivelled back to Steers just in time to see his right fist rushing toward her.

CHAPTER FIFTY-ONE

Clocks ripped through the entrance to the Royal Surrey County Hospital and screeched to a halt in the nearest parking space available. The two men stepped out just as another car pulled up beside them. Clocks locked the door and started to walk away.

'Excuse me!' The driver of the car leaned out of his window.

Clocks turned. 'What's up, pop? We're in a rush.'

'You haven't displayed your badge.'

'I know. I ain't got one.'

'Well, then, you'll have to leave. It's for disabled people, that space.'

'Is it? Oh, well. They'll 'ave to find somewhere else to park.'

'If you don't move it, I shall report you.'

'Right you are, then. Crack on.' Clocks turned and walked away.

'You! Young man. Did you not hear me?'

Clocks looked back over his shoulder. 'No. I can't 'ear you. I'm deaf. Thinkin' about it, that's a disability, ain't it?'

The old man scowled at Clocks. He watched him continue to walk away then hauled himself out of his car and hobbled off to find the car park attendant.

Paterson suddenly stopped walking in the middle of the car park and Clocks had to pull up short to avoid crashing into him.

'The fuck . . . Whassamatter? What'd you stop for?'

'John. It's him!' He pointed toward a black Ford and the man who was easing himself into the driver's seat.

Clocks followed Paterson's finger and saw him.

'Shit!'

They were a good fifty yards away.

Both men broke into a run.

Steers turned over the engine.

Paterson saw Steers's hand drop down. The reverse lights came on.

The Ford began to back out of its parking space, left lock on.

Thirty yards.

They split. Paterson to the driver's side, Clocks to the passenger's.

The Ford reached the end of its manoeuvre.

Fifteen yards.

The car straightened up. Steers looked to his right. His eyes widened. Satan was coming for him.

Five yards and closing.

Paterson slammed into the bodywork, bounced off and punched at the window.

Steers rocked backward as a shower of glass sprayed the inside of the car. Paterson's punch caught him on the cheek. Clocks smashed the passengers window with a sweeping blow of his right hand and shoved his torso inside.

Paterson reached in and grabbed Steers by the hair. Clocks grabbed at his arm.

Steers stamped on the accelerator.

Clocks was jerked backward by the force of acceleration, lost his footing and pushed himself backward out of the window and rolled across the ground.

Paterson clung on to Steers's hair as the car shot forward. Steers screeched at him and struggled violently to throw him off. With his hands off the steering wheel, the car lurched sideways and headed toward a line of industrial waste bins. In front of them was a cycle rack.

Clocks shouted something to Paterson that he couldn't make out. But he sensed danger. Turning his head, he saw. Holding tightly onto the clump of hair, he pushed himself backwards, away from the car. Steers screeched again, this time in serious pain as Paterson ripped his hair from its roots. Paterson rolled along the floor several times before coming to an undignified halt just shy of the cycle rack. He watched the Ford hit the bins, straighten itself up and shoot off toward the exit.

Pulling himself up he ran back toward their car. Clocks was ahead of him. The game had begun.

CHAPTER FIFTY-TWO

As Monkey Harris turned his car into the entrance of the hospital, he panicked and wrenched his steering wheel violently to avoid the Bentley coming toward him at speed. 'Shit!' He stamped on the brakes and the passengers, Dusty, Jackie and Tommy, were thrown forward forcefully.

'Is that the guv's?' said Jackie. 'Gotta be.'

'Yep!' Monkey threw the car into reverse and screeched the car around. 'Give 'em a call, someone. Pretty sure they didn't even see us.'

'I'm guessing they just missed Steers.' Dusty hit a button on his phone and waited. 'Was Clocksy driving?'

'Yep,' said Monkey.

'Oh, fuck . . .'

* * *

'Dusty!' Paterson's phone was pressed against his ear. 'Yeah. Just missed him. Nearly did for me again. He's in a black Ford. Not sure what model. Two smashed windows. We're behind him.'

'*Want me to call the locals for some backup, guv?*'

'What? Do I fuck! Do not call the locals, you understand? Stay with us. Just inform the locals that we're in pur-
suit and to assist with pedestrian and traffic safety. Under no
circumstances are they to interfere with this operation.'

'*Yessir.*'

'And Dusty . . . get someone to call the hospital. See if
he's done anything to anyone there.'

'*Sir.*'

Paterson hung up. 'Do not lose him, John.'

Clocks had a look of intense concentration on his face.
'John?'

'I won't.'

'If he does—'

'He won't.'

'He can't escape agai—'

'Said he won't. Now, shuddup!'

Paterson clung onto the hanger strap and dug his feet
into the footwell as Clocks tore through yet another set of
red lights. 'Make sure you don't crash either.'

'Really? I was hoping I could.'

'Funny.'

'Laugh a minute, me. Now stop shootin' yer flapper fer a
minute an' lemme concentrate.' Clocks glanced over. 'Fuck's
that in yer 'and?'

Paterson looked down at the clump of Steers's hair he'd
pulled out and was still gripping tightly. 'His hair.'

'Why you still got that? You thinkin' of puttin' it in a
locket or summin'? Fuckin' chuck it away you 'ol romantic.'

Paterson opened the window and dropped it.

* * *

Steers pushed the car faster. The adrenaline that spiked his
body helped him to ignore the pain. He glanced at his bloody
knuckles, evidence of the damage he'd inflicted on Doctor
Young. *She lied.* By the time security arrived, he was long
gone, down the corridor and out of the nearest exit. *Let them
point at him.* Confusion would aid his escape.

Once out of the building it was an easy matter: straight into the car and back to London. He would tend to his own wound, however crude it would be. And if he ultimately died, then he was ready. His mind, though, burned with thoughts — with doubt. *NO! You will not control my mind, Satan. NO! How did you find me, Satan? Why did my Father not tell me of your arrival? Did He want me to be caught? But I escaped. He was looking after me. Why then are they so close behind? Is it Thy will that I be captured? Is that Thy will? Confused! So confused . . .*

* * *

'C'mere, you fucker!' Clocks physically pushed himself forward in his seat, willing his car to go faster. He drew closer to Steers. 'C'moooon. I'll fuckin' 'ave yer. C'mere. Lemme give yer a little kiss.'

'Steady, John.'

Clocks ignored him. He was close to tagging the car now. Once he did that, touched the back of him, it was just a matter of thirty seconds or so. Once a fleeing driver felt the bump of a police car on his tail, something psychological happened. Unless he was a career criminal with experience of being chased, that touch caused him to panic suddenly, and with that panic came a slight loss of control. But, at high speed, that slight loss was usually enough for them to either give up altogether or stack it into the nearest stationary object. No one really knew why.

'Yes!' Clocks rammed into the back of Steers's car. He kept going. Normal rules did not always apply. Half a mile later, the car swerved violently off the main road and tore along a narrow country lane. Clocks stayed with him. Paterson saw the road lights ahead suddenly disappear into the dark of night. He braced himself. High-speed chases along dark country lanes invariably ended in disaster for someone. And Clocks was driving.

Clocks flicked the headlights onto full beam. ''Ave them, son.'

Clocks swerved out to the right. A small gap had opened between Steers and a hedge. He wanted to wedge himself into it, but he missed and dropped back in behind. The two cars tore through the dark at sixty miles an hour. When the road straightened out, Steers pushed it to seventy. So did Clocks. Back into the curves, Steers kerbed it and the car lifted slightly.

'Gotcha!'

Steers kept the car under control.

Clocks smacked the top of his steering wheel with the back of his hand. 'Oh, you lucky bastard!'

They shot over a hill, all four wheels leaving the road for a second. The cars twisted and turned for another mile before Clocks realised the road was opening out ahead of them. He floored the accelerator, swerved out into the opposite lane and managed to get the nose of his car just level with the back wheel of Steers's car. Clocks wrenched his steering wheel hard left and the two cars collided with a loud bang.

Steers's car quickly turned sideways in front of them. Clocks kept his foot down, pushing Steers along the road amid a cacophony of screeching tyres, showers of sparks and the smell of burning rubber. Steers turned his head toward Clocks, a look of burning hatred on his face. And then he was gone in a sudden explosion of movement.

Clocks's forward momentum had moved Steers's car into an awkward angle that was just enough for it to launch into a hard roll. With Steers gone, Clocks fought to bring his car under control and stamped on the brake, his advanced driving training forgotten. The Bentley skidded to a halt amid the crashing sound of metal as Steers's car rolled down a small embankment.

The second they stopped, both Clocks and Paterson were out and running back to the crash site. He would not escape this time. They ran across the road. The car landed upright, gently rocked from side to side, then stopped and the boot popped open. Drawing level with the driver's side, Paterson could see Steers was still inside, head down. In his peripheral vision he noticed the car was ten feet from a small river. His hand went straight in through the broken window and grabbed Steers by the hair. The man was semi-conscious, mumbling incoherently.

Paterson ignored him and pulled at his hair, desperate to get him out of the car this time. 'Come out, you bastard!'

Clocks joined him. 'You alright, Ray?'

'He won't come out! Get out! Get the fuck out, Steers!'

'Want some 'elp?'

'Fuck off! He's mine!'

'Charmin'.'

Paterson punched his man in the head, frustration and rage boiling over.

'Can I give yer a suggestion, mate?'

Paterson was still tugging at Steers's hair.

'What? No!'

Clocks chuckled. 'Undo 'is seatbelt, Ray. That'll 'elp. You're gonna scalp 'im at this rate. Might 'ave to start calling you Geronimo.'

'What? Fuck!' Paterson wrenched the door open and undid the belt. He dragged Steers out and dropped him onto the grass face up. He noticed a cut on his face and two swollen eyes: airbag trauma.

Steers moaned as Paterson and Clocks looked down at him. 'Said we'd get 'im, Ray.'

'Yeah. Good job, Clocksy. Good job.' Paterson stepped over Steers and stood one leg either side of him. He bent down and, with an almighty slap across his face, shouted, 'Steers! Get the fuck up!'

'Ooooh!' Clocks cringed at the crack the slap made. 'Bet that woke a few cows up.'

'Steers! You hear me? I said get up!' Paterson slapped him again.

'Ray. If you're gonna get all rowdy on 'im, do it like a man. Punch the fucker. Don't be goin' all Will Smith on 'im.'

Steers's eyes snapped open. 'Satan! Begone!'

Paterson slapped him. 'You no-good murdering moth-erfucker . . .'

Clocks cocked his head to one side. Something was bothering him. A sound. He walked to the back of the car to where the boot was open and looked inside. 'Oh, shit! Ray! Ray!' He leaned in when he heard the girl moan again. 'Ray! Stop fuckin' about with 'im. There's a girl in 'ere! 'Elp me!'

Paterson smacked Steers hard in the face, stunning the man completely, and dragged him back to the damaged car by his feet. He dropped one of them onto the foot well and stamped down hard. Steers screamed in agony when his leg broke in two at the knee. He continued to shriek, writhing around on the ground. 'Let's see you run away now, fucker.'

Paterson ran to Clocks, who was staring into the boot. What he saw shocked him. A young girl in her early teens was curled up inside. She looked in a bad way. 'Oh, Christ! She alive?'

'Ray . . . Did I . . . ?'

'Just give me a hand to get her out, John. Carefully.'

The two men lifted her out of the boot and laid her gently on the grass. Paterson guessed she was no more than thirteen . . . fourteen. *How did she get in there?* He winced at the sight of a large hole in her forehead, her blood running black in the dark. Her eyes were glassy and her chin was convulsing. Paterson had seen that convulsion once before at the scene of a car accident when he was a rookie. Car versus railings. The driver, drunk, had ploughed into railings at the side of the road and suffered massive head trauma. She never survived. He wasn't hopeful for this girl.

The girl gasped a few times then went silent. Paterson dropped onto his knees. 'Two breaths in, John. Wait for it!' He hit the girl on the chest once, hard, then started the first thirty chest compressions. When he stopped, Clocks put air into her. He wiped her face, slippery with blood.

'Come on, treacle. Back you come . . . come on!'

Paterson pushed again. Thirty times.

Two breaths.

'Come on, kid!' Paterson shouted. He pushed again. The girl lay still. He carried on.

Clocks shook his head. 'She's gone, Ray.'

Paterson kept on. Counting in a whisper.

'Ray! She's gone, mate. C'mon.'

Paterson snapped his head back and stared at Clocks. 'Fuck off! Just fuck off!'

He took over the inhalations as well as the chest compressions. Clocks stood and watched him as he fought an already lost battle. She wasn't coming back.

Paterson eventually stopped and shook his head. He whispered to her. 'I'm so sorry. So sorry.'

'This was my fault,' said Clocks. 'I did this.'

Paterson stood up. 'Don't be stupid.'

Clocks dug the heels of his hands into his eyes and groaned. 'Fuck! Fuck! Fuuuuuccck!'

When he finished, he opened his eyes. Paterson was marching off toward Steers. Clocks watched him. He'd seen him go off the rails before, but this time he could see by the way Paterson was striding toward Steers, something bad was about to happen. He watched Paterson grab the screaming man by the hair and start to drag him off toward the water.

'What's 'appenin, Ray?'

'I'm shutting him up.' Paterson dragged Steers into the water. Grunting with effort, he dragged the man out into the middle of the river.

'Ray? Ray?' Clocks called. 'Why am I gettin' the feelin' this ain't gonna be a christenin'?'

'Stay out of this, Clocksy.'

Clocks put his hands on his hips and lowered his head. 'Ray . . .'

With both hands around Steers's throat, Paterson pushed his head under the water and held him there. After a few seconds, Steers started to struggle violently. His hands grabbed at Paterson's arms, and he flailed wildly to break his death grip. Steers was strong. Paterson, fuelled by adrenaline and rage, was stronger. 'Try to drown me, you dirty fucker.

Yeah? Want to see God, do you? Well, I'm gonna fucking send you home to him!'

Steers kicked out with his one good leg and reached out, grabbing at Paterson's face. He turned his head away as Steers struggled. Paterson dropped his weight onto him, both knees on his chest. He stared down into the water, to see the panic on Steers's face as he died. 'Not fucking saving you now, is he? Come on, you dirty, no-good bastard! Just fucking die!'

Water splashed everywhere as Steers's legs and arms flailed in his last few seconds. 'Good boy,' said Paterson, through gritted teeth. 'There you go, there you go. You're fucking nicked!'

Steers slowed and his struggling weakened, then slowly sputtered out. His arms splashed down into the water. Paterson held him there for another twenty seconds just to be sure. Satisfied that Steers was dead, he let him go and looked down at him. Justice. He wiped his nose with the back of his hand then turned to Clocks. 'We good?'

Clocks shrugged. 'We're all tickety-boo, mate.'

A soaking-wet Ray Paterson nodded and trudged out of the river.

'You okay, mate?' said Clocks.

Paterson nodded. 'Never better.'

'Ray?'

'What?'

'*Did* I do that?' He nodded toward the girl.

'Did you do what?'

'The girl. Did I kill 'er?'

'No. You didn't kill her.'

Clocks rubbed his forehead then wiped his face. 'I didn't know she was in there.'

Paterson shuffled over to him. Now the adrenaline rush had died down, the girl's death was sinking in. 'Mate. It's rough on you. It's rough on us. I get it, but this isn't on you. He took her and put her in the boot. You couldn't possibly know she was there.'

'But . . . those injuries. Was that because of me?'

'Look. Just stop, alright? Stop. You don't know those injuries weren't caused by Steers. We won't know until the autopsy results come in, so don't go around blaming yourself, John. No good will come of it.'

'But—'

'No buts, mate. Enough. Now listen. We've got to get our stories straight before it all kicks off. You up for it?'

Clocks nodded. 'Tell me what 'appened an' that's what 'appened.'

CHAPTER FIFTY-THREE

Paterson and Clocks sat themselves down on the grass. For a good five miles in either direction they were surrounded by darkness and quiet. Paterson looked over at the girl's body. He shook his head. 'I had to do him, John.'

'I know. No argument from me, bruv. Didn't know we were *really* gonna murder 'im though.'

'Really? Seem to remember you saying something about killing him back at the swimming pool.'

'Ah. Well, yeah. You remember that, then?'

'I do. Anyway, *we* didn't murder him. I did.'

Clocks shrugged. 'I didn't stop you, did I? So, I'm just as much to blame.'

'If it helps, I could knock you spark out and claim I did it while you were out.'

Clocks chuckled. 'You? Knock me out? In yer dreams.'

Paterson looked across to him and shook his head. They both knew Clocks wouldn't last five seconds with him if it came to it.

'So, what do we do now?'

'To be honest, John, I don't really know. I seriously overstepped the mark this time. I don't know how we're going to get out of this one. I'm sorry.'

'Crap. I was 'opin' you might 'ave an idea runnin' around in that big nut of yours.'

'I got nothing, mate.'

Clocks sniffed. 'Right. Listen up. It won't be that difficult. Trust me.'

'Go on, then. I'm all ears.'

'What do you see when you look around?'

'Nothing.'

'Exactly. Not a single witness. So, the only sensible thing to do is to chuck him in the boot, drive away and get rid of his body. Can't leave it in the river, can we?'

Paterson shook his head.

'Look. If we don't dispose of it, we're proper fucked mate. Forensics'll be all over it like a rash an' then they'll be all over *us* like a rash. Won't take Einstein to work out you drowned 'im. It's gotta go. You know it makes sense.'

'Think about it though, John. Other people knew we were chasing him. It's gonna seem a bit odd if all we've got is an overturned car in the middle of nowhere, by a river, no body to go with it and I'm soaking wet. Don't you think it's gonna look a little bit strange?'

Clocks shrugged. 'Don't matter what it's gonna *look* like, alright? We can turn around and say that we tried to save the girl and while we were busy tryin' to do that, the slag 'ad it away on his toes again and we made a choice. We could either go after 'im and let 'er die or we could try and do the very best we could to save 'er life, which *is* what we did. No one needs to know that you took 'im for a swimmin' lesson, do they?'

Paterson shook his head. 'No. They don't, but why am I wet?'

Clocks shrugged again. 'I don't know. Sexually excited around me, maybe.'

'Very funny.'

'What about we say that before we realised the girl was in the boot, you an' 'im 'ad a little tear-up in the water. I called for you. 'E limped off. There you go. Job done.'

'Might work.'

'Might? It's genius, mate. Clocksy saves the day again. Hoorah!'

Paterson gave him a little smile.

'So, we bung 'im in the boot, call for backup: the girls' dead and Steers 'as done a runner. They send out a search party, can't find 'im, they come back, we all do our bollocks 'cos 'e's escaped again — *tch*, the bastard. Then, when everyone's gone 'ome, we get rid of 'im.'

'And how will we do that? Bury him?'

'Nah, fuck that. I know a man.'

'Course you do.'

'We slip 'im a monkey an' problem solved.'

'A monkey? Why would he want a monkey?'

'Oh, you muppet. You really don't know what a *monkey* is? 'Ow long we been knockin' around together now?'

'Too bloody long.'

'A monkey is five 'undred quid.'

'Why not just say that?'

'I dunno. It's the way we ferals talk. It's just more fun to say monkey.'

'You trust this person? This monkey man?'

'Actually, I do. I mean, there's consequences if 'e says anything an' 'e knows that. So, it's not in 'is best interest to say anythin'. Besides, in 'is game, discretion is important. Last thing 'e'll ever do is tell the police.'

'He does this regularly?'

'More of a side hustle.'

'And you're okay with that?'

'With what?'

'With . . . monkey man disposing of bodies.'

Clocks sighed. 'Makes no odds to me. The slag gets what's comin' to him, an' my mate gets a few 'undred squiddly-diddlies — that means pounds to you — in 'is pocket. Everyone's a winner. Now, you want me to give 'im a bell or not? Up to you, but there's no fuckin' way on God's green earth that I'm diggin' an 'ole to bung 'im in. I've got a bad back and tiny delicate 'ands.'

Paterson chuckled. 'Best give him a bell, then.'

'Ray?'

'What?'

'What'd you pay for that car?'

'Don't remember. Upwards of three hundred grand, I think.'

'Fuck me blind! Well . . . thinkin' about it . . . gettin' rid of 'im's gonna cost more than five 'undred quid.'

'Why's that?'

'Car's gonna 'ave to go too.'

CHAPTER FIFTY-FOUR

Paterson called it in. In the ten minutes it took for assistance to arrive, they had their story straight. The area they stood in was now brightly illuminated by headlamps and red and blue flashing lights. The dead girl was covered by a sheet and Clocks was busy explaining to Monkey Harris and the others what had happened.

'I managed to give 'im a nudge an' 'is car rolled an' ended up off the road. Steers pulled 'imself out and we saw 'im. But as we got near, the boot popped open. Didn't think much of it and we carried on after Steers. The guv'nor wanted to nick 'im 'imself an' they ended up havin' fisticuffs in the river there.

'But summin' felt off to me, so knowin' the guv can take care of 'imself, I decided on a little peek-a-boo and 'ad a look in the boot. There she was. I 'ollered to the guv an' we pulled 'er out. Steers went on 'is toes somewhere — dunno where, wasn't lookin' at that point — and we started the ol' first aid bit. Pointless, as you can see.'

'So you don't know where he went to? Which direction?' said Gunn.

'Nope. The girl was more important.'

Gunn nodded. 'Yeah. Course.'

'The guv's gonna sort out the locals to do a search of the area. You guys give 'em some backup, yeah?'

The team nodded and broke away.

'Monkey . . .' said Clocks.

'Yes, guv?'

'What 'appened to you lot?'

'How d'you mean?'

'You were behind us at one point.'

'Yeah, I know. I just lost you, sorry. Must have been a bit too far behind when you turned off. Just shot past you.'

Clocks nodded. 'Shame. Coulda done with you all. Fucker'd be in cuffs now.'

'Yeah. Sorry.'

'Don't worry about it. Go an' 'elp the others for me.'

'John . . .'

Clocks was a bit wary. Monkey never called him by his first name. 'What?'

'Are you okay?'

'What d'you mean?'

'The girl. In the boot . . .'

'What about 'er? You thinkin' it might be down to me?'

Monkey nodded.

'Me too. But I can't deal with that right now. I can't. Just go do what you 'ave to do an' don't worry about me. Thanks, though.'

'Okay. Take it easy, though.'

Clocks watched him lumber off. Lying to Monkey didn't sit right with him but it was a necessary evil. Prime him first, he'll tell the others and so it goes. Seeds planted. He looked around at the scene. There was a lot riding on whether Paterson could influence the locals to go tramping off across the fields in the pitch black to look for a man who was already dead. Paterson could be very persuasive, but this was a whole different level of lying and it required strong nerves to pull it off. He watched Paterson smile and thank the duty inspector, Thomas Hewson. He went over to him. 'Alright, mate?'

'Yeah. All good with them. He's gonna get things under-
way. There is a slight problem though.'

'Of course there is. Let's 'ave it, then.'

'He's called in search dogs.'

Clocks's eyes widened. 'Dogs? The sniffy kind? The
sniffy find-a-body-in-the boot-of-a-car-with-no-problem
kind?'

'Those are the ones.'

'Why didn't you stop 'im?'

'And say what? "Don't worry about dogs, we'll all go
traipsing off in the dark across a five-mile stretch of land and
find him ourselves"? You don't think that sounds a little bit
. . . odd?'

'Fuck!'

'Fuck indeed.'

'We gotta get outta 'ere a bit lively.'

'Yep.'

'If Scooby Doo an' is mates turn up, it ain't gonna take
'em long to work out that they ain't gonna get too much exer-
cise tonight, is it? They start stickin' their bugles around the
boot of yer car an' we're just gonna 'ave to shout "Surprise!"
an' look a bit embarrassed when it's opened.'

'I'd rather not.'

'Plan?'

'I think it's time we leave them all to it and nip back to
London. Tell them we've had a call and we've got to report
to the commissioner in person. That sound reasonable?'

'Thin, but it'll 'ave to do.'

'Thin it is, then.' Paterson turned to look for the duty
officer, who was busy corralling his officers together. 'Mr
Hewson!' Inspector Hewson looked over. Paterson held up
a finger and nodded. 'Start the car, John, and let our troops
know we're out of here, will you?'

'On it.'

Paterson marched over to Hewson. 'Listen, I'm sorry to
leave you in the lurch but we have to go. We've been summoned by the commissioner for an urgent briefing. He wants

a full update. You know what the bigwigs are like. Always wanna know everything.'

Hewson nodded slowly.

Less than five minutes later, they were heading back to London, passing the dog unit on the way.

CHAPTER FIFTY-FIVE

Paterson and Clocks drove back to London in near silence, both locked in their own thoughts, both imagining what the future held for them. The first task was to dispose of Steers's body. Clocks had already made the call and that was to be their first stop. The second problem was to visit the commissioner and brief him.

Paterson knew he would have to hold a press conference to inform the public that yet another girl had been killed and also to reassure them that the service was bringing all its resources to bear. They would find themselves under the spotlight again, right when they could do without it.

'Whereabouts are we going, John?'

'Arse end of Woolwich. There's a scrapyard tucked away down one of the side streets near the ol' railway line. Unless you knew it was there, you wouldn't know it was there, if you catch me drift.'

'Yep. Is it just the one man there?'

'Should think so, this time of night. It'll be fine.'

'Do they have CCTV anywhere?'

Clocks shook his head. 'Never used to an' I can't see 'im 'avin' it now. Height of stupidity for someone in that game.'

'Well, these people are not usually the brightest bulbs on the Christmas tree, are they?'

'No. They're not. But then, they're not likely to shoot 'emselves in the foot either. The last thing 'e's gonna do is 'ave any film of cars drivin' in but never drivin' out. If 'e gets a tug from us lot, then 'e's sunk. So, no. No CCTV.'

'Good to know. Listen, how do you know this guy?'

Clocks said nothing. He squirmed in his seat.

'John, how do you know him?'

'Used to date me mum years ago, alright?'

Paterson turned to look at him. 'What?'

'Used to date me mum.'

'Really?'

'Yeah. Then 'e married 'er.'

'*Fuck off!*'

'True.'

'Are you telling me he's your father?'

Clocks grinned, put his hand over his mouth and breathed deeply as he spoke. 'Yes, Skywalker. He is my father.'

Paterson smiled.

'Anyway, I bleedin' 'ope 'e is or some stranger's been seein' to me mum right under me nose for years.'

'Bollocks, Clocksy. You're winding me up again.'

'I ain't, mate. Definitely me dad.'

'Christ. I honestly thought you were born under a stone in a dark forest somewhere to a wolf. Hold on . . . wait a minute! Didn't you once tell me your dad was dead?'

Clocks glanced over at him. 'Did I? I don't remember.'

'I'm sure you did.'

'Well, he ain't. So, if I told you 'e was, then I was tellin' you a porky pie, mate. The ol' boy's alive an' well.' Clocks shrugged. 'What you gonna do 'sides? That's why it's only five 'undred quid. Friends and family discount.'

'You better *not* be winding me up again, Clocksy.'

'*Would* I?'

'Er, yeah. When wouldn't you?'

Clocks chuckled softly. 'Look, we'll be there in ten minutes so just chill, put the record player on or whatever it is you have in this car and prepare yerself to meet the family.'

CHAPTER FIFTY-SIX

Clocks turned off the main road and onto a side road marked by a line of burned-out cars. He switched off the headlights. The street was dark, all lighting extinguished by expertly thrown stones and bricks. As he drove along the deserted street, he resisted the sudden urge to lock the doors. There was no need. No self-respecting yob would be roaming the streets this early in the morning.

Some of the cars had windows smashed or dents on the roofs and bonnets where the local yobbery had danced the night away, and bottles of wine and crushed cans of beer littered the road and gutters.

He'd been gone from here for years now but this was still his old stamping ground. He hated to admit it, but this place somehow felt comfortable to him. It always had. It always would. The streets were still the same: rough with a side helping of dangerous. The few friends he had from the old days were still dotted about here and there together with one or two members of his family, but by and large everyone had moved on to greener pastures. This wasn't the old Woolwich he once knew and loved.

The Royal Borough of Greenwich was constantly working hard to sell the lie that Woolwich was the place to be. 'Up and coming,' they said at all the town hall meetings. 'Invest with us,' they told the property developers. And invest they did, all along the riverfront and what used to be the Royal Arsenal, a large munitions factory that operated at its peak during the Second World War, dormant for years before the developers moved in and turned the old factory and offices into luxury houses and flats. They made millions, a few members of the council did well and the rich unwittingly moved into a war zone. Clocks had heard that someone once said that Woolwich was the only borough to be twinned with Beirut.

Now it was part gentrified, if that was the right term, and the other parts were still untamed, occupied by people of every stripe imaginable. Clocks would joke that even people in wheelchairs were just as likely to mug you here as an able-bodied person, but now, driving along this road, it seemed that it was more than a possibility.

At the end of the road, he saw a man standing behind two big iron gates. A plume of smoke drifted upwards from his vape machine. As they closed in, the man pulled open one of the gates and gave a curt nod as the car drove in. In his rear-view mirror, Clocks watched the man loop a chain through the gates and secure it with a hefty padlock.

Paterson was the first out. He turned to greet the man, hand extended. The man nodded and ignored the offer of a handshake. Clocks stepped out.

'Alright,' he said to the man.

'Yeah. Not bad. 'Ow's you, Johnny boy?'

'Mustn't grumble. This is Ray. My guv'nor. Ray, me old man.'

Paterson guessed that the man was in his seventies. He was about the same height as Clocks, otherwise it was a strain to see a resemblance between the two. There was a slight kink in both their noses and the jawline was similar but that was all he could make out in the half-light.

'Ray,' Paterson said. The two shook hands.

'Bloody nice motor, mate. Very nice. Me boy tells me you've got yerselves in a bit of bovver?'

239

Paterson nodded. 'Hmm, you could say that.'

'You're all wet.'

Paterson looked down at himself. 'Yep. Been a funny old night, I'm afraid.' He peered closer at the man. 'I'm sorry but . . . can I ask? Are you really his dad?'

The man wrinkled his forehead. 'Er, yeah. I really am. Why's that? What's the fucker been sayin' about me?'

'Nothing. That's the thing. John plays his cards close to his chest. Don't know much about his family at all.'

'No, don't s'pose you do. An' that's good. I don't want you to, either. When 'e joined up, I weren't too 'appy about it an' told 'im so. None of the family or 'is mates were 'appy either. But 'e wanted to, so we 'ad to be a bit careful an' not flaunt it in 'is face.'

'Flaunt what?' said Paterson.

Old man Clocks weighed him up before answering him. Perhaps he was thinking that if he worked with John, he'd be alright. 'All the stuff we got up to — robbin', stealin', bur-glaries, that sort of shit. Didn't want 'im to be, whatchacallit . . . *compromised*. He went 'is way, we all went ours. All I said to 'im was to keep 'is mouth shut an' gimme an 'eads up if 'e knew anything that would affect me or mine.'

'And has he?'

The old man smiled at Paterson. 'What? Given me the 'eads up? Ah, Ray. I'm not gonna be tellin' tales on me own flesh an' blood, am I?'

'No. No, I don't suppose you are. Listen, I didn't see you at the wedding.'

'Nah. I regret that but there were a few tickets out for me.'

'Warrants?'

'Yeah. Them. An' the place was gonna be crawlin' with ol' bill, so I gave it a swerve in case anyone spotted me. Didn't wanna fuck up 'is big day, y'know?'

'Yeah. Probably best.'

'What I thought. Anyway, enough of the chit chat. What you got for me, boys?'

'You been keepin' up with the news, pop?' said Clocks.

'Yeah. Why?'

'Front pages, last few days. Mad vicar. We got 'im.' He nodded toward the car.

'Nice. Proud of yer, boy. An' you Ray. I 'ope the pair of yer gave 'im a bloody good 'iding before you did fer 'im.'

'We did indeed,' said Paterson.

'Good. No fuckin' loss to the world, is 'e?'

'None whatsoever. So, if you'd be so kind, I'd be grateful.'

''I'll 'ave to do the car too. You know that?'

'Yeah. We know.'

Old man Clocks shook his head. 'Oh, fuckin' liberty, that is. Brand spankin' new Bentley. Must be worth, what . . . three 'undred an' fifty grand?'

'There or thereabouts,' said Paterson.

'Seems a shame. Still, every contact leaves a trace, eh? Best to get rid of it completely in case one of those fuckers in the white paper suits finds a bleedin' molecule or somethin'.'

Paterson nodded.

Old man Clocks jumped in the driver's seat and pulled the car over to a large crushing machine. He dropped all of the windows and hopped out, and secured two big heavy chains through the open windows. Then he jumped into the cab of a small crane and pulled a few levers, and the boys watched the car leave the ground and swing lazily from side to side before being dropped into the crusher, where it landed with a loud, hollow bang.

'Wanna do the honours, Ray?' said the old man.

'I really don't. Lovely car, that was.'

Clocks smiled and walked over to the machine. He punched a red button and the crusher groaned into life. The sound of creaking metal and smashing glass mixed in with the noise from the crusher echoed around the yard. Clocks looked up at the surrounding flats. There were a few lights shining on different floors of each of the tower blocks. But even if there were witnesses, it wouldn't be wise for them to speak out.

Nobody wanted to fuck with old man Clocks and certainly not with Johnny. Their reputations preceded them. Difficult to know which of the two was worse.

Finally, the machine finished its programme and the yard went deathly quiet. Paterson looked at a four-foot cube of metal that used to be one of the most beautiful cars he'd ever owned.

'Sorted,' said the old man. 'Fuckin' cryin' shame about that motor, though.'

'I keep tellin' 'im to drive around in an ol' banger, but does 'e listen? Does 'e bollocks.'

Paterson kept on looking at it.

'Cheers, pop. What'd I owe yer? Monkey?'

Old man Clocks looked at his son with his head cocked to one side. 'You takin' the piss, boy? Fuck all. I don't want yer money, an' certainly not on this one. *This* fucker is a pleasure to get rid of. No. This one's on me.'

Clocks nodded. 'Cheers, pop.'

'Yeah. You two off now or you wanna cuppa?'

Clocks looked at Paterson, who shrugged back. 'Up to you, mate. I'm not in a rush.'

'Yeah, why not? Be nice to catch up for a few minutes.'

'Come on, then. Ray, I've an 'eater in the cabin. You can dry yer togs off on that if you want.' Old man Clocks led them toward his office, a rundown, grubby little portacabin secured with a steel door and metal grilles on the two small windows.

'So, 'ow is everyone?' said Clocks.

The old man grabbed a kettle from on top of a filth-covered fridge, shook it and held it under the tap for a few seconds. 'Yeah, y'know, ploddin' on.'

'Mum all right?'

'Yeah. Sweet as a nut. You should pop in from time to time. See 'er a bit more.' He sighed. 'Look . . . she probably ain't got that much longer, if I'm honest.'

Both men looked at him.

'What?' said Clocks.

'It's 'er lungs, innit?'

Clocks swallowed hard. 'Why didn't you tell me it 'ad gotten worse?'

Old man Clocks shrugged. 'Why? Can't do fuck all about it, can yer? Is what it is.'

Paterson looked across at his friend. It may have been a tear that glistened in his eye. With Clocks, it was difficult to tell.

'I know you're busy an' all, but try an' pop round, eh? When you can.'

'Yeah, of course. I'm sorry.'

'Don't be sorry, son. Shit 'appens. Ain't none of us gettin' out of 'ere alive, are we? Anyway, 'ow's married life?'

Clocks pulled himself upright and sniffed. 'Yeah. So-so. Don't see much of each other, to be honest.'

'Fuck me,' said the old man. 'That was quick.'

Clocks looked annoyed. 'Whatcha mean *that was quick*?'

'Just thought it'd be a bit longer before you ballsed it up.'

'Oh, thanks. Appreciate that. You didn't 'old out much 'ope for it to work, then?'

'Look, Johnny boy, we both know you're your own man. It was never gonna be easy for you, an' I've met Lyndsey, ain't I? She's strong-minded too. *Bloody* strong-minded, so . . . y'know? Anyway, where is she, then? What's she up to?'

'Workin' away.'

'Away? Where?'

'Dunno. Top secret.'

The old man scoffed. 'Top secret. Silly sod.'

'Alright, if you must know, she's teamed up with a few old colleagues an' she goes around shootin' people in the nut for money.'

The old man spilled some of the hot water he was pouring into a cup. 'What?'

'You 'eard.'

'That true, Ray?'

Paterson, who was holding his shirt over the heater, nodded.

'Fuck me! I never 'ad 'er down fer that. Good gel. Ha! Best you stay in 'er good books, son. Don't wanna be dippin' yer lollipop in someone else's bag of sherbet then, that's fer sure. What else been 'appenin'?'

Clocks made a *phut* sound with his lips as he breathed out. 'Nothin' much. Oh, wait a minute . . . you're a grandad an' soon to be a great grandad. Yeah, turns out I've got a boy too. And, you'll like this . . . 'E's an armed robber. *And* the fucker wants me to keep 'im out of jail. *And* I'm goin' to nick 'im an' bang 'im up. There you go. That's me. All caught up.'

Old man Clocks handed the teas around and waved a packet of Jammie Dodgers at them both. 'Fuckin' 'ell. Never a dull moment with you, is there?'

Clocks smiled at his father and reached for the biscuits.

'You say 'e's an armed robber?'

'Yep.'

'What's 'e robbin', then?'

'Post offices. Buildin' societies. The usual, *if* you were a robber in the seventies. I think 'e's tryin' to revive the genre.'

Old man Clocks sniffed. 'Sounds like a right thick little bastard.'

CHAPTER FIFTY-SEVEN

Old man Clocks dropped the boys at the bottom end of Parry Place, a five-minute walk from the Woolwich Arsenal DLR station, and they said their goodbyes. Paterson checked his watch. 7:17 a.m. He figured they'd be at back at Tower Bridge police station within the hour.

'Interesting man, your dad,' said Paterson as they set off.

'Yeah, 'as 'is moments.'

'Look, John . . .'

'Leave it, Ray.'

'Why didn't you tell me about your mum?'

'Didn't want to. Can't do fuck all about it, can I?'

'No, but . . . fuck, mate. You've been carrying that around with you all this time.'

'Don't matter. As the ol' man said, it is what it is.'

'You have to go and see her.'

'I know. I will. When I'm ready.'

'If you don't, you'll regret it.'

'Ray.'

'What?'

'Shut the fuck up, eh? I said leave it, so leave it. Please.'

Paterson nodded. 'Okay. I'm sorry. Didn't mean to upset you.'

'I'm not upset. I'm fuckin' angry, okay?' He stopped walking and shook his head before letting out a big sigh. Paterson could see his eyes were moist again. 'I didn't know she'd got worse. It's fuckin' killin' me. I dunno what to do.'

Paterson stood in front of his friend, upset for him. 'Look. Whatever she needs, okay? You know that. You should have said earlier.'

'No, mate. You've done more than enough for me as it is. 'Sides, it's incurable. Money won't help. Nothing will.' He started to sob.

Feeling awkward, Paterson put his arms around him and let him cry.

After a few seconds, Clocks sniffed and shook his head. 'Ray . . .'

'It's alright, mate. Let it out.'

'Ray . . .'

'What?'

'We're in the street.'

'And?'

'And if you don't stop cuddlin' me right now, I'll kick you right in the twins. Now, be a pal, an' get the fuck off. There's a good gel.'

Paterson immediately let go and stepped back. 'Sorry. I just—'

Clocks held up a hand. 'I know. You were just being an' ol' woman. Either that or you were trying to cop a feel of me arse. I know what you're like. Just let me deal with it my way, mate.'

'Yeah. Of course. Sorry.'

'C'mon. We've got shit to deal with.'

They walked in silence for a few minutes until they got to the station.

'John?'

'Better not be about me mum.'

'It's not.'

'Go on, then.'

'I have to ask. All this with your dad disposing of bodies for the local villains — you clearly knew about it, yes?'

246

'Dunno what you're talkin' about.'

'John, this is me. Be sensible.'

'I am being sensible. If anyone asks, all I know is that 'e's a scrap dealer. That's it. Don't see 'im very often. We don't talk about work or anything. Nothing. Best that way.'

'I get that, but how do you square it with yourself?'

Clocks took on a look of bemusement. 'Square it? Really? That's a piece of piss, mate. We both know that sometimes the criminal world 'ave to do a spring clean an' they like to take out their own rubbish. Trouble is, the ol' shallow grave thing can be a bit iffy. Dogs usually find 'em an' so on. Sometimes these people end up doublin' up as a bit of ballast in concrete posts, usually on motorways — don't even ask 'ow many there are in the Dartford flyover — but that's only if there's a big build nearby. But, if they've 'ad to do a bit of *urgent* cleanin' and there ain't any buildin' goin' on, Dad gets a call.'

'Hmm. I can see that. A noble profession, I guess.'

'You got a problem, Ray? 'Cause it's too late to go back and pull him out of that four-by-four cube of steel.'

'No problem, John. Just getting it straight in my head.'

'Is it straight?'

'Yep. I can see where you got your sparkling personality and wit from.'

Clocks sniffed. 'Can yer?'

'Yeah. I'm curious though as to why you went the other way, y'know? How come you never went a bit . . .'

'Criminal? That the word you're lookin' for?'

'That's it.'

'Jesus, Ray. What the fuck 'ave we been doin' for the last few years, eh?'

'What?'

'It takes a crook to catch a crook, eh? You 'eard that? I mean, it's not like we're livin' in a fuckin' fairy tale where everyone says, "It's a fair cop, guv. You got me bang to rights. I was just tryin' to feed me perishin' kids, copper. I'll come quietly officer." Is it? No. We fight fire with fire and *you*, you of all people, know that. *Especially* after tonight.'

They dodged in between a couple of cars that had got an early morning start to beat the rush hour that was coming.

'You make a point.'

'Where we goin' after the nick?'

'Back to the Yard. See the commissioner and bring him up to date. He won't be happy when he finds out that our boy's gone "missing" again.'

'Well, we'll deal with that. At least we know the fucker won't be 'urtin' anyone else ever again. I'm good with that.'

'Yeah, me too.'

CHAPTER FIFTY-EIGHT

Tommy, Jackie, Monkey and Dusty were sitting around a large oblong table in the canteen of Tower Bridge police station picking at a large bowl of heavily salted chips.

'All I'm saying is that something doesn't ring right,' said Gunn.

'Keep your voice down,' said Jackie. Dotted around the canteen were a number of uniformed PCs either on their breaks or writing up reports or both.

Gunn lowered his voice. 'Look, you know I'm right. You were there, same as me. That search turned up nothing. The dogs turned up nothing. Don't you think that's strange? Dogs can't find any scent in an open field? Think about it.'

Dusty shrugged. 'Maybe he ran along the river? Wiped the scent out?'

'Oh, yeah. Because he'd have the presence of mind to do that, wouldn't he? He's as mad as a mongoose, yakking on about God and the Bible, but he's aware enough to think, "Oh, I know. Just in case the coppers bring in a dog or two, best I run along the river in order to throw them off my scent."'

'Maybe he did just that,' said Jackie. 'The bloke had dogs of his own. You don't know what goes on in someone's mind.'

249

'Look, come on. Think about this. There was no trace of him. Paterson was wringing wet and him and Clocks took off from the scene when they should have been helping with the search. You all know that.'

'So, what you saying?' said Dusty.

'You know what I'm saying.'

'No, I don't. And before you clarify it for me, keep your voice down. Again. Okay?'

'Alright. I'll say it. I'm saying that I think they did him in and chucked him in the boot. There. Satisfied?'

Jackie chuckled. 'Silly bastard.'

'Okay, then. Go get your coat,' said Dusty.

'What?'

'Well, that's you finished on the squad. Go get your coat.'

'Excuse me?'

'It's about loyalty, you little prick. Look, I know you've had a rough time of it. You're gonna carry a scar on your face for the rest of your life and no doubt a few on the inside too. You saw a colleague get killed. I'm gonna put it down to shock and a bit of the old soul searching, but you don't ever go around banging on about some conspiracy theory that involves the guv'nors.

'You've just shown us that you can't be trusted. Can't keep your mouth shut. And to think that you'd even consider they'd do that shit? Well, I'm done with you, mate. I'm not gonna work with you again.'

Jackie smiled. 'That's two of us.'

'For fuck's sake! Wake up and look at the facts!'

'I'm wide awake,' said Jackie. 'All I see is that the fucker got away. Again. It happens. Get over it.'

'I know that but *how* did he get away? That's what I can't get my head around. Can any of you? No, course you can't if you're being honest. Come on . . . dozens of coppers . . . sniffer dogs . . . open fields. You ain't gotta be the Brain of Britain to do the maths on it.'

Dusty dug into the chips and pushed a handful into his mouth. He chewed them for a second. 'Give it a rest, okay. You got a problem? Talk to them about it.'

Gunn pushed his chair back with his feet. The loud scraping sound caused a few heads to lift from their tables. 'Oh, yeah, right. 'Cos they'll put their hands straight up, won't they? I mean, you just kill someone and then cop to the first person that pulls you up on it. I'm sure they will. You all know their reputation for violence. Fuck me, the whole Met knows of it. Paterson's killed before. Don't know about Clocks, but it wouldn't surprise me. Man's a fucking lunatic.'

Monkey Harris had been unusually quiet up to now, but things were getting a bit out of hand. 'Yeah. Alright. You've had your fucking say. Now that's enough. Just shut your trap like you've been told. Go upstairs and type out your resignation.'

'What'd you say?'

'You heard.' Monkey stuffed a handful of chips in his mouth, chewed them quickly and swallowed hard. 'You're done now. You've made a serious, *serious* accusation against the two best coppers I've ever known in my life. They're my friends too. You're obviously thinking whether or not you should report your suspicions and you're testing the water with us because you want us to support you.

'Only you've fucked up. No one's going to go along with your little fantasy. So, spot the writing on the wall, mate. You're not wanted on this squad anymore. Certainly the guvs won't want you if you're going around thinking and talking shit like that about them. And, if you put in for a transfer, I'll make it my mission in life to see you *don't* get wherever it is you want to go to. I'll be putting in phone calls to make sure you don't get taken on *anywhere*. Can't be trusted, see? So, you're proper fucked. Now go and type your resignation like a good little prick.'

Gunn's face turned red and he bunched his fists, an action that did not go unnoticed by Monkey.

'Feel free,' he said. 'Gimme an even bigger excuse to batter the granny out of you.'

Gunn scraped his chair further back and stood up. 'You can't cover this up!'

Monkey pushed the table forward and rammed it into Gunn's legs, knocking him backward. Then he was up and on him before Gunn could regain his balance. Jackie and Dusty, along with everybody else in the canteen, looked shocked as Monkey launched his assault.

He grabbed Gunn by the lapels and in one swift move picked him up and dumped him onto his back on top of the table. Gunn grunted as the air left his body. Monkey shoved his face close to Gunn's.

'Cover *what* up? There's nothing *to* cover up. Now, I told you to shut up, didn't I? Spouting shit like that! Get people into all sorts of trouble.' He pulled him up slightly then pushed him back down onto the table. Gunn hit his head. Monkey cocked his fist but before he could throw the punch, Dusty and a couple of uniforms grabbed him and dragged him off.

'Fuck off! Get off me!'

Jackie helped Gunn up. 'Best you go,' she said. 'Before he really loses his temper.'

Gunn fought to get his breath back and nodded at her. 'I'm not frightened of him.'

'Not a question of being frightened, love. More a question of you not having to take your head home in a bag.'

'Monkey! Enough! Calm it down!' Dusty was pushing Monkey backward as he tried to advance on Gunn again. The two PCs stood by looking nervous, unsure of what to do.

'You were supposed to be one of us, you *fucking* piece of shit!' Monkey yelled at him. 'Get outta my sight before I fucking do you!'

Gunn held a finger up. *Wait a minute.* He finished taking a deep breath, shook himself out and looked at Monkey. 'Come on then, big boy. Let's go.'

As soon as the words left Gunn's mouth, Dusty's eyes widened, and he was forced to push even harder against a now enraged Monkey Harris. Monkey shoved him aside and headed toward Gunn, who raised his fists.

''Ello, 'ello, 'ello. What's 'occurin' 'ere, then?' said Johnny Clocks.

Monkey and Gunn stopped in their tracks. Paterson and Clocks stood in the doorway of the canteen both wearing concerned looks. Everyone else looked worried.

'You boys ain't 'avin' a party without us, are yer? That's a bit out of order.'

One of the uniformed PCs took the lead. 'You hear that, boys? Urgent assistance shout on the radio.' He grabbed his jacket off the back of the chair. 'We gotta go, sir.' The rest of the uniforms scrambled to get out of the canteen.

'And keep your mouths shut.' Paterson stood aside to let them past. 'All of you.' He turned to the detectives on his team. 'Right . . . seems that things have gotten themselves a bit heated in our absence. You two —' he nodded toward Monkey and Gunn — 'stand down.' They did, albeit reluctantly.

'Right. What's 'appenin', then?' said Clocks.

'Nothing, sir,' said Jackie. 'Card game got out of hand, that's all.'

'Oh, yeah? What yer playin'? Mental poker? I ask only 'cos there's no fuckin' cards on the table. Bit of a giveaway really.'

Jackie rolled her eyes.

'C'mon, spit it out. Let's 'ave it.'

Monkey turned toward Clocks. 'Nothing. He just pissed me off with his mouth and I lost it. My fault. I'm out of order.' He started to walk toward the doorway. Clocks stood in front of him. For a second, Monkey looked uncertain as to his next move. 'Excuse me, sir,' he said.

Clocks looked him in the eye. 'Nah, nah, nah. Not yet, yer big ol' lump. I wanna know what's caused me team to get all arse'oley with each other — an' you know me, Monkey, I won't let it go until I find out.'

'It's on me,' Gunn said.

Clocks craned his head past Monkey's formidable frame. 'Whatcha gone an' done, Tommy boy?'

Jackie and Dusty started to look agitated, both well aware that this could go one of two ways with Clocks.

Gunn shook his head. 'I was questioning what went on out there, that's all.'

Clocks walked past Monkey and up to Gunn. 'Questionin' what?'

Gunn stared directly at Clocks. 'I'm just curious as to why Steers wasn't found. Seems a bit . . . odd.'

Clocks nodded. 'Does it? What's odd about it, then? 'E's escaped before, 'e's escaped again. Don't see the problem meself.'

'That's true, guv. But I can't figure out why the dogs didn't pick up on his trail. Seemed right up their street. After all, that's all they do, isn't it? Their one job.'

'Didn't see no dogs.'

'You wouldn't. You two had left before they arrived.'

'Things to do, places to go, people to see.'

'Of course. Busy men.'

Clocks struggled to keep his temper but his heart was pounding in his chest. 'That's right. Busy men. Now we've established that, make yer point.'

Gunn took a half step backward. Clocks recognised he was getting ready to fight if need be.

'Point is, I don't know why he wasn't found and why you left before the dogs arrived.'

'That's not a point, son. That's a coupla statements that sound like an accusation's followin' on be'ind. So, let's 'ave it. Come on.'

'I'm just wonderin' if, by any chance — any little chance — Steers had found his way into your boot.'

Clocks never took his eyes off Gunn. He stayed silent for what must have been a full ten seconds. Then he nodded as he spoke. 'Well, there you go, boy. You're way too good for us, ain'tcha? You're bang on. We topped 'im an' slung 'im in the boot, just as you thought.'

Paterson felt his heart jolt and the rest of the group's eyes were like saucers. 'John. What are you doing?'

'No. It's alright, Ray. Leave it be. Sherlock bloody 'olmes 'ere is clearly a brilliant detective that we've seriously underestimated.' He continued to stare at Gunn. 'Ain't that right, Tommy boy? So, now you've put it out there, best you back it up. If you think that's what we've done, make the arrests. Go on. Put yer money where yer mouth is an' slap the cuffs on.'

'Don't, sir.'

'What?'

'Don't, sir.'

'Why's that, Tommy boy? Tell Uncle Johnny. What's that? You've what? No evidence to back up yer bullshit claim an' you're just spoutin' bollocks? Well fuck me bandy. Who knew?'

Gunn's face turned a deeper shade of red.

'What? You wanna 'ave a little pop at me too? Go on then, 'ave a little go if you fancy yer chances. You sure you wanna take on a murderer like me? Is that wise? You never know. You might end up in a car boot, eh?'

'Tommy,' said Paterson. 'What's this all about? This isn't like you.'

Gunn tore his eyes away from Clocks to look at him.

'Something isn't right, sir. I know it.'

'Okay, I see where you're coming from but these are dangerous allegations and you know it. So, the question now is, where do we all go with it? Do you intend to take it further?'

Gunn nodded. 'Don't seem to have a lot of choice now. Monkey's just threatened to fuck up my career.'

Clocks smiled at Monkey. *Good boy.* 'Good. If 'e 'adn't, I would.'

'And there we go. So, like they said, I'm gonna leave. I'm done here.'

Paterson took a deep breath and allowed a calm to run through his body. It was the sort of calm that preceded a storm. It was the sort of calm that came over him while he burned the organ harvesting clinics in Mumbai not too long ago. He stepped in front of Gunn and blocked his way. 'Can we have the room please, everyone? You too, John.'

'What?' said Clocks. 'You want me outside too?'

'Yeah, I do. Thank you.'

Clocks frowned as he followed his three teammates out into the hallway. He closed the door behind him.

Paterson held his hand out. 'Sit down, please.'

Gunn eyed him warily but slowly pulled out a chair, letting it scrape loudly across the floor.

'Well, this is a mess, Tommy. I don't know where this is coming from but I expected better than this from you.'

'Why's that, sir? I'm a police officer. If something's not right, I have a moral and legal duty to speak out. You understand that.'

'That's true. It absolutely is. But if you really think that's what we did — and clearly you do — why didn't you think to discuss it with us first? Or the troops?'

'That's what I was trying to do, but then Monkey got all lairy and started in on me.'

'To be honest, it sounds like you deserved it.'

'Excuse me?'

'Well, you haven't handled this well at all, have you? You've known us a while now. And in that while, we've been nothing but good to you, haven't we? We took you on under the impression that you were a solid officer. Reliable.'

'Have I not been reliable?'

Paterson nodded. 'Yeah, you have. Until now. I thought you understood us, the way we are, the way we work. I accept we're a bit sketchy and that we've had our run-ins with upstairs but . . . y'know, we're decent enough.'

'Look, sir. I know that. I know all of that, but something's wrong here. Nothing adds up.'

'Okay. I get that. I understand what you're saying.' He looked into Gunn's eyes. 'But look at it from another point of view. So what?'

Gunn looked rattled. This was not the sort of thing he had expected Paterson to say.

'Pardon me?'

Paterson shrugged. 'Look . . . we didn't. But even if we did do what you think, so what? You think his life is worth saving? You think he's worth a trial and incarceration? He tried to kill me twice — no, three times — and Clocksy too. He's killed children, a baby, blew a fucking bus to bits and killed and maimed young girls, murdered colleagues of ours, raped a nun and God knows what else *and* he slashed you into the bargain. You got lucky. Could have been you instead of Tetley lying in that road. You don't think he should have paid for what he'd done? Is that it?'

'No. That's not it, sir. You know that. It's just that he has to pay the right way. Not some cowboy, outlaw justice. That's not right.'

'Okay. I can see you're upset—'

'No sir, I'm past upset, and you wanna know why?'

'Go ahead.'

'*For what he'd done.* That's what you said. Not what he *has* done. What he *had* done. Past tense. So, I think now, even more than ever, David Steers was dead in your boot when you left the crime scene.'

Paterson tensed up. He gave a slow nod. 'Tch. You know, you would have made a good detective but—'

'I'm sorry. Is that a threat coming? Are you threatening me?'

Paterson took a deep breath. 'No. I'm not threatening you. Look, you do what you have to do, but be careful. These things have a way of coming back to bite you in the arse. Do you understand?'

'I understand a threat, sir. That I do.'

Paterson's hand shot out and he gripped Gunn by the throat. He squeezed so hard that Gunn's eyes bulged. He struggled and kicked to get away but Paterson's grip was like steel. Gunn couldn't manage to prise open a single finger. 'Listen, Tommy boy, John and I are always in trouble and it's getting boring. Now, you breathe one fucking word of your little theory to anyone and I will slice you up the middle and pull your heart out of your chest. Got it?

'See. *That's* a threat, Tommy boy, and if you want to test my sincerity, well, you know what to do. Now, before you leave here I want your phones, personal and work. Can't have the possibility that you've recorded anything, can I?' Gunn's eyes were streaming and he choked out a few unintelligible words which Paterson took to be his agreement. He stared at him for a few more seconds before his rage began to fade.

Clocks opened the door and poked his head in. 'You okay there, guv? Thought I heard a bit of a kerfuffle.'

Paterson let his man go. Gunn coughed and spluttered. 'Yeah. All good thanks. We're getting on like a house on fire. Just coaching Tommy here with a few tips on how to be a better team player.'

Clocks nodded. 'Need any help?'

'Oh, what do you think?'

Clocks smiled and closed the door again.

CHAPTER FIFTY-NINE

Paterson stopped at the traffic lights on Lambeth Palace Road, a short distance from New Scotland Yard. He'd already made the call to the commissioner and informed him that they were coming to brief him fully on the night's events. Sam Morne had already been given bits of intel from various sources, but he was not the sort of man to rush to judgement.

The way Paterson saw it, his point of focus now was Tommy Gunn. He had seen the look in his eye, worried but defiant, and he clearly wasn't one to be easily intimidated. The thing he had to decide was what to do about him. Of course, he hoped that his appeal to loyalty and the brotherhood and the threat to split him up the middle would be sufficient, but he really wasn't sure with this one. Times had changed and threatening him had been a stupid move.

Clocks had often told him about a more 'golden' era of policing when coppers relied on each other. Everyone had each other's backs and to inform on a colleague was the greatest sin. Such behaviour would have seen you ostracised not just from your team but from every aspect of policing. If you needed urgent assistance, it would be slow, *very* slow, in coming. If you were at court giving evidence, you might find that your colleagues decide that they didn't in fact see what you put in your statement. Perjury used to be a real fear.

Those days were long gone and things were different now. The youngsters coming into the job had a totally different mindset: not one dedicated to keeping the peace and catching criminals but one that was fixated on changing the system; people dedicated to ferreting out grass roots, working-class police officers in favour of those with a more liberal view of policing; officers who joined the job at a high rank with no idea of what it meant to police the streets. Nowadays the copper sitting next to you was probably working out how to get rid of you. But for now, at least, Paterson and Clocks had each other.

'Ray, we're running out of time. We have to decide what to do about Tommy.'

'I know that. We've been talking about it for the last half hour. It's not easy, is it?'

'No, it's not, but if he goes the wrong way and grasses us, we're in trouble. Why the fuck did you threaten to kill him?'

Paterson shook his head. The light turned green and he pulled away. 'I don't know, John. I got the dark again.'

'The dark? What the fuck's *the dark* when it's at 'ome?'

'You know what it is.'

'Do I?'

'Yeah. You tell me that every so often I change . . . become cold . . . menacing. Like I'm not myself.'

Clocks sniffed and wiped his nose on the back of his hand. 'Blimey. You've named it now, 'ave you?'

'I think that's what happened there. I could feel myself . . . separating almost. Like the real me was being pushed away. Pushed into the background and a smaller version of me, helpless, could only watch what was happening.'

Clocks turned to him. 'Jesus! That don't sound good.'

'I know it doesn't. But there it is, okay? I had to tell you.'

'No, you didn't.'

Paterson pulled up at another set of red lights. 'What?'

'You didn't, but I'm glad you did. You need to get it out in the open. Chat about shit.'

'What? Like you?'

'We're not talkin' about me, are we? But know this . . . whatever you say, there's no way on this earth that I'll be cuddlin' you. Not at any point. Okay? Just sayin'. I don't do that. Look, we've both been through some shit, seen some fuckin' awful things. Done even worse things. And that's bound to fuck us up in the 'ead.'

Paterson nodded. 'You back on the drink, John?'

'What?'

'Apart from the odd glass in the office, are you back on the drink?'

Clocks squirmed in his seat then lowered his head. 'Yeah. You back on the sniff?'

'I've done a few lines.'

'What's a few?'

'More than a lot.'

'Oh, shit.'

'Thing is, I don't care anymore. About anything, anyone — apart from you and Lyndsey, of course. I don't *feel* anymore, John. I look at people with their petty problems and I reduce them to mere . . . nothings. They're nothing to me.'

'Come on, Ray. That's not true. Your *thing* is kids, isn't it? You lose your shit when it comes to kids being hurt.'

'Well, yeah. I do, but what I mean is . . . the scum of this earth . . . I feel only hatred for them. Rage. I *want* to hurt them. So bad. I want them to pay for their crimes. For the pain they've inflicted on others, the hurt they've caused, the damage they've done. I despise them with every fucking fibre of my being and I want to stop them. *Have* to stop them.

'With Steers, I had no intention of nicking him and every intention of doing him in. I was way past thinking of the law, the right and proper thing to do. This darkness took me, John. And when he fought back, desperate, I just became more enraged with him. I wanted to not just drown him but to push him into the ground, right into the ground, deep. I wanted to bury him too. Does that make sense?'

'Kinda.'

'I'm losing the plot, mate. Big time.'

'Ah, you lost the plot ages ago. You lost it when Adam Walker killed yer missus. That's when it all went tits up, bud. Didn't that Met-appointed psychiatrist help you at all?'

'Eileen? No. Not really. To be fair to her, I wasn't very forthcoming. I didn't want anybody snooping around in my business. She helped you though, didn't she?'

'A bit. Got me off the drink for a while, but you know how it is. I like a drink. Always have.'

'Meeting Lyndsey was the best thing that ever happened to you, though. She put you on the straight and narrow. Got you sober and clean. Good girl, that one.'

Clocks shrugged. 'Yeah, she is. But look where we are now. She's gone off-piste to go and work with Wol and 'is little firm, travellin' around the world. We ain't seen too much of each other since we got married. I dunno. Maybe I was wrong to get married.'

'Bullshit, John. Plenty of women go out to work and plenty work away from home.'

'I'll grant you that. But plenty of them don't shoot people in the bonce for money, do they?'

Paterson started laughing and worked himself up so badly he had to pull over, much to the annoyance of the traffic that piled up behind him.

'What's so funny?' said Clocks.

'It just suddenly hit me how much our lives have changed since the day we met. My wife is dead . . . yours is an assassin. I'm on the coke, you're on the booze. We fight with coppers. We're hated by the higher-ups. We're going no further in the job — this is it for us. We have no regard for the law anymore and we've killed people, for fuck's sake. Killed people. And those we didn't do ourselves, we sanctioned. We are *fucking terrible* people, John. *Terrible.*'

'Speak for yerself, mate. I'm still the loveable rogue I always 'ave been. Apart from the killin' an' the sanctionin' and the drinkin' bits. Yeah, apart from that, I'm lovely, me.'

'I don't know what to do anymore. I can't trust myself.'

'There is an answer. We've spoken about this before, over and over. Walk away if you want. That'll get you out of the front line, but the reality is, you'll always 'ave an itch you can't scratch. You *need* to do this, Ray. You 'ave to. Same as me. It's a drive that's inside of us. A drive to put this poxy world right, to stand up for what's right an' to 'elp people get some sort of justice an' comfort. But — an' I do agree with yer — we do tend to go about it in a dodgy way. Lyndsey once said we're a pair of 'orrible fuckers with 'earts of gold.'

'But we're doing wrong.'

'To do right. An' you can't make a sausage sandwich without bread, can yer? No, yer can't. Otherwise you'd 'ave a plate of sliced up sausages an' greasy, tomato-ketchupped fingers. So . . . we 'ave to accept that this is where we're at. This is the way our lives 'ave gone, an' we accept it or we walk away from it. Don't know about you . . . well, I do know about you. You won't walk an' neither will I, so we need to find a way to control our shit properly or we'll end up dead from drink or drugs or we'll top ourselves some other 'orrible way.'

Paterson nodded. 'You're right. I know you're right. But I don't know how to get my shit together. One minute, I'm okay with how I am. I'm confident in myself. I don't give a damn about what we do or how we do it, who we hurt or don't. I sometimes feel . . . untouchable, powerful, y'know?'

Clocks nodded slowly.

'And other times, like now, I'm wracked with guilt, self-doubt.' Paterson tapped his temple. 'Two different people living in here now. Two *very* different people, and every day, every fucking day, it's a war and I can't for the life of me figure out who will win.' He shook his head. 'No, that's not true. I know who will win in the end. The dark. It's consuming me and, if I'm honest, I kind of want it to. It'll ease the pain if I let it take me.'

'Fuck me Obi Wan. You *'ave* got some shit goin' on in yer noodle, ain't yer? You 'ave this every day? Christ! It's a wonder you get out of bed an' come to work.'

'I know. D'you not feel like this some days?'

'Yeah. Course. But you know what I do?'

Paterson looked at him. 'Go on.'

'It's really, really simple. I give a little whistle. And always, *always* let my conscience be my guide.' He chuckled.

Paterson didn't.

CHAPTER SIXTY

Less than thirty minutes later, Paterson and Clocks, hot drinks in hand, sat themselves down in Commissioner Sam Morne's office. Morne was dressed in full uniform, looking sharp. In front of him on his desk was a cup of peppermint tea to ease the acid build-up he'd developed since meeting these two.

'Thanks for coming in, gents. I hear you had a . . . busy night.'

'Yes, sir,' said Paterson.

Morne blew onto his tea before taking a sip. 'I understand another young girl died. In the boot of his car, wasn't she?'

Paterson nodded. 'Sir.'

'What do we know about her? Where did he take her from?'

'At the moment, we have no idea,' said Paterson. 'It's most likely that he picked her up on the way to Guildford. Maybe he snatched her from outside a school or a motorway station. Nothing is confirmed yet as far as I know. I would expect that my team are trying to trace her movements and her family as we speak.'

'Hmm. Do we know how she died, exactly?'

'No sir, not exactly. We'll have to wait for the pathologist to determine cause of death. I'm hoping later today.'

'John . . .' said Morne.

'Guv?'

'I understand you swiped Steers's car. Sent it rolling.'

'Yes, sir.'

Morne rubbed his face. 'Christ. Why did you do that?'

'To stop 'im getting away. I didn't know the girl was in there, otherwise I wouldn't 'ave done it, would I?'

'No. Of course not. I know that. Are you alright?'

'No. Not really. *I* mighta killed the poor little cow an' I 'ave to live with that.'

'Hmm. We can get you help if you want it.'

Clocks scoffed. 'Oh, yeah. Another shrink who'll want to know about my mummy and daddy and if I shagged my sister an' wanked over 'er dollies while I was growin' up. No thanks. I'll talk it over with Johnnie Walker.'

'Get some proper help, John. I mean it.'

'Right you are, sir. I'll just finish me tea first.' He took a gulp of his drink. 'Then I'll be on me way.'

'John, this really isn't the time for your sarcasm. We have a fucking huge problem here. Not only did a girl die perhaps because of police action, but that bastard Steers escaped again. Tell me what happened, Ray.'

'It's blurry still, but the upshot is I had him — physically had hold of him. We were fighting in the river when John called. He shouted something about needing help — there was a girl or something. I managed to smack Steers in the nose and I watched him stumble backward, then I went to John. I saw the girl and helped him take her out of the car. We laid her down on the ground and immediately started giving her first aid, best we could. I could see she was in a real bad way, and at that moment, she was my only point of concern. Steers was secondary right then.

'I remember hearing him run, water splashing, but I didn't think he'd get far. Not with his bad leg. Help was coming. As I said, he was not my main concern at that point.'

Morne drummed his fingers on his desk. 'What happened when you realised she was dead?'

'I determined to go after Steers, but by that time, or shortly after — I can't quite remember the timeline of events — my team and a bunch of locals had arrived. Ambulances too. I told them what had happened, liaised briefly with the local duty officer, filled him in, and he organised a search.'

'And then what happened?'

'We left.'

Morne frowned. 'Left? Why did you leave? Why didn't you join the search?'

Paterson shrugged. 'A couple of reasons. We needed to get back to brief you. My team were capable of working with the locals and, to be honest, I thought it best that I didn't get my hands on him a second time.'

'Meaning?'

'Meaning I'm not overly fond of child killers, sir, and I didn't trust myself not to, shall we say, *manhandle* him. We do have a reputation for violence sir, don't we? And I think, given the circumstances, I may well have proved my critics right if I'd gotten hold of him again.'

'But you did have him, didn't you? Once, you said. Is that correct?'

Paterson took a deep breath. This didn't feel right. The tone of this meeting was *off* somehow. He couldn't work out where Morne was going with this. Was he supportive or did he know something else? Had Gunn already done the dirty on them? He fought to remain cool.

'Yeah. Correct. I think it's reasonable to say he deserved, at the very least, a smack or two in the face.'

'I hear he almost killed you and the Morgan girl too. Yes?'

'Yep. John sorted it all though. He and the others rescued me.'

'And, John . . . you shot him, didn't you?'

'I fired at 'im, yeah, but wasn't sure if I 'it 'im. Turns out I did. One in the leg. Bastard lived, though, didn't 'e?'

'It would seem so.'

'We'll get him, sir,' said Paterson. 'I promise.'

Morne eyed him. 'Hmm. With respect, Ray, he seems to have got the better of you both so far. The press are howling for an arrest and we have to tell them that, once again, he escaped and another girl was killed in the process. Doesn't look good.'

Paterson shifted in his seat. 'Is this what this is about, sir? Optics? How it looks to the world? Because if it is, I don't give a shit. Yes, he has got away from us, more times than I care to admit, but he won't escape forever. We'll catch up with him soon.'

'Tell me about his injury.'

'Whose? Steers? Not much to tell. The locals called to tell us that he went into A and E and was clocked immediately. They played it all normal to keep him there, took him in for treatment and, at some point, it seems he turned on the doctor attending to him and attacked her. He punched her in the nose, knocking her over, then set about beating her. He escaped before security arrived. That's all I know so far.'

'Is she okay, the doctor?'

'Not happy, sir. I understand her nose is broken and she'll have a couple of shiners no doubt, but apart from that and a few fractured ribs where he gave her a kicking, she'll be peachy.'

'Do we have a report from the hospital yet with regards to the extent of *his* injuries?'

'No. Not yet. Doctor's not ready to make a statement. Shock and all that.'

'I'm not worried about a statement. I'm more concerned with what she said, if anything, in relation to her thoughts on his condition. I mean, are they life threatening? Is he likely to bleed out somewhere? Flesh wound, was it?'

'I don't know, sir. I can make some more enquiries for you, but I would have thought if he was going to bleed out then he'd have done it running away from us.'

Morne rubbed his eyes. 'John . . . when you shot him, he could still run, yes?'

Clocks shrugged. 'I'd say it was more fast limpin' than runnin', guv.'

Morne nodded. 'I was rather hoping you might have taken out an artery. Make it really difficult for him to stay on the run — or to stay alive.'

'Didn't get much chance to take proper aim, guv.'

'You'd have missed anyway,' said Paterson. 'Let's be fair.'

'Ooh, you bitch.' Clocks smiled at him.

'You realise you're both going to face a substantial investigation on this one, don't you?'

They both nodded.

'There's nothing I can do about it. This isn't a witch hunt. This is legitimate.'

'I know, sir,' said Paterson. 'And I'm sure when the facts come out, you'll see we've done nothing wrong. Again.'

'Ray . . . I sincerely hope you're right and I sincerely hope you're being straight with me. If you're not, then now's the time to tell me.'

'We've done nothing wrong, sir. Straight as an arrow.'

'Close the door on your way out please, gents.'

The two men rose to leave. At the door, Morne called out. 'Ray!'

'Yessir?'

'We both know that sometimes an arrow can get knocked off its course, don't we?'

'Sir,' said Paterson with a nod. He closed the door.

CHAPTER SIXTY-ONE

Clocks stepped into the empty lift. 'Why do I get the feeling he don't believe us?'

Paterson pressed the ground-floor button. 'Because he's not stupid, is he?'

'No, I s'pose not. You think Gunn's already put the knife in?'

'I bloody hope not.'

'Yeah. Me too. Soon now, I reckon.'

'Hmm, hmm. They won't wait long on an allegation like this. Especially if this one is police backed. The little shit.'

'He's six foot three.'

He grinned at Clocks. 'The big shit.'

The lift stopped and a woman got in. The head of the Diversity and Cultural Unit. Clocks's face lit up. 'You all right, love?'

Paterson shook his head. As if they weren't in enough trouble.

The woman, Leanne Sax, glared at him with contempt.

'Can't stay away from me, can yer? Proper man, 'ere. That's what does it. Sheer animal magnetism. Must be a change for you, babe. Being around a man that smells of masculinity instead of some poncey perfume. Bet that floats yer boat under yer nightie, eh?'

'Don't speak to me, you troglodyte.'

'Oi, oi! That's not nice, is it? I thought you lot were all s'posed to be non-judgemental up there in the . . . what was it? Cultural and Diversity mob. You can't be callin' me names like that. I'll report you to yerself if you keep on.'

Leanne Sax bristled at him. 'You are not funny. You think you are, but you're not.'

'Oh, so now you're attacking me character as well as me looks.'

'What? I never attacked your looks!'

'Called me a troglodyte. What's that, then?'

'What?'

'You're thinking of a gargoyle, John,' said Paterson.

'A what?'

'A gargoyle.'

'Am I?'

'Think so. A troglodyte used to mean a person who lived in a cave but nowadays it's a person who is regarded as being purposely ignorant or old-fashioned. A gargoyle is a stone carving. You see them on churches and old gothic buildings mostly.'

'Oh. Okay, then. Sorry, sweetie. I stand corrected. You weren't 'avin' a go at me looks. Just so you know, though, I'm not bein' *purposely* ignorant or old-fashioned, I'm naturally ignorant and old-fashioned.'

She glared at him. 'Yes. You are. Can you think of any more derogatory names to call me?'

Clocks wrinkled his nose. 'Derogatory. I'm not bein' derogatory, treacle. These are nice names that we men 'ave for you birds. They're terms of affection. You want me to run a class for yer? Teach you all about being lovely to people?'

She let out a loud sigh.

'Oh, come on, love. Loosen up. It must be really 'orrible for yer to walk around with that big self-righteous stick up yer arse all day. I know it's in yer job description to 'ate everyone who thinks an' talks sensibly about things, but pull it out an' lighten up a bit. You don't really need it. Not with us. Ooh. I tell you what . . .' He pulled out his phone. 'I'll do you a right favour. Bang yer number in there an' I'll give yer a bell sometime. Take you out to the café or somethin' an' we can 'ave a lovely chat about bein' sensible. That'll cheer you up.'

She looked horrified at the thought. 'Never in a million years would I—'

'Do us a favour, though. Keep it quiet in the office just in case anyone there knows me missus. She gets a bit funny about this sort of thing. She'll think you're tryin' to bang me or something.' He looked at her. 'You're *not* are you? I mean, you're a lovely girl an' a fantastic conversationalist, but yer tits are a bit on the small side for me. No offence.'

Paterson grimaced. *Too far, John. Too far.*

Leanne Sax stood there, her mouth open in horror.

'Ooh. Best not leave that open around me, babe.'

By the time the lift stopped on the ground floor, Leanne Sax was ready to explode. Nothing would come out though.

Clocks stepped out of the lift and held his arm across the door for her, a last silent dig.

'After you, princess. An' don't forget . . . gimme a bell.'

CHAPTER SIXTY-TWO

A flash of lightning distracted Tommy Gunn from his thinking. It wasn't often you got to see a bolt of lightning streak down from the heavens somewhere into the streets of London. At least that's what it looked like from where he was on the thirteenth floor of New Scotland Yard. A few seconds later, a peal of thunder rumbled across the city. A storm was on its way.

'You were saying?' said Commissioner Morne.

'What?' Gunn snapped back at the sound of Morne's voice.

'You had got to the part where you believe — but have no direct evidence of — Paterson and Clocks having killed David Steers. Please, go on.'

On Morne's desk was an A4 pad of paper and in his hand a Waterman fountain pen, his preferred choice of writing implement. There were a few notes scratched on it. Morne did him that courtesy at least.

'Yes . . . sir. Sorry . . . lightning . . . beautiful. Yes, well, that's it. As you said, I can't prove it. They're way too clever for that. But, when you look at it from a distance, it's all there.'

Sam Morne put his pen down onto the pad and made sure it was straight before he leaned back in his chair. 'I'm sorry, detective. But I'm not sure I'm seeing the same things you are. I don't see anything as being "there". I take your point about the dogs and them leaving the scene, but those things do not a murder make.'

Gunn nodded. 'I know. I get that, sir. But can you at least open a covert investigation on them?'

'A covert investigation. I take it you mean one that's off the books, eh?'

'No, no. Not off the books, no. Just on the down-low.'

'I'm sorry. What exactly is a *down-low*? I'm not familiar with the expression.'

'Sorry, guv — sir, I mean. It means to do something on the quiet.'

'Oh, I see. You mean like any other investigation into police officers, then. They're all pretty much on the *down-low*, aren't they? Probably wouldn't do to let them know they're being investigated, would it?'

Gunn felt his face flush hot. 'Er, no. Sorry. Silly thing to say. Sorry.'

'That's okay. You're upset. I'm sorry too. I didn't mean to sound rude. Is there anything else you want to tell me or is that all?'

'There's a bit more, sir.'

'I thought there might be. Please, go ahead.' Morne leaned forward, picked up his pen and listened as Tommy Gunn moved on with his story for another five minutes in which he explained how Monkey Harris had assaulted him, how the team promised to ostracise him and how they would also spike any sideways move he tried to make. He also told him about Paterson's threat to his life.

'And that's all of it, sir.'

'Good. Thank you. Can I ask . . . you said that Superintendent Paterson grabbed you by the throat, yes?'

'Hmm, hmm.'

'Did you see a doctor?'

'Er, no. Difficult to see these days.'

'Tell me about it. Did you or anyone call the divisional surgeon? They're doctors, aren't they?'

'Yes, sir, they are. And no, I didn't. I should have.'

'Indeed. And did you pop along to the hospital by any chance?'

Gunn shook his head. 'I wasn't in pain, sir. I didn't want to use up valuable resources.'

'Very commendable. Do you have any marks at all? Let me see.'

Gunn edged forward in his seat and pulled his collar open. There were a few faint but visible marks.

'Okay. Thank you. You say that Superintendent Paterson then verbally threatened to, let me see . . .' He consulted his pad. 'Ah, yes. To "slice you up the middle and pull your heart out of your chest". Is that right?'

'Yessir. His exact words.'

'And did you believe him? Were you in fear of your life?'

'Yes, sir, I was. I know what Mr Paterson's capable of. He has a temper on him.'

'Yes, yes, indeed. Mr Paterson is indeed a formidable foe. I wouldn't like to upset him.'

'Then you'll look into it?'

'Of course I will. The Met have been after these two for a long, long time, as I'm sure you know. This could be the thing that finally nails their coffin lids shut. Now, is there anything else?'

Gunn shook his head. 'Not that I can think of, sir. No. I'll leave it to you then, shall I?'

Sam Morne stood up and held out his hand. Gunn did the same and they shook. 'I'll get the ball rolling. Can I ask that you hang around for —' he looked at his watch — 'say, an hour or so? I'll need to contact Professional Standards, fill them in on what you've told me, and they'll no doubt want to grab a detailed statement from you. There's a nice little café across the road.'

'Or I could use the canteen on the ninth floor, sir.'

Morne nodded. 'You could but it might be best if you weren't seen sitting around the office. You never know who sees what, do you? I'm thinking of you.'

'Fair point. Thank you.'

'Get yourself something to eat and I'll call you when Standards get here. That okay?'

'Yes, sir, of course. Thank you for listening to me. I'm so sorry it's come to this but I can't leave it. I never once thought I'd be going on record talking about my fellow officers, but . . . these two aren't right.'

'Of course. You did the right thing. Absolutely. Should be me thanking you. You've given us the chance to get on top of and over these two. I can't say too much, of course, but they are, shall we say, due for a tug, as I believe it's called. Go and get something to eat. Go on. I'll call you once I know what's happening.'

Gunn smiled and headed out the door.

Sam Morne walked over to his safe and pulled out a laptop. He set it on his desk, sat down and typed in a password. The screen turned green and showed a simple flashing cursor. He typed in the words: *Meeting request. Urgent.* He leaned back in his chair and waited.

A few seconds later the screen split into five boxes. Four had faces, one was blank.

'Sam,' said the only woman at the meeting. 'What's this about?'

'I need authority.'

'Go on.'

'Where is Leonard?'

'He has a thing at his son's university. His absence was discussed in advance and we are able to agree or disagree in his absence. He will vote with the majority.'

Morne nodded.

'I have a problem.'

Over the next twenty minutes he outlined his problem. At the end, he got what he wanted.

'Your resolution is authorised,' said the woman.

'Thank you,' he said.

Sam Morne closed the computer's lid and shook his head slowly.

CHAPTER SIXTY-THREE

Tucked away in a booth in the nearest pub, Paterson and Clocks each nursed a pint of beer. Clocks was on the second half of a cheese and ham baguette. Both men were in a sombre mood.

'We need to talk, Ray.'

'About what?'

'You know what. What're we doin' about Tommy boy?'

'How d'you mean?'

'Word is he's not goin' to let things lie and he's gonna grass us up. That's not good, is it?'

'Nope. Where'd you hear that?'

'Bouncin' about the nick. Monkey and Dusty 'ave both 'eard whispers.'

'Is it solid information?'

'The boys think so, yeah.'

Paterson sat quietly for a moment, regretting that he threatened to kill Gunn. He sighed. 'Leave it with me.'

Clocks swallowed a bite of his sandwich. 'What does that mean, *Leave it with me*?'

'It means I'll sort it out.'

'An' 'ow you gonna do that?'

'I don't know yet. But I'll make sure he doesn't open his mouth.'

Clocks scowled at him. 'I 'ope you're not thinkin' of . . .'

Paterson ignored him.

'Ray, no! Don't you even think that. Don't you fuckin' dare.'

Paterson looked bemused. 'Excuse me? What are you suggesting?'

'You know exactly what I'm suggestin'. Do . . . not . . . think . . . about . . . it. Fer fuck's sake, 'e's one of our own.'

'Is he?'

'Well . . . no. Not now. Not if he does this, but that's no excuse to—'

'Of course I won't.'

'If you do anythin' dodgy, we'll be double-fucked then. I mean, 'ow obvious would it look if 'e turned 'is toes up? The world an' 'is brother knows what's goin' on. It wouldn't be a big stretch of the imagination to put us straight in the frame, would it? *You* can't take 'im out or '*ave* 'im taken out. Understood?'

'Don't worry about it, John. I'm not bloody stupid. Look. I'll try to make it right between us all. I'll go and see him, apologise profusely and we'll take it from there. It'll all work out. Trust me.'

'Hmm.' Clocks settled back in his seat. 'Make sure it's done right, then. I'm worried about that little dark thing you've got goin' on inside yer. Oh, and then, of course, we've gotta come up with some answers about Steers. Sometime down the line, someone will wonder where the fuck 'e disappeared to, won't they? When 'e doesn't show 'imself between now and, er, *never*, someone's gonna ask questions and it'll end up circling right back to Gunn the grass and 'is allegations. This really ain't good, mate.'

Paterson rubbed his face for a few seconds and nodded. 'I will sort it out. That's all you need to know. Finish up that sandwich and let's get out of here.'

'Two other things . . .'

'Yep. Go on, then.'

'Yer car. What's the plan for that not bein' around anymore? People know you were drivin' it that night, an' the investigators will want to 'ave a nose around it, won't they?'

Paterson thought for a moment. 'I dunno. I might say it was my sister's an' she's got it now. Gone to live in Algeria or something.'

'Oh, yeah. That's a cracker, that is. They call it "the long arm of the law" for a reason. They'll go an' check.'

'Hmm. Good point. I'll just have to report it stolen. Car like that would be in another country by now with a whole new ID.'

'Well, that'll explain why you can't produce it. But no investigator worth 'is salt will believe it.'

'Might not believe it, but can't prove otherwise, can they?'

'Okay, then. That's that sorted, I guess. So, what we gonna do about ol' Dick Wakker an' Vicar Codd an' all 'is churchy mates?'

Paterson sighed. 'Well, first up, we'll have him charged and then we can pop over and nick the vicar, and then I was thinking we'd open up an investigation into the church itself.'

'What? All of it?'

'No, you spanner. Can't do all of it, but it'll be fun to throw the cat among the pigeons, won't it?'

'Be even funnier if the cat was a choirboy.'

Paterson laughed and spilled his drink. He wiped off the beer from his trousers and looked up at Clocks. 'It'll be a hell of a can of worms to open up, though. Think of all the senior officers and ministers who'll get the raging hump over that. Can you imagine? I can hear the fury in high places now.'

Clocks smiled. 'Bagsy I get to nick the Pope.'

CHAPTER SIXTY-FOUR

Forty-five minutes after his computer meeting ended, Sam Morne stood at his window looking down into the street. He watched the raindrops drizzle their way lazily down the glass before pooling on the aluminium frame. The cup of coffee in his hand left a vaguely conical mist on the window.

He took a sip of his drink before pulling his mobile phone from his trouser pocket. He dialled and, while he waited for an answer, took another sip from the cup.

'Gunn? Yes, it's me. I've spoken to Standards and their officers are on their way. Should be with us in twenty minutes or so. If you've finished eating, pop up and we'll get cracking as soon as they're set up. Do you want legal representation with you? No? Okay. How about the Federation? No to them too? Okay. That's fine as well. We can get started quicker. See you in a minute.'

He squinted at the screen as he hit the 'end call' icon with his thumb, glanced at his wall clock and went back to looking out of the window. It was panning out to be a doozy of a storm.

Looking down into the street, he felt himself tense when he saw Tommy Gunn leave the café and walk out onto the pavement. He watched the man look first to his left and then to his right before stepping off the kerb and into the road. He watched as a motorbike, large and heavy, roared into view from Gunn's left. He watched the rider stop, pump five bullets into him and screech off around a corner and out of sight.

He watched the pedestrians react in horror and run across the street to him. From the thirteenth floor, Morne sipped at his coffee and watched Tommy Gunn die.

THE END

THE JOFFE BOOKS STORY

We began in 2014 when Jasper agreed to publish his mum's much-rejected romance novel and it became a bestseller.

Since then we've grown into the largest independent publisher in the UK. We're extremely proud to publish some of the very best writers in the world, including Joy Ellis, Faith Martin, Caro Ramsay, Helen Forrester, Simon Brett and Robert Goddard. Everyone at Joffe Books loves reading and we never forget that it all begins with the magic of an author telling a story.

We are proud to publish talented first-time authors, as well as established writers whose books we love introducing to a new generation of readers.

We have been shortlisted for Independent Publisher of the Year at the British Book Awards three times, in 2020, 2021 and 2022, and for the Diversity and Inclusivity Award at the Independent Publishing Awards in 2022.

We built this company with your help, and we love to hear from you, so please email us about absolutely anything bookish at: feedback@joffebooks.com.

If you want to receive free books every Friday and hear about all our new releases, join our mailing list: www.joffebooks.com/contact.

And when you tell your friends about us, just remember: it's pronounced Joffe as in coffee or toffee!

ALSO BY STEVE PARKER

Lightning Source UK Ltd.
Milton Keynes UK
UKHW041006010323
417851UK00004B/250